MW01610174

Cycles of the Phoenix

The Whole Interlaced Souls Series

Table of Contents

4

Book I

Sanity's War

NICÉPHORE

About Nicéphore

When the imminent battle commences, you may
wonder which side will attain victory, the heroes or
the
opposition?

This is a story of a grand scale yet it is of a
personal one as well.

They parted their lips to scream but their voices were soon consumed by the damask and flaxen flames that shot forth from their decaying mouths. There was still life in them as the inferno wasted time in cutting the thread connecting them from life and death but eventually it triumphed. Their existence was sacrificed to the fire's ultimately suicidal desire as mine continued to swim in recently dissolved ice. Their ivory innards decomposed within the bowels of the killer, metamorphosing into stark ebony ashes. You and I were left alone yet you knew not of my presence. A deluge rushed to wrap you in its eager embrace. By the end, you and your subjects were nothing.

Kazimar gingerly folded the scroll after he studied the most recent entry, written from the moment the author awoke. His jasmine tinted eyes slowly ascended to inspect the woman seated across from him. "I am so sorry, Aveline, I didn't realize that you have so much trouble coping with your stress."

Aveline's cheeks alighted crimson when she heard her name spoken by the King. However, those raging red rivers rapidly slowed as she perceived her betrothal's pronouncement. She hoped the details of her dream would elicit a different response. "Kazimar, I'm terrified for you and this Kingdom, what if this dream is an omen?" Kazimar opened his mouth yet his words died within him as Aveline continued, "I felt blood rise from my throat as I yelled, as I struggled, yearning for my body to overcome paralysis. I vomited when I couldn't stop the winds from bringing me the smell of death. I. Watched. Everyone. Whom I love. Die. It wasn't JUST a dream, it's a prophecy."

"Aveline, you know very well, that prophecies are nothing more than fantasy. Dreams are reflections of our fears, our desires, even our pasts but since when have they predicted the future?" She struggled to hold his gaze within her emerald eyes. "Do we really have to keep him here Kazimar?What's the worst that could happen if we returned him to those monsters? Surely, there's a chance that they could hold off and if they still attacked us, would it really be much worse if one more person joined the horde?" Kazimar took in a deep breath before quietly and sternly responding, "Now, I have treated him very fairly but I will not exonerate a terrorist." He softened his tone, displaying hurt in his voice as he proceeded, "We should hold onto logic as we prevent fear from triumphing over our compassion for the innocent. Certainly, you should realize this Aveline. That is my final word on the matter."

Aveline bowed her head, still terrified but ashamed for her outburst. She felt guilty as she thought of Kazimar, full of nobility, failing to bring up the trauma he received from the traitor. How could she even dwell on the thought of persuading the King to trade a piece of his empathy for the preparation of a dream, birthed by compounded tension? Aveline had been terrified of experiencing her first battle. Kazimar's scouts confirmed that only twenty-one more nights would remain between this Kingdom's army and theirs, if they proceeded with the latest plan. She knew it would be precarious, at this moment, to relay the vision which immediately proceeded this one for it hadn't manifested death yet it was just as disturbing.

"Aveline?" She saw slender, callused hands trembling in her lap as her surroundings came back into focus. Four boots, two beige and two milky, sat on the face of the bleached stone floor. Two uniforms embraced them, hers scarlet, his snowy. A glossy cherry wood table stood between the soldier and royalty. She clenched her fists and within moments, she grasped onto composure. Her lover called her name again as he inquired, "Please let me know what I can do for you." He got up, knelt beside her chair, and placed a hand on her knee. "Aveline, I love you and nothing will change that," he reached up to brush a strand of hazel hair from her face. "That is why it is particularly hard for me to forgive him."

She took a fleeting moment to silently admire his tanned, perfectly chiseled features. Curly, graying, raven colored hair graced his head. His arms, chest, and legs seemed to strain against the seams of his clothing. It amused her that he still found time to maintain his clean shaven face. His sheepish smile, reserved only for her, worked further to calm her nerves.

She looked into his eyes, "I'll be okay." A cursory chuckle proceeded her words, "I'm sorry for freaking out and delaying the procedure. By the way, since I probably won't get an opportunity tomorrow morning before I leave, I've made up my mind. I'm ready to go in now." Her betrothal tenderly rubbed her arm, "Are you sure, Aveline?"

She would not give up this chance to see Nicéphore stripped of his power, within the confines of a foreign Kingdom. She nodded, "It would give me some closure." Kazimar and Aveline briefly held hands as they crossed the threshold to the adjacent observation room.

"Please bring Nicéphore in for questioning," Kazimar requested when he tapped his earpiece. The gratefulness and apprehension which tumbled inside of Aveline exploded, the moment was here. Though she couldn't watch the interrogation, since she did not yet hold a lofty position, the King was gracious enough to allow her a view of the nation's most wanted criminal. She braced herself, though she knew how he looked, this would be the first time that she saw him in person, not counting the moments with him in her runaway memories. She remembered the abundant representations of him that circulated before his capture. There was one constant in the textbook illustrations, the paintings, and the graffiti. He was portrayed with piercing jet-black eyes, a haunting sneer, and a bare torso, which allowed the viewer to behold his impossible strength. The warlord was often shown with a sword slitting a child's throat, a representation of his crimes and never ceasing desire to destroy what is pure. Those scenarios always shared space with a metaphorical promise, a visual of the glorious King stabbing Nicéphore through the heart as the fount of daylight rose behind them.

Aveline turned towards her fiancé and smiled. Kazimar reflected her expression but it quickly changed as he pressed his earpiece. He brought his vision towards the pane of glass in front of them and a baritone voice escaped from his lips, "He's here."

Eighteen days had arrived and disappeared since that event. She parted linen curtains, sewn with emblems of golden wolves, and stepped outside. Aveline tilted her head towards the heavens as she witnessed an inky darkness spill through an undulating, silvery, murky mass. A charcoal hued behemoth ascended from the fog, which embraced Kazimar's Kingdom, and begun its eclipse of the amber sphere that hung on the firmament's ceiling. The creature turned to the east and Aveline felt a delicate breeze after the legend passed over the jagged mountains, which sat perpendicular to the antagonistic regions. Aveline glanced at her comrades, many of their eyes still pointed towards the direction of the hushed creature's flight, most were set on the direction from which it came.

He was the only one left in the world and they were taught that though myths greatly exaggerated the physical capabilities of dragons, their sightings were still to be considered an omen. Exultation and terror warred within Aveline since she knew that throughout history, the sighting of a dragon resulted either in the utter triumph of the witnesses' enemy or their destruction, in moments which came close to equaling each other in occurrences. Her nightmare detonated into a memory and she ran towards the General's tent.

As Aveline sprinted around individuals, tents, and supplies, she skidded to a stop, barely avoiding a collision with an obstacle which leisurely moved towards her. The prodigy held up a hand, "Calm down Aveline." She bowed her head, and took a few moments to rapidly slow the rate of her breaths before she spoke. "Redd, brother, please listen to me. If we continue our course it will only result in our massacre, by their hands."

The General gently propped his relative's head so her eyes could look into his. "Aveline, this isn't like you. Is it the dragon that has caused you so much distress?" Aveline responded, "If it had just been the dragon, I would be just as horrified as I am now yet uncertain as I was before." She took a deep breath, hoping that her next phrases wouldn't sound as preposterous and dishonorable to him as it seemed to her. "I had a nightmare, a prophecy which King Kazimar already knows about." She pressed on, speaking over the laughter of Redd and those within earshot. "He didn't take me seriously either but that was before this harbinger flew over us! He might understand the situation with more clarity now, perhaps he saw the messenger as well. Please send a message to the King, warn him that we need to return Nicéphore to his subjects and tell him about the dragon in case he missed it."

Redd's expression turned grim, "Sister, what's gotten into you? Did your 'vision' really show you that our lives were in danger because we were holding him prisoner?" A whisper escaped Aveline's lips, "Actually, he wasn't in it but I had the dream the night before we left. I feel, no, now I know that if we release him, we can avoid a disaster that this Kingdom will not be able to recover from."

The general shook his head, "Dreams have never predicted the future, no matter how devastating the catastrophe, history shows us this. Look, we are going to be okay, I have a plan that I'm going to announce to all the garrison. I don't want to hear any more of your panic inspired thoughts and you better make sure no one else is privy to them." He glared at the onlookers which compelled them to make their distance from the conversation a great one. "Aveline, when I'm finished, I suggest that you get as much sleep as you can, it's going to be a long day tomorrow. Now, if you excuse me, I have a speech to make." He hastily brushed past her as he made his way to the center of the camp.

A journey begun by the light of dawn. No breaks for rest. They would snack and drink on the

move. If anyone had to relieve themselves, it better be an emergency and it better be quick since no one would wait behind for them. They would continue their trek through the night and attack the enemy by the following dawn, surprise would be their advantage. The strength that rest would grant the enemy would not matter much since Kazimar's army had practiced combat while sleep deprived. Though not ideal under other circumstances, it was the best plan at present, considering that their armies were evenly matched. Staying focused on one objective, victory, and a flare-up of adrenaline would largely make up for what they lost during their walk. In the end, they would have the greater advantage. The dragon was a herald of their victory. Do not fear. Aveline ran through these main points of Redd's speech, even as she turned around in her cot to look through the slit in the drapes, letting the twinkle of her favorite star, a brilliant lavender one, lull her to sleep.

Someone vehemently shook Aveline awake,

"Wake up!" It felt as if only a moment passed since she had closed her eyes. When she opened them, she saw one of the medics, an elderly man, with eyes infected with horror. His face was inches away from her own when he shouted, "Get up, get ready, they're here!"

Her words tumbled over themselves, "What, what are you..." terror crushed her soul in its icy hands as she slid past the elder and leapt out of her bed. She threw back her tent's partition and shielded her eyes from the photosphere as it crept up from the horizon. As her eyes adjusted, she saw some of her colleagues gather weapons and running farther from their Kingdom and closer to the enemies'.

The elder exited the tent with armor and shoes in his hands. For a moment, Aveline was thankful that it was required for soldiers to sleep in most of their uniform. Aveline's emotions went numb as she mechanically placed the straps of her shield on her left arm and placed her right hand on the hilt of her sword as the medic helped her into her beige boots. "Aveline, GO!" the medic shouted.

She darted for the hills before her, the place where the army watchers had set their tents. When she reached the apex, she paused. Horror flooded away her anesthetized state. The enemy was no more than three miles from Kazimar's warriors. Aveline took in an immense breath and sped towards the growing front line.

A dark skinned man was seated on a steel chair as the wardens proceeded to chain his handcuffs to the top of the polished table. They didn't follow through when they saw their leader shake his head.

"I told you, that won't be necessary. Presently, I doubt he has enough energy to be of particular danger." They untied and removed the sackcloth that hid his countenance and the earplugs which were designed to be soundproof, save for a convict's thoughts. Kazimar nodded to the two guards who had brought the prisoner in and they left the room. Aveline's fiancée swiftly removed his adversary's gag since there was no wavering soul to persuade. Kazimar beamed at the other King as he sat across from him, pulled out a handkerchief to wipe the sweat from his brow, and removed a few splotches from his white boots. "So, has your decision changed?" The interviewer waited for a response but received none.

"Nicéphore, I'm so sorry, I overestimated the effectiveness of pain when it comes to granting a supplier's desires. Deep down, I knew that it wouldn't work with you, it never works on people of your character. However, I needed to get some things off of my chest though it wasn't as cathartic as I had hoped, as I'm sure you already knew. Anyways, it didn't hurt for me to try, right?"

The prisoner slowly opened his eyes to let his vision settle on the voice's source. Maroon liquid dripped from the lacerated skin on his forehead, down and from his shattered nose, into and out of his disconnected jaw. His long matted hair partly hid the blood which seeped from his left temple, trickled from his ear, and onto his discolored cheeks. The King's tousled beard mostly concealed his skinned chin. The inmate's clothes concealed the rest of the damage. Kazimar spoke over Nicéphore's silence, "Yes, I got quite passionate but can you blame me? I mean, can you really fault me after everything that you have done to me?"

The condemned didn't make an effort to speak so his antagonist decided to carry on. Kazimar removed his gossamer gloves, revealing his scraped knuckles and his engagement ring which was capped with a milky pearl. He placed both of his hands onto the other's, gripping them in place, as he asserted, "Please, if not for me, your own brother, then do it for the people. If you truly have compassion, then at least you would do it for your daughter, your beautiful Aveline."

Kazimar let go as he pressed his earpiece once, "Go ahead." The General gave him an update which was confined within a sentence. Kazimar responded, "Victory is imminent Redd, thank you." He tapped the audio communication device in his ear three times and spoke over her, "Thank you Avice, Redd has already informed me." He pushed the apparatus and held it for a couple of seconds, in order to change the setting to a standby mode.

He stared into Nicéphore's mahogany eyes. "The armies are a mile away from each other. Confess that the source of all their catastrophes were acts committed by you. Then, if you still desire death, tell me and I shall finally give you what you want, for I am generous. That's all that you have to do, nothing more, nothing less. If you promise to do this, I will call off the battle and each army will raise their white flags. If you continue to do nothing, every death will be on your conscience. Don't you see that we can save them all? Some of them still struggle with doubt but there can be peace. You need to give me an answer now."

Kazimar smiled as Nicéphore set his hands on his mouth and struggled to reset his jaw. After three attempts, a loud and moist crack announced success. The convict used his palms to silence his scream.

When Aveline reached the mile long army's front, she compartmentalized the memory of the dragon and focused on the monsters closing the gap between them. She imagined dodging and parrying their attacks as she eliminated every one that exposed vulnerability. She envisioned victory for Kazimar's Kingdom and she steeled herself as she caught her breath.

Time seemed to slow as she waited but it still

didn't feel sluggish enough by the time the opposition halted. Aveline was lean and sinewy, just like the men and women who stood at her sides. The individuals in front of them appeared genderless. Their identically burly and immense bodies were partly concealed by charcoal tinged uniforms. Copious amounts of fluid mucus oozed from their sepia skin and through their clothing. Curved five feet long necks sat on top of six feet high shoulders. Their massive circular mouths opened to reveal seventeen rows of compact, triangular, serrated teeth. Aveline knew that she and her comrades could make up for the gilthers' strength and pearly whites with their speed. She felt one of the gilthers expose her soul to its disgust as its black irises and colorless pupils glared into the windows of her soul. Aveline drained the minuscule of empathy that she had for the enemy and she sustained her stare as she gritted her teeth. Despite the circumstances, she was thankful that she would be able to spot some human faces on the other side. A baritone screech resounded from about a mile behind her. General Avice quickly retorted by sounding her own horn and Aveline permitted her instinct to take over.

Some of the knee high wheat appeared to bow before them, many seemed to keep their heads upright to see the outcome, while a few gave the impression of turning their faces as the armies braced for collision. A deafening clang reverberated through Aveline as she broke her run and slid under the gilther's advancing legs. She rapidly arose to her knees and swung her torso in time to plunge her steel blade into the creature's side, allowing it to stop within the middle of its gut. Black liquid sprayed from the crevice and onto her hand as the blade withdrew. She heard a soldier approach from behind and she brought her shield above head to prevent a blade from piercing her skull. The enemy's blade ricocheted off before submerging halfway into the ground. Before he could remove it, Aveline stood, revolved her body and stomped on the hand which held the hilt of his sword. She drove the blade all the way into the earth and raised her other foot to gain a level position. The spirit flew from the gilther behind her. Aveline was able to maintain her balance as it fell from its knees and onto its torso.

Aveline angled her sword to avoid breaking any of the man's bones, before bringing it through his throat and down through his vital organs. As he fell to his knees, she sat on his shoulders, which forced him to fall backwards. She closed her eyes and mouth as she heightened her hearing when she brought her sword into the open. A crimson geyser hit her as she used the tip of her blade to break the diaphragm of a dazed soldier who had fallen on her back across from her.

Aveline heard two of her comrades fall while two victors stepped towards their next target. She arced her shield above her, hoping the enemies' blades would connect, as she used the back of her right hand to wipe the blood from her eyes. She felt her left arm tremble as the first blade deflected and when she opened her eyes, she caught sight of the second sword as it impacted the bottom edge of her shield. The edge of the second sword had stopped two inches from Aveline's throat. She lay on her back as the gilther leaded in the reattempt on Aveline's life. Its blade flew to pierce her while the man's tried to behead her again. The opponents' swords met above her while she held her shield over her upper body, her blade parallel to her lower and she used her feet to pull herself forward. Aveline swiftly rolled to her right a few times, used her heels to push herself back twice and she stood to face the gilther. It thrust its sword towards her heart and she began to push her shield forward, so the power of the blow could be lessened, while she launched her blade towards its thigh. Her heart dropped when she realized that the gilther had feigned, its blade rocketed towards her throat.

The top extremity of her shield hit the creature's blade as she panicked and launched it with all of her strength, yet her maneuver wasn't enough. The gilther wasn't able to puncture her throat but its blade struck her right cheekbone as she turned her head and briefly witnessed her second opponent appear at the creature's left. Aveline shrieked as the sword traveled in synch with the shield, unable to halt the momentum that coursed through her arm. During this moment, the gilther was able to bring its shield down on Aveline's sword and prevent the rupture of its right leg. She closed her right eye to prevent additional blood from reaching it. She sidestepped to face the creature's shield, before the man could deal his blow and to avoid another from the gilther. The sepia tinged individual held its shield in place and twisted its torso to position itself for another strike. Aveline saw as the gilther prepared to launch its blade towards her throat and realized it may have been another feign but it didn't matter whether it was or not. At that moment she rotated sideways and slid through the space between the creature's arm and the edge of its shield.

She lowered her head as she lunged her sword towards the gilther's right arm and through its elbow. The man was able to adjust his attack when he realized what Aveline was doing, for this she was thankful. The human's blade made its way towards Aveline's side and the gilther's left arm quickly moved towards her as its screeching, rotating, mouth dove for her head. In one motion, Aveline bent her torso, thrust her spine back, clinched onto the man's wrist, used her steel reinforced boot to snap his kneecap, and added to his forward momentum by pulling him close to the gilther. His sword pierced through the bowels of the creature as its mouth fell over the man's head. His muffled screams were brief. Man and beast collapsed into each other, paralyzed.

Aveline could hear the creature struggle for breath as black blood trickled from its most recent wound. She could see the man's chest rise irregularly as his crimson blood, mixed with black liquid, flowed from the creature's mouth. Aveline walked over to the gilther's lengthy sword, which lay on the ground, crouched down and grasped the silvery hilt as she prayed that neither enemy would be able to retaliate. Aveline stood up, placed herself behind the man, positioned the sword, and drew her arm back. When she felt as if enough strength had gathered, she placed her hand on the gilther's head and plunged the sword. The force carried the blade's tip into its upper mouth, through the man's submerged neck, to the other end of the creature's mouth, past the gilther's upper spine, and out into the air.

Aveline took a few steps back from the lifeless bodies as she wildly look around and listened to make sure that the individuals within her vicinity were still preoccupied. She stooped to hide amongst the wheat stalks. Aveline spat out the liquid which found its way to her mouth, looked down to blink away as much of the blood as she could, appreciative that the blade had missed her eye, and raised a hand to feel her laceration. She used the man's sword to swiftly and gingerly cut

one of her red pant legs off. Aveline set her recently acquired weapon on the ground and
she bandaged her wound with the piece of cloth. She lifted her head and as she ran to rejoin the fray, damask and flaxen lit the corner of her vision.

Kazimar hung his head. "It's such a shame that you will have caused so many deaths." The man in white stood, pushed his chair back, and made his way to a side table. "My dear Nicéphore, though this path isn't ideal, you still have lost. Soon, you will have confidence in this truth."

The speaker picked up a pitcher, full of water, and poured some of its contents into a glass as he turned to smile at the man in vibrant lavender prison garb. "My 'King,' do you know the three most powerful emotions in the world? People foolishly yearn for it but love is not one of them. Allowing oneself to love another is self-destructive, it is deceptive, and it benefits no one. Look at what you have done, you claim that you love these people, yet you have left them to fend for themselves. You weren't even willing to lie, to sacrifice your status in order to save them. Your decision allows my doubters to remain, so what? I will root them out as I have always done."

Kazimar made a show of relishing his water before he sat back down in front of the prisoner. He dabbed his wet lips before he continued to speak. "Fear, trust, and greed. Those are the strongest emotions.

For those who followed you, I found them and I wiped some of them out. Of the survivors, I kept those whose love for you really turned to fear of me. I was able to find those who lust for power and I was able to bring them to my side by giving them everything that they wanted, except my title of course. I made sure that they trusted me to lead them into eternal victory but I also continued to instill fear so they would never betray me. The team who finally apprehended you were made up of those people and your capture was the motivation I needed for this battle." Kazimar displayed mock sympathy as he continued, "By the way, this was the same group who took your daughter when she was a little girl.

To those who wavered, I showered them with

what they interpreted as love. I exploited their desire for acceptance by showing them kindness, and they grew to trust me. Certainly, they thought, there was no way that I was the enemy. Surely, there was a mistake. Controlling information by constantly bestowing fabrications as truth, concealing facts, making legends of the seemingly impossible, this further cemented their feeling of comfort in their belief.

To the north, I found a directionless people, their Queen had taken her life and she left no descendants. I treated them just as I treated yours. So you see, whichever side 'wins', triumph will be mine. This battle will dispose of the physically weak, some of my power hungry subjects are the best warriors. Thus their egos will be satisfied when they see that though other greedy followers will have lost their lives in battle, they were powerful enough to survive. The survivors who lust for power, from each 'side,' will execute the prisoners on the battlefield so no trace of rebellion remains. I will finally have the best army in the world to help me conquer the larger nations far to the west, the ones who don't know who to trust, and I will expand the size of my Kingdom."

Nicéphore used his hands to wipe away the tears that had been falling, "It grieves me to see that you have stooped so low, Kazimar. Fortunately, my people will be saved." He looked towards the left wall and at the clock. "My army will be arriving soon."

Kazimar guffawed, "Your army? Were you not there as I burned your subjects? Did you not learn of the Kingdoms I razed, the ones who supported you? Did you not hear what I said just now, that the survivors are now loyal to me? Last night, I gave the armies a sign, and I made time to admire my work beyond the Terae Mountains. There is no one left on the other side."

Nicéphore responded, "You haven't found all of my followers." Kazimar sneered, "I'm quite sure that my ability granted me a faultless vantage point." Kazimar's sneer intensified. "If you do have an army, are you planning to join them to victory? You don't have enough energy to transmute, I made sure that you were injected with a customized inhibitor when you got here. You certainly can't escape or even kill me in your present state." He exhaled with annoyance, "Pardon me, my son and Avice want to speak to me." Kazimar tapped his earpiece, "What is it Redd?" The tyrant turned pale as he brought his vision to the floor. After his son spoke, he rapidly pressed a sequence into his device to contact the leader of the opposing army. "I heard from Redd, Avice, is it true?" After hearing her pronouncement, the King swiftly gave permission for the Generals to immediately initiate the execution stage.

Horror choked Aveline by exhaling into her soul. From the sky and beyond the mountains standing to the east, a legion of seemingly sentient flames swiftly approached. Aveline noticed that a few warriors stood mesmerized.

Confusion mixed with her terror when she witnessed a number of soldiers break from their fight and flee; the northern division of the Kingdom bolted to the south and the southern to the north.

A blood curdling screech snapped Aveline from her transfixed immobility, "Aveline, run!" Aveline turned her head and saw an elderly woman fight with a man in scarlet. The woman behind her yelled again. The rest of the commotion within her view slowly registered. Aveline perceived the armies fighting members of their own and murdering one another. The woman who had alerted her fell to the ground, her head twisted too far to the side. Nausea and guilt permeated through Aveline as she ran from the approaching killer. As she joined those who were fleeing to the west, she turned to look at the north and

saw a similar advancing chaos. She maneuvered around the humans and creatures who quickly filled the gap.

Unable to completely overcome the mayhem that clouded her senses, she tripped over a recently slain body. Aveline landed on her face and she bit her lip to keep from screaming as fresh blood seeped from her cut. She heard a metallic crash above her and she rapidly turned around to see that a gilther shielded her

from her pursuer's sword. It proceeded to use its shield to crack the skull of her attacker and it ran to the east to save another endangered life.

A man with auburn hair and blue eyes ran diagonally, towards her vicinity. Their eyes met and she noticed that he looked frightened as he yelled,

"Don't stand there, let's go! We need to get out of here!" Briefly, Aveline felt as if somehow they could escape. Despite her loved one's continued commands, she waited for him, at that moment a shelter from the raging storm which enveloped them. Her smile faltered as he got closer. Panic and desperation emanated from his eyes.

Redd shouted as he grabbed her wrist, "What are you doing?" Before she could respond, she witnessed a movement she couldn't comprehend. Pain erupted within her and the liquid which rose in her mouth tasted like metal. She looked down at the blade as it retreated from her gut, as it entered her diaphragm and skidded against her spine. She tried to scream but nothing came out. Tears flowed from her eyes as the General caught her. "Do you really think that your engagement means that much to the King? Kazimar esteems me more than you." Aveline shook as she desperately tried to breathe. "Did you know he's your Uncle? Yet, you mean nothing to him Aveline, he deemed you too weak to be included in this plan. I am better than you. I will reign with him in the improved Kingdom. I won't mourn your loss." As flames seemed to flood her vision, General Redd withdrew the blade and aimed it towards her heart.

Aveline was snatched into the air, enclosed in talons. Above her, she saw a colossal winged creature, clothed in radiant golden and ruby feathers. It kept her secure in its talons as it brought her close to its chest. Aveline thought that the creature's warmth was pleasant. She turned her eyes to the sides and witnessed many others cradling additional people and gilthers as well. She also saw numerous winged beasts circling overhead the flying rescuers. Aveline's vision turned black and her limbs went limp within the creature's embrace.

As Kazimar stood back, he asked questions which had touched his mind since his Generals contacted him. "How did you know that this battle would take place? How do you know which ones to rescue?" The answer came to him as soon as he had asked it. "You have spies in my Kingdom." He stared at the bloodied King before him with abhorrence and dread. Nicéphore shook violently, some new blood had splattered on the wall behind him. The innocent's face was concealed in it and it dripped from Kazimar's knuckles.

Nicéphore spoke, "Now they know your true character and everyone will know mine." Kazimar scoffed, "You better not think that I'm going to kill you over this. You will not be able to escape my gaze and I will make sure that you don't end up a martyr!"

"Kazimar, you say that fear, trust, and greed are the most powerful emotions but they are not. Love is the most powerful. I despise your atrocities but I still love you, my brother. I never stopped hoping you would return to be the kind person that I once knew. I tried to warn you of your future through your dreams and by granting Aveline an abridged version. Yet, you convinced yourself that they were lies. Your pride has blinded you, selfishness continues to motivate you. Everything that I do, I do out of love."

"I hate you," hissed Kazimar. Nicéphore peered past the deceiver and nodded at the mirror. The door separating the observation and interrogation rooms flew open. "How did you get in here? You're not supposed to be here!" Kazimar spat as he walked towards the intruder. The security officer raised an unfamiliar metallic object and pulled a lever. The adversary froze as thunder erupted in the room. Kazimar paused for a couple of seconds and turned around. A small trickle of blood fell from the inflicted wound in Nicéphore's head. An explosion of luminous white light burst from the deceased's body and instantaneously enveloped the world.

Aveline felt electricity briefly course through her. She looked around as she gasped for breath. She sat up and looked around but darkness was the only thing that met her vision. Aveline felt no pain, she touched the areas where she had been injured but her wounds were gone. She stood up and light flooded the darkness. She shielded her eyes and waited for them to adjust. The moment in which she found herself was just like the dream which proceeded her nightmare. She looked up and saw Nicéphore and a beautiful woman, kindly holding her four year old hand and laughing with her. She felt warmth flood her and tears stung her eyes. He picked her up and held her tightly as he and the woman spoke their love to her. This is where her dream had ended but at that moment the vision continued.

As a selection of moments flashed before her, a realization hit her. This wasn't a dream, it was her past, and these were her suppressed memories. Time went by and her perspective changed to a third-person view. This allowed the moment she was kidnapped to not feel as horrific as it did then. The out of body experience helped her to gain a new perspective as she saw herself being indoctrinated by propaganda and by the preliminary seduction of Kazimar. Once all of her repressed moments transformed into unadulterated memories, darkness returned to her sight. Aveline fell down and cried, the truth of who truly loved her had made itself apparent. Remorse and disgust tore through her. She regretted the lives she took and the individuals she hurt for Kazimar, her Uncle. She awoke and she slowly opened her eyes. Her mind was healed.

Kazimar awoke in the field where the battle took place. He stood up and noticed that his son stood at his right hand side. He looked around and saw the rest of his loyal subjects standing there. The sacrifice of the faultless King had healed all of their wounds and restored the lives of the deceased. Nicéphore appeared before them in his metamorphosed state. As his ebony form stood on the hill, his vision alighted onto the eyes of his former friends and brother. His voice boomed so everyone could hear. "Do any of you have regrets and wish to return to my Kingdom?" He looked into the eyes of the others. "Would any of you like to join my side?" Nicéphore lividly stared into the eyes of the righteous King. He looked around him and laughed. How foolish, he thought. "You realize that you didn't take my people's weapons?" He looked back towards his servants and yelled, "Let's show him who's more powerful. Attack!"

Kazimar speedily metamorphosed as his message was carried down to those in the rear. Nicéphore sank his head low as his eyes moistened.

Flames shot forth from the mouths of phoenixes and fire enveloped Kazimar and his army. Kazimar looked up to discover the source of the flames. He screamed as he flew up towards them. Kazimar was unaffected by fire while existing in this form yet the unfolding defeat scorched his ego. Kazimar exhaled his fire towards the creatures but his flames seemed to rebound in midair. He turned to face Nicéphore and shrieked as realization dawned. His brother had somehow set up a one-way containment field around him and his people.

Kazimar gathered up as much breath as he could and let loose his fire, not caring if it ricocheted off the walls and towards his loyal subjects, unconcerned if any of them were still alive. He only yearned to murder the brother who threw him out to protect the minds of his Kingdom. Yes, Nicéphore had pleaded with him before banishing him but he deserved better he thought. He craved the same level of loyalty that Nicéphore's followers gave him, despite the love that his brother and his people gave him. He wanted absolute power, power which wasn't his. Besides, he lied to himself, couldn't his brother see that he was wiser, he would be a better ruler.

Kazimar roared, "I promise that I will get out of here and I will cripple you. I will make you watch as I slaughter every mother, father and child that is faithful to you. I will start with Aveline, her death will be extraordinarily slow and painful." Nicéphore looked up, his grief filled eyes looking into Kazimar's empathy starved ones. The King pronounced, "Goodbye." The phoenixes stopped raining their fire and flew west to join their comrades. Nicéphore flew above the dome and opened his mouth to emit a torrent of water. The heat within the dome had been so intense that no evidence of Kazimar's followers remained, the swift deluge was for his brother alone. It didn't take long for the dragon's life to succumb and Kazimar's body reverted to human form.

Nicéphore scratched the dome to free the water as he caught the lifeless body and flew high into the sky. Once he broke the pinnacle of the topmost clouds' barrier, he breathed fire onto his brother. Nicéphore held him close, his colossal lion like body immune to the flames. In the end, no trace of Kazimar remained.

Aveline had heard everything that took place between the winged animals who had lived within the earth, Kazimar and his followers, and her father. She was grateful that the Ereaith Mountains had obscured the deaths of Kazimar and his loyal adherents and thankful that the clouds concealed her Uncle's body when it burned. The deceiver would no longer have control over her life or her true friends. Not even his form remained to haunt them. There was no more reason to fear, they were free.

Aveline broke from conversation with a phoenix and a gilther as she turned to see a man and woman walking towards them, clothed in white. Her mother carried no sign of the illness which had taken her. Nicéphore bore not even a scar from his recent experience, save for the one over his heart, the source of the light which reached out to heal everyone. She ran towards her father and mother and they embraced each other as they cried tears of joy. Nicéphore's pain began to subside as he lifted his head to look at the rest of his family. Whether they were related by blood or adopted, he loved them the same. Every one returned his gaze with tears in their eyes and smiles on their faces. All was well.

NAYATI

About Nayati

If you struggle with self-worth, look through the
eyes of those who love you because you are
amazing.

This is a nontraditional story that is partly abstract
and semi-non-linear.

"May I tell you a story?" The question was a dove, who had spread its wings at the edge of his lips before maturity. Unaided by the currents of an approval, silence induced the request into a free fall. The sun, already flushed with embarrassment, began to hide his face. Nervously, crimson rays initiated her slow retreat from existence, without heed to the two individuals in her path. A breath liberated from the elder's thoughts became one with the soft breeze, compelling gravity to loosen its grip on the writer's inquiry. "Yes, I do love stories. But how long are you going to leave my questions stranded without a companion?" The younger man's eyes rose to meet the vision of Apenimon, only to quickly avert them afterwards. "It is the easiest way for me to tell you the truth because...I...," hesitation interrupted Nayati. A parchment painted with words again found its way to the writer's hand and exited the pouch from which it resided. He slowly swiveled his eyesight towards the elder, finding a small yet reassuring smile displayed across his face. "Believe. Allow doubt to run away and tell your story, I am eager to hear it."

* * *

"Do you want to hear a story?" he asked barely feigning nonchalance, excitement was in competition, desiring to be revealed. His friend appeared eager as the following words jovially danced forth from their host's lips. "No. Had you fooled when I said yes, didn't I? Stinks for you!" The recipient of those words had an expression of loss as he exclaimed, "What, but...you said...," "Muahahahaha! Seriously Carl, was that the answer you were looking for? Clearly it wasn't 'yes'," Hanna gave her explanation, flavored with a laugh which joined the chuckles of Carl. The warm air, lucid sky, and the aroma spiraling from the roses helped to nurture the childhood friends' joy. A dove flew between them, slamming their hearts with a brief jolt of adrenaline, as if to keep their joy in moderation. "Wait a second, Carl, do you even have a story to give me? You certainly seem to be delaying." "Actually...um no." Shock quickly took two candles, promptly placed them behind Hannah's Cobalt-blue eyes and proceeded to push her chin, which allowed her lower lip to drop from the upper. Elation quickly overtook her. "Jerk!" she laughed. Carl was prompt in his response, "Just kidding!" "Jerk!" reiterated a laughing Hannah. She gave him a push that wasn't supposed to overtake the receiver's balance, unfortunately Carl was in the process of sitting down and gravity gleefully initiated its tackle. Thus Carl was about to tumble down the side of the hill. "No, I'm sorry!" cried Hanna, who grabbed his wrist, much to gravity's delight. They awkwardly embraced as they rolled away from the summit, laughing like there'd be no tomorrow. You see, the hill's slope was a gradual one, its crest only reaching nine feet into the sky. When they reached the bottom, they held their embrace for a moment times three, overtaken by the giggles. After breaking contact, and amidst subsequent failed attempts at coherent conversation, time was the one who eventually conquered their chortles, finally winning back most of their sanity. The tears staining Carl's face only heightened the look that took place of the thrill before. "Thank you. Thank you for being my friend." "Hey, are you okay?" asked Hannah. "Yes, I'm ready to tell you my story," Carl finally replied.

"It's about time," she smirked, joy unable to mask itself from her features. He straightened his back and puffed out his chest, "Once upon a time..."

Nayati had reached the end. Nostalgia continued to hold him in her embrace. When he walked through his memory, the cracked dirt received the brunt of his delicate laughter, as if it were in on the secret. The tears that soon accompanied the end were incompatible to what came before. The author carried the fragment of a story back home as the constellations swam before his vision. Since Nayati had silently traveled through his story, Apenimon had not let his sight wander from the writer. Yet, he was still able to gather textiles from his treasure chest of memory. It was when Nayati hid his eyes to all but the heavens that the elder and experience began to sew. "Pain does not know the difference between a secret and its guardian, Nayati. Though hurt will never be absent, do you know what decision pain is terrified of? Confession. When we sacrifice our secrets to the presence of the trustworthy, pain's power is weakened." Apenimon let the breeze carry the quilt of comfort to Nayati. The masked perspective was chased by vulnerability as the author inched his face away from the summit of the sky and towards the lined, warm face of the sage. Nayati pulled the insulation tightly around him as he sunk his torso a bit lower and released the breath that he had held captive. "I remember when...

...Innocence was present and Time was patient. Memory has lost the moment that I first awoke but they comforted me, singing memoirs of the purpose I birthed to them when my vision first met the world. Though I spent too many seconds away from them in latter years, having exhausted it upon my supposed friend, my parents always welcomed me back when I knocked on our door. It's funny, whenever I pulled out the documents that describe my life during those years, the joy that I felt in the presence of rebellion is absent. When that fire broke out in the library, some years ago, I was consumed with confliction. Ecstasy was mine when I found that the flames had disintegrated the pages that detailed my moments with Ignorance, yet I was terrified when I found that it consumed the sheets which held the exactness of those early occasions between my guardians and I. However, my cursory observation only revealed distorted truth. I was stricken with regret when I found that not all chronicles about my parents and I were touched by the inferno. Even so, the only record that remains incorrupt is the one detailing my final moments with them."

Instinct led the parchment into the palm of Nayati. His hand embraced the item as a current of distress endangered to overwhelm him. The transcript defied that which had convicted his hope to silence.

A gust of wind emanated from Hannah's nostrils, "A-Choo!" "Gesundheit!" countered Carl.

"I'm so sorry!" she apologized. "It's okay," he laughed. "There needed to be a relief from all that tension." His look became worried, "I need to tell you something." Hannah froze in uncertainty. "There's a bat, begging to be freed from his cave." Confusion inspired the look on her face, before the arrival of realization, "EW, Carl!" Laughing, she dug into her purse for the remedy. When all was fixed, Carl continued.

His fingers sure have a funny way of dancing. I like him though, he's keeping me warm. Whoa! Did he just wave at me? I think he did, I think he did! Can he read my thoughts? He must have, he did! "Hi, Mr. Fire! Look Mommy! Look Daddy! He waved back!" I laugh and I clap. Mommy and Daddy are laughing with me too, how can we not be excited for a miracle? Mommy is still laughing as she brings me in closer and tightens her embrace. I like when she does this, her warmth makes me feel even safer. Daddy is the first one to

run out of laughs. "Though winter be born, summer shall never be taken from our hearts." I don't always know what Daddy is talking about but I love when he speaks because it sounds like he's saying something very important. "This is a perfect setting for a bedtime story. What do you think, Innocence?" "Absolutely, Time. What do you think, Nayati?" I excitedly move my head up and down, "Yes, please!" I love listening to Daddy and Mommy's bedtime stories, I think Mr. Fire will love it too. Daddy leaves his rocking chair and sits down with Mommy and me. Me, Daddy, Mommy, and Mr. Fire, as happy as can be. I see Daddy and Mommy looking at each other with love. They lean towards me and I can see Mr. Fire dance in their eyes. Mommy speaks first, "The title of this story is...she pauses for a second, letting Daddy join her..."You are loved." The door falls down. We jump. The wind brings in something wet and hot and I scream. Why is Ignorance walking in? Why is he smiling? Did he break the door by accident? He's not supposed to be hear. I see something else behind him. Daddy makes fists and walks away from us. A monster walks in and I scream. Mommy takes me far away from it. She covers me. The monster hits Daddy, I *scream louder. I can't hear what Mommy is telling the monster. I see Daddy bleed. I can't stop shaking. I see the monster smiling and Mommy kisses my head. I hold onto her as tight as I can. I see something metal. I close my eyes. I still see something bright and I hear a noise that hurts my ears. Mommy falls and I do*

too. The monster and my friend laugh at me. Mommy is bleeding. She fell asleep. I try to wake her up, why won't she wake up? They continue laughing. I see Daddy waking up. Daddy looks at me and Mommy. He screams and cries. The monster takes my hand and he takes me outside and Daddy runs after us. It's too late.

Shaking, Nayati brought his hand out of the shadows, opening the fingers which embraced what was left of the letter addressed to him. He needed to tell Apenimon this story, he needed to stop running. If anyone could fulfill his hope, it was the elder. Finally composing himself, he stepped back out into the twilight kissed desert, and found the elder still waiting for him. Still feeling fearful, Nayati took one more look at those words which assured him that hope is still alive. You are loved. Returning the parchment to his pocket, Nayati wiped the evidence of pain from his face. As he sat across from Apenimon, he asked, 'May I tell you a story?'"

...Nayati paused. The emotions that had cradled the boy within his imagination had broken into reality. Apenimon placed a hand on Nayati's shoulder. "It's going to be okay." Nayati's tears continued but...

...a smile became present." Carl tried to hide his shaking hands but Hannah already saw them. Holding them in her own, she looked at her friend, her teary eyes mirroring his own. He was worried that she would see the truth behind the story, part of him hoped that she would. He was tired of keeping his vulnerability a secret. Hannah held onto her friend and assured him, "Everything is going to be okay."

NEHA

About Neha

"Neha" is a Sanskrit name which translates to 'loving'.

Dear reader, you are about to enter a story which takes place in India, though it is not a traditional Bollywood tale.

"If you had the opportunity to bring someone comfort, to inspire their dreams, when you knew that you would have to experience a nightmare, would you do it?" Neha's eyes rose from the most recently written words of her story and she allowed her vision to rest upon two of her family members. "What do you think of my story?" Neha asked them. Arya and Sharma kept their eyes on the road ahead and remained silent. "Why are they being so unusual?" Neha wondered as she bit her lower lip. She looked at the window beside her, proceeding to peer past the rain which lashed against the barrier. Blue-gray skyscrapers whizzed past her view. Outside one of these, she briefly viewed a mother cradling her baby, both were laughing, oblivious to the misery cascading upon them. Neha smiled despite the clinging sensation of emptiness as she looked ahead and inquired, "When are you coming to pick me up?" Silence. She witnessed an emerald light rapidly approach them as she hugged her lavender coat closer. Yellow beams overtook the emerald's intensity. Neha quickly looked out her window in time to see a dark red truck closing the inches between them. Her body gave way to the impact and for a moment she felt flames consume her from within. Darkness followed.

Neha gasped for air as her torso rapidly left the bed. The sound of cascading water was a member of the three which prominently met her senses upon awakening. She quickly looked towards the pane of glass beside her, a protector hidden from view, a sheet of ebony preserved her and him from eyes on the outside. Fear obliged her to observe the door and listen. Nothing. Yet, hope collided into the tension within her, compelling her to turn to him who lay next to her. She tried to stabilize her trembling hand as it came to gingerly rest on his forehead. Neha wiped the perspiration away with her sleeve before she gently pulled the sheets tighter around Nishant. Her watch revealed that only two hours had left existence, approximately three hundred sixty minutes remained. Quietly and quickly, she traversed the distance from the double bed to the meager bathroom. The past recruited around three more minutes by the time Neha submerged herself in the same element which continued to dive from the sky. The intended effect fully kicked in, once her head lay at the bottom where clarity diffused her disorientation. Her coverings parted from the twin pools which contained a hue of raven, chestnut, and ivory, while the frigid achromatic liquid encompassed them.

She reviewed her dream, dividing truth from fiction and Neha began by altering the weather. Rain vanished in an instant while sunshine illuminated her vision. She looked out her window and the dark red truck, uncomfortably close, instantly dematerialized. Her family's sedan reached the end of the four-way, unimpeded. Neha traveled to earlier scenes, looking for the woman and the child but soon realized that they weren't there amongst the bustling throng of individuals. She reversed from there and turned her head to behold her family. Indeed, silence was there. However, within a moment it was drowned by a tenor voice, followed by two more that were on the higher end of that range. They sounded happy, and she realized that they were commending her but for what? She looked down, yes, she did write a story. Neha paused the image to read the last line. It was blurry but eventually a few words came into focus.

"Bring...comfort...inspire...experience...nightmare...

would you do it?" She was able to remember the intent of the message from these few words but something was wrong. The last sentence did not exist then but came into being just a couple of hours ago. Suddenly, she rose from the pit of the tub to inhale the air which her lungs cried for. She had been so focused on deducing that she had not taken notice of the warning signs. After the pain disappeared, Neha reentered the vision and focused on the individuals in front of her. Her Dad wore a khaki uniform while her Mom wore an embroidered black leather jacket...no, she had a lavender jacket and snow white jeans. She knew, in reality, that her father had made many a glance into the rearview mirror to look at her and that her mother had turned sideways to do the same. Why though, she wondered, was her memory failing to conjure up the details of their faces? Impulse drove her foot forward and her heel slammed into the far wall of the bathtub. The source of frustration changed as a loud thump rung out. Neha turned her eyes toward the door and strained her hearing as much as possible. Nothing but strained snores journeyed from the main room to the bathroom. She realized Nishant's cold was severe but she knew he would be able to overcome it. Neha revisited the memory and refocused her observation on the person sitting next to her, a brother whose face she too had trouble recalling, until she met Nishant. As Nishant came to the forefront of her thoughts, an amalgamation of emotions flared within her. Some images of her shared experience with the boy flashed by.

Running away with his hand entwining with hers, letting the moon and stars guide them on their path towards freedom. Moments before that, seeing him for the first time, his hushed cries inspiring her to risk her life by running towards dying innocence. Their first train ride together, praying no one noticed them, dreading that someone would stop their progress. His story to her, that his innocence was gone before that night when she arrived for him. Showing sympathy and building trust by sharing with him her history from the moment she arrived at that place where wrath and selfishness formed the basis for intimacy, rather than love. Relief comforting her as she discovered that she hadn't spent nearly enough of their manager's cash to prevent them from acquiring a haven for most of the night. Holding him tight as she fed him a few snacks, helping him sip water, and giving him the medicine that she had acquired. Giving in by retelling him about the moment when a stranger lent her a cell phone and revealing the details of the call; in essence they have no reason to fear, he was welcome where she was going. Watching over him as he nodded off and trying to win her own fight against sleep but failing within minutes.

Neha stared at the soiled tiles in front of her for a short time before she gave into the memory of her capture. She didn't remember their faces nor what any of them were wearing, save for one. She remembered a dark red shirt...a whisper on the opposite side passed through the wood separating her from Nishant.

"*Diidii?* Where are you?" Neha grabbed one of the ivory shaded towels as she called out, "I'm right here Nishant, hold on." She hurriedly wiped herself, redressed, and turned the lock, all within the progress of sixty seconds.

"Hi there, is everything okay?" Neha asked through a disarming smile as she made her way towards his bedside and sat next to him. Nishant gave a generous smile as he sluggishly replied, "I don't think I can go back to sleep. I had a dream where I wasn't sick anymore. You and me were in your family's home and we were all laughing together. You were sitting right next to me and we were laughing the hardest, and we didn't have anything to worry about. I know you're stressed now but we'll be home soon and we'll be free. Don't worry." Neha's smile widened as she bent down and embraced him. It was right then that she noticed that his temperature was on a higher scale than the last time she checked. She tightened her hug.

How could she tell him that she was still afraid of their rescue not arriving? She still worried that she failed to meet her parents' expectations since she skipped school on her last day there. She was convinced that it was her fault for getting kidnapped. Yes, her father cried but he sounded happy on the phone or did she actually hear the tone of disappointment accompanying his sobs? Would her parents change their mind about arriving for her and Nishant? Would they really take in a boy that they didn't know? Her parents may not love her anymore after all that she had done, they certainly would no longer trust her, since she felt, no she knew, that purity had left her.

She pulled back from Nishant's arms as she playfully tweaked the end of his nose and said, "Hey, I think it's time for you to take more medicine. Don't you think?" Neha grinned as she remarked, "Your nose is a bit wet." Neha reached over for a tissue to wipe the phlegm from her hand. "That's gross", laughed Nishant. Neha grabbed a good amount of tissues for Nishant as he proceeded to protest, "You told me the box's instructions say to take a pill every 6 hours. I don't think I've been asleep that long and besides you gave me two so that should cover me for about 12 hours total. Besides, I'm starting to feel better now." He blew and wiped his nose as she replied, "Yes, but your cold is a bit stronger than normal, and I don't think it would hurt to take another now, it should help." "No, no more." "Nishant, please", Neha entreated. He shook his head. Neha's shoulders slumped forward as her head bowed but she was careful to allow her dimples to remain as she kept her eyes on him. At that moment she noticed the sounds of familiar movements and passionate whispers coming from the next room.

She swiftly spoke while grabbing the tissue box, "How about we move to the floor where it's cooler? I think you've sweated out your cold for long enough." Nishant nodded. Patiently, she led him towards the far end of the bedroom and down to the frayed carpet. His shivering became more pronounced as they sat there. "I can grab the sheets from the bed..."

"It's okay, I felt smothered under all those covers anyway", interrupted Nishant. A substantial shiver coursed through him, "But I am just a little cold, can I lean back on you?" Neha brought Nishant close to her, "Of course." They stayed like that for a few moments, his back to her chest, while Neha stroked his hair, trying to ignore the increasing fever. She felt an urge to call the medics but she worried that they would be brought in for questioning. She remembered her superiors repeatedly telling her it would be useless if she found a way to call the police. She was tirelessly informed that despite any news to the contrary, the truth remained, all cops were dirty and some even preyed off people like her. She was sure that many of them were her clients. But what about her Dad and his friends? Surely, at least he was a good cop amongst corruption and he did warn her about the police in the area. It probably didn't matter if he was a good officer since she was also informed that her family had not truly loved her, even if they weren't mad, they had definitely forgotten about her. As time wore on, she was assured that if her family still loved her then they would have searched for her, they must have given up if they did search for her from the moment she was lost. If they were really driven, they would have already found her.

Nishant transformed the silence with an inquiry, "Neha, I know it's a bit late but can I please hear a bedtime story?" She noticed that his speech was more slurred than before but she pushed that observation to the recesses of her thoughts. Thankful for a compelling opportunity to redirect her mind, she looked towards him.

"Hmmmm..." Neha muttered as she prepared herself. "Close your eyes. What do you see?" "Darkness," Nishant replied. "Yes, you're right, it is dark, I can't see anything either. Wait Nishant, I think I see something beautiful, making its way toward us." "What is it sister? I can't see it." "Oh, bhaii, it's a tiny but bright, blinking, glowing yellow light and it seems to be getting bigger."

"I see it," Nishant joyfully whispered. Neha

took note of his response, a voice which had been frighteningly more feeble. A tinge of guilt stabbed her. "Shhhh, rest your voice now, *bhaii*", Neha stated as she brought herself even closer to him.

Nishant slowly and briefly brought his arm straight in front of him and pointed. Neha stared ahead of them and noticed nothing unusual. A moment later, she looked down and saw that his eyes were still closed. "Nishant, that's amazing, you found another light! Do you see the one I found? Look up a little bit." Nishant did and his smile grew ever so slightly as he gave a barely perceptible nod. "Whoa, another one appeared below yours, and wait there's one next to mine and one more next to yours, there's a bunch appearing closer and closer and...Wow! There must be at least a hundred now!" Nishant gingerly turned his body to the right, lowered his back to the floor and placed his head onto Neha's lap. She saw his eyes widen behind his lids as he grinned. He kept his arms on the ground, as he raised his hand and pointed skyward. She gave a hushed gasp when she looked above them. "So that's what they are." She raised her hand, "Let's see if this one will land on my finger." She gently took one of Nishant's hands in her free one and she placed her bent finger next to his.

After a moment she gently cupped her hands underneath his head and lowered it to the ground. Afterwards, she slid down and lay on the ground with him, placing her body next to his. "These are the most adorable fireflies that I have ever seen and this is definitely the most enchanting place that I have ever been. It's so warm out here, as if we went inside during a snowy day and sat in front of a fireplace. The air smells slightly sweet and it smells fresh, away from traffic and far from the crowds. I think we're the only ones up on this hill, the first to experience this gentle wind. The clouds are beginning to move away...finally! Oh, Nishant, I've never seen the moon look so big and bright, neither have I seen the stars appear so brilliant! The clouds sure were thick."

Nishant unhurriedly turned towards his still curled digit and slowly, very slowly, he turned his face heavenward while he straightened his finger. Neha uttered, "Aw, she's looking especially great, flying within the moonlight." Neha brought her palm to Nishant's forehead to make sure her perception was correct. She bit her lower lip and swallowed. Neha carefully took Nishant's left hand

and placed it upon her forehead. "Aren't I a bit cold, Nishant? I know what could completely warm us up!

"Let's do this together. The first step is easy, we just have to continue laying down in this incredibly soft grass. Now, we'll have to use our imaginations without moving a muscle, letting our mind take over. Okay, now turn your body to the left while I turn mine to the right and we'll both lay on our sides.

"Wow, you're doing it Nishant! You really are my *bhaii*, we're on the same wavelength, inside each other's imaginations! Let's bring our knees close to our chest, there you go. We'll bring our arms to push our upper bodies up and continue lifting until we are both sitting. Nice! Now we just have to bring our feet underneath us and stand. Awesome, now the hardest part is done and here comes the fun part. Place your hands in mine and take two steps back, now two steps forward, there you go! Let's take two steps to the left and then two steps to the right. Great job! Finally, we'll repeat from the beginning, take two steps back..."

They continued with their steps for a few times. Nishant's breathing was less strained now but it was barely audible. Yet, Neha was relieved that his smile was still apparent. "I didn't know you were such a great dancer Nishant, you're a natural! May I please hug you for a little while now?"

Nishant moved his head down and up in a manner that was barely noticeable. She closed her eyes and they held each other as they moved through the grass, underneath the moon and stars, with the breeze, while the fireflies accompanied them. "I love you, Nishant." They remained in that moment for as long as they could. Neha left when Nishant became silent. She faced the ceiling and opened her eyes. She didn't look at him until his body started to cool.

Her cheeks became moist by the flood of grief which she could not keep at bay. "Nishant?" She sat up and lay a hand upon his chest. She tenderly lay two fingers on his neck, checking for a pulse. After a few seconds, she lost control. Her body convulsed as she gasped for air and her tears continued to descend. Neha inclined her body closer to his and she wrapped her arms around him. She sat up while she continued to hold him. "I love you so much Nishant, you didn't deserve this."

Neha had realized that though he didn't know his age, he seemed to be around 9 years old.

His own family didn't care about him, only for the money he could bring. He didn't even have a proper name when she first found him. Who was going to bury him? He didn't deserve this. "I love you *bhaii*." Why did he have to receive the desires of those sadists? "I miss you so much, Nishant." Why was his innocence stripped from him? Who weakened his immune system? He was just a boy. "Nishant, we still have to go home, please come back." These thoughts and similar ones afflicted Neha as she continued to rock back and forth.

She didn't know how much time had passed when the sun's rays started to peer around the edges of the thick jet-black cloth but it was around the time that her sobs began to subside. Neha and Nishant were supposed to move at dawn if no one had arrived for them. The sunlight's power had increased substantially by the time Neha settled on a decision, she had to risk it.

There was no feasible way that she could take him nor was there any chance that she would leave him here. She looked at her watch, an hour after deadline. She started to stand while she lifted him up and she fell. She gritted her teeth, tried again and succeeded. She wrapped his left arm around her shoulders as she held him tight. Time seemed to decelerate as she dragged him to the bed. She stumbled a couple of times but she made it. Neha sat on the bed's edge with him and slowly lowered his torso to the bed. She inhaled a considerable amount of air as she wiped her brow. After a short while, she stood up, picked up his legs, and brought them onto the bed so he would be laying horizontally. She brought the covers up to the edge of his chin and as she looked at him, fresh tears formed in her eyes. She grabbed the phone and called for the ambulance.

"Please, my friend is having a seizure and it keeps getting worse, nothing is working. What? No, please, we don't have a car, please..." Neha sighed with consolation. She gave the dispatcher the address and the room number. "Okay thank you so much! What? My name is...I'm sorry, my name is Esha and my friend's name is Harsha. You said the ambulance just left right? How long before it gets here? Thank you."

Neha didn't wait to hear the dispatcher's next sentence when she slammed the phone down. She didn't have much time. She bent down and kissed Nishant's brow. "Goodbye, baby brother."

She ran down the cracked concrete stairs and arrived in the lobby. She was terrified that she might have been too late, she didn't dare look at her watch. She saw the man she had paid stand up from his stool. "Just in time, my shift is about to end", he gruffly told her. Neha gave the most brilliant smile that she could muster and asked, "Sir, may my friend and I have two more hours? He needs some rest and I need to go out to get him some more food."

"Sure, if you pay me for the 5 minutes for which you're overdue and pay me double again for the additional time. Actually, pay me triple." "But sir..." Neha began.

"Listen, *kuthri*, I know you two are refugees and I hate the cops but you're going to have to give me a little more motivation for keeping you underage kids in here." Neha didn't have time to waste, she reached into the confines of her clothing and paid him the requested amount. She had one bill left. After the employee gave her clearance, she ran. As the front door slowly closed, Neha heard him shout at the others to let her and her friend out the back when their time was up. Her feet pounded mud and she saw a blur of cruel, tired, dejected, and obliviously joyful faces. She heard an ambulance siren and some solace found its way to her heart.

She briefly stopped running when she found an elder. She asked him to make sure that she was on the way to her destination. She was careful to weave in and out of crowds, avoiding alleyways and the sparsely populated areas, just like her father taught her. When she arrived at the brink of a place with only a few people, she either waited, hidden, waiting for the crowds to move in or she turned into an area that was still occupied by them. Finally, she arrived at the train station. Not the same one that Nishant and her got off of but it was close. This one was a major one, the one her father told her to go to because of the bustling crowds. They would have preferred the airport but there was no way she would be able to make it all the way there, the closest operating one was close to 30 miles away from the hotel. She made her way around the multitude and to a bench where a family was sitting. She could catch her breath at last.

Neha frantically looked around, focusing on each face that she laid eyes on. She forgot how her parents' faces appeared but she was sure she would recognize them once she saw them again. Her father had told her that he would be making his way through the crowds to look for her. He planned to meet her and Nishant in the hotel room but he urged her to make her way to this train station by dawn, if he hadn't arrived yet. Amidst his tears and spoken prayers of gratitude on the phone, he warned that the hotel was far but he and Neha's mom would try their hardest to get there in time. They would definitely be at the train

station, he promised. Neha had left much later than planned though, would they still be here? Are they not here yet? Were they ever going to come? Neha turned to the lady next to her and asked if she could borrow her cell phone.

"Sure, sweetie, I'm not sure if there's reception in this area but you are welcome to try." She handed Neha her phone as she asked, "Is everything okay?" Neha forced herself to grin and jubilantly nodded her head. "My parents are on their way, I just need to ask them something." She dialed a number and waited. No signal. She tried three more times before she handed the phone back, smiled, and thanked the woman.

Neha looked at the incoming train. Neha

watched as the woman smiled at her while the family made their way towards the train. She wondered how far this track went. She pondered whether she would feel any pain if a locomotive hit her, would she die before she felt any pain? She could follow the track. She could lay down when she found a spot on the track where she deemed the train would have gathered enough power to take her life. It couldn't be too far, she'd walk an extra mile just in case she stopped too soon. She got up and started to walk with her face downwards while she kept her sight on the tracks.

"Neha, Neha?!" She stopped. Someone here knew her name, impulsively she felt fright but she recognized that voice.

"Neha!" She knew that voice too, no, it couldn't be. She lifted her head and saw a familiar man and woman pushing through the crowd and waving at her. "Daddy, Mommy?" Neha whispered. She stood there while her parents continued to push through the crowd and then she ran towards them. Soon they were wrapped within each other's embraces. She felt tears falling on her head and face. She gently pulled back and lifted her face. She reached out and gently touched her father's and then her mother's faces. Tears fell from Neha's eyes as she pulled herself closer to her parents.

A

WAR

FOR A

DREAM

About A War for a Dream

This is a tale of a passionate platonic love,
haunting memories, and a creature who can shatter
his victims' realities.

The warmth emanating from within coursed and sparkled through their souls like electricity. His twin charcoal hued lakes shimmered along with the oak tinged beaches which enclosed them. The bonfire's light only enhanced the effect of those sparkling eyes, the tears which rained from them captured the light and enhanced its luminosity; until the salt water shattered upon the vibrant soil. His smile was the gateway that allowed his joy to channel into her heart, increasing the joy within, causing it to overflow into her soul. The flames' reflection and their shadows jubilantly danced with them and their friends. Farrah forcefully yet playfully pulled him close to her so their loving souls would be pressed up against one another. They interlocked their arms across each other's backs for a moment before they raised their right arms and Mahli twirled his friend to her next dance partner. As his tear streaked face turned towards his next friend, Farrah took the fleeting moment which passed to look into his eyes where peace reigned with exaltation. Her eyes began to sting as they moistened for him and she blinked rapidly. Mahli was finally free. That event was a week ago and it only took place within Farrah's mind as she slept.

Cloven hooves pierced through the ivory blanket which laid upon the remains of spring's children. Tears from the sky met warm streams, which flowed past the windows to the rider's soul, the heaven's fractured upon colliding with her and her steed; hers were already broken. Healthy gusts of mist tumbled from the stallion's nostrils, which accompanied his master's lesser ones within the frigid air. A whisper propelled by a fragile hope, fraught with sorrow, and caressed with fear, reached forth from her hoarse throat. "Hang in there".

When the rider left the campground, a few hours ago, the Sun had begun its descent towards its habitual death. The land started to eat that star alive by the time Farrah briefly and firmly tugged on the reins. As she kept her legs on Shun's sides, he eased to a trot and the wind's whistle began to ebb from their ears. Farrah proceeded to gently pull on the reins as they approached the border to the Viraag wasteland. She tightened the scarf around her nose and mouth. At the opposite edge of the plain, an unnatural protrusion poked into the sky.

The rider was grateful for that mountain's distance since it granted her the inability to make out the details of the skeletons which formed it*.

The driver slid off the saddle once she and her equine friend entered their destination. Farrah could hear her heart as it rapidly drummed against her chest and she could feel her throat constrict as her eyes searched for an answer. Farrah bit her tongue and trekked on. Only a sliver of the Sun remained by the time Farrah found a possible confirmation to her hope.

Farrah re-mounted her steed and guided a galloping Shun towards what appeared to be a tiny heap which stuck forth from the snow covered earth. She reached for her torch from the rear loops of the saddle. The driver struck a match against its head and when the light fell across the mound, flames of happiness, crippled by anxiety, blossomed within her. She coaxed Shun to slow his pace to a halt. Farrah leapt to the ground and thrust her torch into the land. Finally, Farrah was beside the form which had caught her attention, the reason she had arrived at this desolate place. Her hands shook uncontrollably as she struggled to place her extra coat around the inert figure. She spoke as she placed her face up close. Relief materialized within her soul and the resultant flood poured from her pores, when she saw thin clouds rise from the entity. "I'm here Mahli. Everything is going to be okay."

A dragon hide canopy slowly came into focus as he opened his eyes. Pinpricks of pain shot through the ends of his appendages and what felt like daggers hacked the inner walls of his skull. Mahli bit his lip and forced his focus upon the light which danced across the tent's ceiling, before he gingerly tilted his head in order to behold the woman next to him. Her right arm lay across his chest, her hand placed above his heart. He noticed that his friend still wore her intricately woven bracelet. He looked down at the matching rahki bracelet that she had made for him.

Beginning to awake, her moist cheeks began to rise as a smile began to form. She tenderly spoke his name and she looked into his eyes after she wiped her own. Farrah held Mahli's gaze, as she raised herself into a sitting position. His face, injured by fear and guilt, peered back at him from her golden eyes. However, the compassion which radiated forth from the windows to her soul outshone the doubt which had exuded from him. Farrah leaned forward and gently held him, he gratefully returned her extended embrace. They remained hugging each other even as he broke down sobbing. His anguish crushed her resolve and this caused her tears to flow anew.

It had been a few minutes after their tears were spent when she gingerly pulled herself away and entreated, "I love you. Please, you need to share your story with me Mahli, doing so will help grant relief to you. You already know that secrets don't murder pain, rather they torture those who guard them and they

leave a canyon between loved ones. I'm strong enough to handle it, I promise. "

Mahli replied, "I'll tell you everything. I've never held back in relaying what happened. It's only truly difficult to tell others exactly what happened since I don't know if they would be able to handle my sorrows."

"Mahli, telling your story hasn't brought you enough solace. You need to show me."

Mahli slowly shook his head as his hands commenced to shake. Farrah took her best friend's right hand in hers and stroked it as she placed her other hand onto his cheek. "It's going to be okay", she whispered. He placed his free hand on top of the one which caressed his and after a few moments transpired into history, Mahli nodded his head. Farrah placed her head to his quickly beating heart and she began to hum their song, in order to loosen his anxious nerves. The vibrations of the tune, its history, and Farrah's proximity, compelled Mahli's heart to slow its pace. He lightly placed his hands on top of Farrah's head and he set his gift free. The scenery around them transformed in an instant.

A woman with long auburn hair, and light hazelnut eyes lay next to Mahli and she stroked his uncovered arm. Amber moonlight illuminated the room. "Abigale", Farrah whispered. "You get weaker every time that you return, Mahli", Abigale whispered to her husband.

"I am at the edge of losing control Abigale but I know that I will win. I assure you that this will be the last of my annual excursions. I am terrified not because I think I will fail but because of this final battle which has to take place, before serenity arrives to stay."

"My Love, if you won't let me fight with you

then please show me exactly what you're up against. You know that you can't keep this burden to yourself, share it with me. It will make the fight easier for you."

"No, my sweet Abigale. Telling you has sufficed. To show you what happened would cripple you".

Abigale quietly pleaded, "Don't you have faith in my resilience Mahli? I'm worried about you, please..."

"Daddy? Mommy?", the voice of a young boy interrupted Abigale's entreaty. He slowly walked away from his adjacent shadowed room. When the moonlight struck his face, Farrah gasped as she placed her hand over her mouth. She had suspicions that Mahli had a son, despite his gentle yet firm denials.

The boy entreated, "I know that I already asked this but can I please go with you on your vacation tomorrow? It's rare that someone goes outside of the city and I want to go with you. I promise to do my chores with extra passion and earning".

Knowing what he meant, his father gently laughed through his mask of a smile, "yearning, not earning. This vacation is especially suited for me but I promise that you and your Mother will accompany me on the next one. Before you ask your next question, which I'm sure was going to arrive, I can't avoid this trip to stay with you for a little extra time because it would be selfish of me. Our lives will be made better because of this particular trip."

"Because after your trip, you will get a bigger celery?", asked the boy.

Mahli laughed kindly and freely, "I won't get a bigger salary but I promise you that things will be better. I can't yet explain how but I assure you that you can trust me, Joshua."

"I know daddy." The four year old boy with flowing auburn curls ran to give his Dad a hug before he slid in between his parents and underneath the sheets.

"It's okay Mommy, don't cry. Daddy will be back before you know it, it's only going to be about two weeks after all," Joshua softly spoke.

Abigale tweaked his brown freckled nose, which resembled her own, and she gave words to his delicate ears, "I know dear but I will still miss him during the time that he is gone. But you're right, he will be back before we know it."

Joshua turned his dark brown eyes away from his Mother's and smiled as he looked again at his father, an individual with a headful of trimmed ebony curls and deep brown irises. He then turned his face towards the ceiling and shut his eyes. Each parent placed a hand on top of his little heart and smiled at each other, Mahli's expression tinged with an inner turmoil and Abigale's infused with worry.

The scenery transformed again and Farrah had a conviction that a week had passed since the moment she had witnessed before. She saw Mahli standing alone in the center of a clearing within the woods, just a few feet away. Farrah observed Mahli as he used his power of re-living memories upon himself. Her friend fell to his knees and shrieked. Farrah fought against the urge to run to him since she knew that memories could not be changed, only the perspectives which accompanied them, yet only he had that power.

Mahli searched for all his mental traumas and frightening premonitions as he held on to each one that he had brought back into clarity. He was forcing himself to relieve every detail which had now formed his chain of horrific experiences, making this moment his most painful thus far. Despite the logic that assured her of the outcome, Farrah took a couple steps forward and moved in to hug Mahli. Her arms went through the projection and enclosed across her chest. She could now see a sharpened knife and a journal in front of him. The journal contained a record of heartwarming moments and convictions to heal his shattering mind. Farrah took a couple of moments to brush away a few stray tears and stepped away for an optimal view of this point in time.

She didn't think it was possible for him to scream any louder but her expectations were defied as his outcry escalated. Her innards seemed to freeze over. Mahli didn't stop until he violently coughed drops of crimson, for it was then that his head was brought low and his vision laid upon the objects that he had lain in front of him. He had been lost within his anguish but he now remembered the rest of his plan. Not letting the intensity of his pain lessen one iota, he grabbed his journal and read to himself those healing words, which refuted his diseased ones, as he forced himself to chain together those triumphant thoughts. He clenched the handle of his blade and touched the tip in between his left ribcage, a self-prescribed failsafe in case it was too late. His plan was to use the collection of euphoria to permanently reframe his harrowing condition. Farrah already knew what would happen. "You can't do this alone my dear Mahli," she intoned.

As soon as his pain completely ebbed away, his focused trauma slammed back into him with full force. "No," Mahli screamed as the pain caused his blade to slip, scraping his ribs, before it followed his journal to the ground. Too weak to re-attempt a thrust of the blade, through his heart, he fell forward. With waning strength and awareness, he slid his arms closer to his torso and placed his hands over his head.

Acting with instinct, he did something he never knew possible. He used his hands to pull the compiled memories and harrowing emotions from his head and used his power to expel them. The lights in the sky vanished.

Blindness only lasted a moment as the shadow rapidly coalesced into the shape of a tactile being. The attributes of a human being gradually replaced the shadow but this entity had vacant eye sockets and decaying flesh. The hair on Farrah's neck stood on end as she collapsed to her knees and shivered violently. She had known of him but, until now, she had never seen Saudade, an entity who appeared to be a rotting replica of Mahli. Terror churned her stomach into unnatural contortions, yet Farrah kept her eyes steady.

The light had left her dear friend's eyes and he was motionless. His emotions and memories had escaped him. He now only had thoughts created from this moment onwards and an inability to feel anything from them. Mahli kept his eyes forward as Saudade inhaled for the first time. The creature brought his vision towards his victim. After a moment, the being pulled back his cheeks, the halves which remained, into a smile. A baritone whisper escaped his lipless mouth.

"Mahli, my sweet dear friend. I am so grateful that you gave me this tangible form." He gazed at his body. Saudade knelt so his vision would align with his opponent. The nightmare incarnate brought a partially skinless hand to his oppressor's jaw. "Tell me, what do you feel?", he inquired as he used his index finger to stroke Mahli's chin.

"Nothing", Mahli responded dryly.

Mock surprise coursed through the monster's voice, "Not even fear of me?"

"No", the interrogated responded, without emotion. Saudade continued to revel within this moment.

"And what of your joy?", the manifestation sneered.

The victim responded in a monotone, "I feel nothing".

"Your euphoric memories are tormenting my mind", Saudade spat as he pushed an index finger onto his temple for emphasis. "Despite our differences over the years, I will now grant you a token of appreciation, my gift to you for freeing me from the cage of your mind. I am going to transfer your happiness and your love back to you. I will also return a copy of your memories but yours will solely be accompanied by every euphoric emotion. You won't have to suffer any more, you won't even feel a touch of sadness. No matter the surrounding circumstances, you will only have these things."

Saudade placed both hands on Mahli's temple. He proceeded to release the emotions at war within his head and into his subject, as he kept horror within his own soul. When the act was completed, Mahli hugged his master. Saudade laughed as he returned his captive's embrace. Though the creature was now incapable of feeling anything favorable, he still had the knowledge and ability to mimic those emotions which he gave up. "Let's go home", suggested Saudade, his hatred and cruel intentions impossible for Mahli to perceive.

Time jumped ahead, a week had passed and it was the dead of night. Farrah saw them at the outskirts of the Shaanti woods and Mahli's city, Khushee. Saudade spoke with conviction, "I must go alone my friend, remember I have business to attend to before you enter. Stay right here until I come back for you".

Unable to comprehend the monster's ill intentions, Mahli smiled as he placed a hand on the wretch's shoulder. "Don't worry. I'll be here when you get back." Saudade seemed to vanish and she discerned that the monster had run at full speed. A second passed as Saudade passed the vast clearing that lay between the woods and the city's open gates. Farrah looked away.

Time, within the memory, proceeded to lapse so that each hour became a second. The blood curdling shrieks continued and they amplified before growing more distant. She witnessed the Sun rise and fall three times before time reached a normal pace again. Still Mahli did not enter, trusting the demon, innocently confused but not in the least bit alarmed by the commotion within those walls. Farrah knew from Mahli's story that none within could escape the monster's rapid speed. All it took was a touch from the nightmare incarnate to drain the hope from the people within Khushee. The one who could help heal their minds remained outside of the city walls.

Saudade left the scene of the massacre with a nausea inducing smile. "I couldn't save the city Mahli but they are now at rest. Yet, I've still kept you family safe. Come with me, we can go see them now".

They walked hand in hand and stepped on those corpses which lay in their path. Farrah saw some of the victims with slit throats and sharp tools in their hands. Others had broken as a result of jumping from lofty heights, some had perished in fires which they made for themselves, while the rest carried no visible marks upon their bodies.

The dead stretched to the limits of her field

of vision. Farrah swallowed back bile as she shook uncontrollably, grateful that visual and audio were the only senses receptive to this trip through his memories.

Mahli just looked around, uncomprehending, unable to feel the appropriate emotions which the monster had kept from him. "Ah, here they are", whispered Saudade as Abigale turned the corner. She was weeping as she led Joshua, while she covered his eyes. She stopped, stunned, when she saw her husband and the mass murderer. The committer of genocide and his unwitting enabler continued their progression towards the two survivors. Keeping her hands over her son's eyes, she looked at Mahli, slowly shaking her head in disbelief and devastation. "No", her quiet voice shook.

Mahli triumphantly spoke, "I brought my friend to meet you. We can live free now, no need to worry about those who hurt or were bound to hurt our minds. I can no longer feel sadness, I can share this with you and my beautiful son. Wouldn't you like that?"

Joshua broke down crying and his mother pulled him in even tighter. "What are you talking about Mahli?", Abigale rasped. "Look around you, innocent people have lost their lives, including our friends and their children! Are you just going to continue standing there with that smile on your face, you monster?!", she shrieked. After a moment, she mumbled, "This isn't you...this isn't...." She moved her focus to Saudade but unable to look into his sockets, she stared at the creature's scabbed feet. She queried, "What have you done to him?"

"I'm sorry," Saudade whispered. "I wanted to save your family too but it's apparent that they don't want what you're feeling, it wouldn't be right to force them to feel happiness. However, I wouldn't want them to go on living without peace, neither would you. They can be at peace with the rest of them", Saudade looked around to view the fallen within their vicinity as he advanced towards Mahli's family.

"Get away from us!", screeched Abigale as she deftly swooped Joshua up into her arms and ran. In her panicked attempt to escape, she tripped over a woman's leg, a few paces ahead, and the mother and her boy fell onto a fellow resident. The evildoer slowly approached, taking his time, relishing every moment.

"Please Mahli, do something!", Abigale cried.

Mahli naively smiled as he turned around to look upon the three. "I am. I'm letting him set you free," answered her brainwashed husband.

Horror froze Abigale's expression as she continued in her struggle to completely rise with her and her wailing son. As she kept Joshua's eyes closed, she and he fell again on the floor of humanity, some who had plummeted from the upper levels of the adjacent tower.

Saudade deftly grabbed Abigale's hair and before she could utter another cry of resistance, he tapped her forehead. Her eyes immediately went pale as she froze in her place. After a brief moment, she let go of Joshua, clenched her hands, covered in the deceaseds' blood, and placed them over her head as she let loose a heart wrenching scream. Joshua, his vision now uncovered, gathered his surroundings and vomited. Crying even louder he pulled at his mother's arms, pleading for her to stop. The healer did nothing but watched, surreally smiling at the scene, only capable of feeling happiness, a corrupted love, and a false faith that this was the best outcome for Abigale and Joshua.

After what seemed to be an eternity, Abigale crawled towards a nearby hunter. She proceeded to unsheathe his knife while hitting and pushing her son who tried to stop her. Joshua shrieked incompressible phrases as he tried to yank his Mother's clasping hands. With a kick that caused her son to gasp for air, she plunged the blade into her body. Doubled over from pain and shock, Joshua did nothing to stop his Mom's continued stabs.

As Abigale, unable to move anymore, lay dying, Saudade silently advanced behind Joshua and touched his head. His screams stopped in his throat and it appeared that all life had drained from him. He looked at his Mom, who stared blankly into the sky while she involuntarily gasped for air. He then looked at the blade which lay beside her...

"I'm sorry, I can't endure this moment", Farrah appealed to her friend. The vision skipped ahead. The boy lay motionless beside his inanimate mother, her blood mixed with his, flowing onto the knife and connecting with the other corpses within their proximity. Saudade grabbed an uncomprehending Mahli by the head and transferred a copy of all negative emotions into his ex-host. Farrah's friend fell to his knees as he stared at his deceased family. Trauma silenced him and shock kept his eyes dry. An indescribable hollowness emanated from within him and it accompanied his anguish. Too weak to stand, he crawled. As he made his way to his family, his hands contacted more than one individual whom he recognized.

When Mahli made it to his wife and son, Saudade placed a hand on the traumatized's shoulder. "Look at what you let happen", sneered the creature. Mahli rapidly turned around and viciously clamped his hands onto Saudade's head. Farrah's friend began to draw the monster back into his mind, not caring that it would exponentially increase his melancholy. It didn't matter to him that his action could ultimately end his life. He thirsted for vengeance, he wanted to join his family in eternal sleep and he was determined to stop this monstrosity from affecting anyone else.

The monster, his hands still clamped onto his opponent's head, tried to take away Mahli's happiness. However, though the creature could kill emotions which opposed him, he could not take them and he had given his victim everything he had...except himself. Nor could he absorb his adversary, only Mahli could since the man had been Saudade's host. A bone shaking wail erupted from the creature as his essence started to dematerialize and flow back into his host. Shaking from the effort and the incremental pain, Mahli held on and continued to reclaim the nightmare incarnate. When Saudade's consistency approached smoke's, he fled from his grasp.

"You will never truly be able to defeat me", wheezed the creature whose frame remained the same. "Nor will you be able to save others from your failure".

Saudade escaped into the wind but not before Mahli's hand encircled the monster's ankle. His hand traveled through and enclosed upon itself. Mahli knew that it was a desperate measure. As Saudade grew smaller in the lone survivor's vision, he collapsed and blacked out. Farrah and her friend came back to the present.

She hugged her friend tighter as she revisited memories of her own. This recollection took place about three hours after Mahli's family perished.

She could make out the solitary survivor sitting stunned amongst corpses, clutching onto a little boy. His wife lay next to him, face down on a shattered body. The rising smoke from Khushee had compelled Farrah and her band of nomads to enter the city.

After a man from Farrah's camp checked for any injuries which Mahli may have incurred, and failing to get an answer to any knowledge Mahli may have had, to who may still be alive and who it was that Mahli was holding onto, Farrah volunteered to take him back. She and her friends would work on his mental recovery and offer him a place in their camp, Mohabbat.

After kissing the sleeping survivor on the forehead, Farrah double checked to make sure the sheets around him adequately protected him from the night air. She stepped outside her tent, into the starry night, and looked upon the once grand city of Khushee. It wasn't long before she saw the existing flames rapidly increase in size and stature. Her comrades had initiated their controlled burn of *the city and its deceased inhabitants.*

Farrah looked back towards the tent, as compassion for him plunged pain into her heart with greater force. Farrah brought the scarf, which lay across her neck, up to her mouth and nose again in preparation for the stench which would come that way. She prayed for more survivors, for his sake.

Three days later, her arriving friends and their horses woke her from her slumber. She leapt from her place of rest which was next to the survivor's. The morning light momentarily blinded her. As her vision came into focus, she surveyed her arriving friends, her hope sinking but surviving. When the closest one to her, from the arriving party, met her eyes, her hope died. He slowly shook his head as he held Farrah's gaze. There were no other survivors.

"Farrah," Mahli's voice brought her awareness from the past into the present. "It was selfish of me to run away, I am so sorry for abandoning everyone. Thank you for allowing me to share my burden with you. I am so grateful that I finally followed you up on that offer. I feel stronger but I'm worried about you. Were my memories too much for you? Please, let me do my best to heal you now."

"No, my dear Mahli. It wasn't easy experiencing a portion of your traumatic memories, especially since I care about you so much. However, I am thankful that you let me help you by leading me through that journey. I wouldn't have it any other way. Let me sit with this until tomorrow morning," Farrah answered before she tenderly placed her quivering lips to Mahli's forehead. "Rest some more now, we'll be ready for you when the day breaks." Farrah rose from Mahli's side and looked down upon him. "We're so relieved that you're with us again. I love you bhaii."

Farrah returned her loved one's smile as she steeled herself from breaking down again. She wrapped her cloak around her and tightened her shawl, before she entered the frigid desert air. Mahli's closest friend silently prayed for him, the others within her camp, and then for herself, as she walked towards her own tent. The cracked ground eagerly drank every tear of hers as Mahli's experiences with horror and her own exploded within her mind. Yet, as she fell to the ground, looked into the rainbow hued constellations and prayed more fervently, a quiet hope returned to war with her doubts. Only a week remained between her camp and the army of Saudade. She passionately held on to the re-growing faith within her as a calming presence embraced her soul. "Saudade will be defeated," she whispered.

As Farrah and her captains went over combat skills with the camp, Mahli spent that week reviewing methods to resist Saudade's mental attacks with them. Mahli also spent the time fighting his urge to leave again. It'd be impossible for Saudade to regain his former strength without the presence of his main opponent. However, in addition to helping his loved ones, the healer was the only one who would be able to utterly destroy his nemesis.

The Sun set on that Saturday, signaling the end of those seven days. The individuals within Camp Mohabbat got into their positions as they anticipated war's imminent kick-down of arrival's door. The last time Farrah sent her scouts out, they had returned to tell her that the army, who required no sleep, was about a two week's journey from them. That report took place two weeks ago from this moment.

They assured themselves that tonight, finality would conquer Saudade and his soldiers or them. Mahli, Farrah, and the rest of the camp held each other's hands for the final time before the opposition arrived. Their minds were flooded with reassurances. For those who forgot how to hope with passion, as the hours closed, they remembered again.

During the last week of preparations, Mahli had held back on the potency of his healing power until this moment. Even as their painful emotions remained, it didn't overwhelm them. Mahli was grateful that his powers were only guaranteed within the moment, for it allowed him to always physically contact his loved ones, and he was grateful that they were contingent upon other's wills, since it allowed the positive form of his powers to operate within freedom.

When he felt everyone had reached a relatively healthy state of mind, given the circumstances, he let go and the others followed suit. No evidence of the Sun's light remained at that point, yet the brilliant multicolored stars and full amber moon provided adequate light.

Farrah gazed at her friend of seven years and she gently rubbed his upper arm. "My dear Mahli, don't forget that you have access to more power than Saudade. You will be able to use the full extent of your gift, I believe in you."

Mahli returned her smile. Thank y..." A dazzling light registered in the periphery vision of his left eye and her right eye. They turned their heads forward as they clutched their swords and tightened their horses' reigns.

Mahli clutched on to the hope that his four years of teaching would be enough to withstand the oncoming onslaught. As five minutes passed from existence, he could start to make out the outlines of the monstrosities that flew in the opposing front line.

In his weak state, Saudade was only able to completely pollute the minds of those beings who were completely blameless. Their bodies, being of the same essence as their minds, had transformed upon Saudade's touch. Mahli had arrived up close to a stray one Farrah killed a year ago. Blackened sockets, absent of eyes, stared at him from a fifty foot long skeletal ivory hued body. The featherless animal didn't resurrect. Mahli blinked the image away as his fear converted into anger. These rare creatures, those which remained alive, were under Saudade's control, it wasn't their fault. Yet, they had no choice but to fight back in order to survive.

"Now!", screamed Farrah when the opposition's front line was approximately nine miles away. Farrah and her soldiers rushed around their most essential warrior until he was within their center. A circle of space, with a half mile area, enclosed Mahli. When seven miles remained between the first line of winged creatures and Farrah and her frontline, she gave a subtle sign which was carried downwards by her comrades. The message of the gesture, a left thumb placed against the left flank of their horses and pointed backwards, reached the destination in a matter of seconds. A line of catapulters, hidden in the shadows of their trench, released the first load of projectiles. A sea of jagged ebony rocks, of various sizes, torpedoed towards diseased phoenixes.

The frontline of Saudade's army dove low when they noticed what appeared to be shadows hurtling towards them. The preceding ranks followed suit but it was too late for the fourth and fifth line to avoid the collision. Skulls fractured, spines snapped, and wings ruptured. Their dive revealed Saudade's location to trained eyes.

When five miles remained between their army and Farrah's, ammunition rocketed from the front trench. This time, the army split down the middle and flew off on either side. The rocks crashed into some bodies but the mortal damage wasn't as prominent. Keeping her composure, Farrah threw her cloak off and leapt off her horse. She bade her steed to go.

She kicked back against the ground as she rapidly enacted a series of stretching her arms out and bringing them up against her sides. After three of these movements, she soared into the sky, followed by those within her vicinity. As each rank set their horses free and moved towards the sky, Farrah, now 100 hundred feet in the air, waved a torch that had been within her cloak, and set fire to it. She fervently waved it and the signal could be seen by all. As one, the soldiers who had remained on the ground, threw off their cloaks. They flapped their arms, to completely unfurl and stiffen their previously concealed artificial wings, and joined her in flight.

"Clever", hissed Saudade. He thought, "What materials have they mixed that gave them the ability to do this? If only the army that I've converted hadn't lost their fire. No matter, their beaks and talons will be sufficient. Once I get to Mahli, I will be able to end them all. They were foolish to reveal him so prominently within their midst."

The flame from Farrah's torch went out and she dropped it to the ground as she withdrew her sword. Farrah remained in front since she was the most skilled in physical combat. Able to control their flight with minimal movements, she and her army soared to clash with their opposition.

As the phoenixes' blood mixed with the first rain of human blood, Saudade slowly moved through his soldiers and Farrah's. Their bodies and weapons were no hindrance to him while he was in this form. He didn't have the power to possess a body but he could injure quite a number as he made his way to Mahli.

He glanced back in surprise. His passage, which should have elicited an increase in mental oppression for the humans, seemed to have no effect except to bring him pain from their joyful emotions. He even glanced at a woman, whom he presumed to be their leader, cruelly and confidently smile at him as he passed through her. Fear choked him when he received this expression as he realized Mahli had adequately prepared his comrades.

Saudade tried to avoid the opposing army's bodies as he frantically searched for his nemesis but with horror, he realized that the army was attempting to keep the battle tightly clustered. Mahli, being of the same mind as Saudade, knew his weaknesses. Mahli's friends wouldn't be able to kill him but the pain he incurred from them was powerful. As a nearby human twirled with a phoenix, he angled their bodies to pass through Saudade's smoke like form. Not able to react fast enough, Saudade felt another jolt of pain.

Farrah's army kept their focus, even when a couple of their friends fell, tattered and lifeless to the ground. However, the world seemed to slow for Mahli when, during his moment of relative peace, a phoenix clenched its claws into Farrah. She had thrust a blade through a weak spot in its armored hide, through its diaphragm.

Mahli flew towards Farrah and her assailant. She and her attacker were far above the rest of the fray, seemingly framed by the circumference of the moon. The chilly air rushed past his face as he speedily made his way to the two combatants.

"Interesting", Saudade whispered as he took notice of the scene and smiled. He braved his trek through a multitude of her soldiers to gain a better vantage point and to be away from the surrounding fray. His hope strengthened when he saw a paralyzed and lifeless body, wrapped in an undamaged suit of

flight, float up into the sky.

Farrah tried to break free from the curved tips of the phoenix's four foot long talons, which remained embedded in her plated armor. She retrieved her blade and thrust it clean through the dying beast's bat like arms, which caused its fingers to splay open. Farrah was in comparative safety again as she recovered her blade. She angled her sword downward, stabbed the blade in its diaphragm again and through its vital organs. She swiftly brought her blade into the open as the dead creature flew away, ending that skirmish before Mahli could reach her. The phoenix began to fall a few paces away from the battle. This all happened within seconds. However, to Mahli, it seemed as if

much more time had passed. Saudade's hollow eyes suddenly appeared inches away from Mahli's face.

Without missing a beat, Saudade grabbed onto Mahli's head, the only being that he could grab onto while he was in this smoke like form. Mahli's painful emotions and memories flooded into his oppressor's starving soul. His was the only mind that Saudade could gain sustenance from. As soon as his body became physical and as he regained a portion of his frightening speed, he grabbed Mahli's sword and viciously twisted Mahli's neck; Mahli's arms which had been rising for Saudade's head, became limp. Farrah screamed as tears broke from their barriers and as her nausea punched her.

"You weren't fast enough," Saudade jeered as he stretched Mahli's rigid arms out and clutched his chest. Aided by the creature's strength, they shot towards the upper atmosphere, far too fast for a pursuing Farrah.

A paralyzed Mahli was awoken when Saudade punched him in the gut. Saudade grinned when Mahli struggled to cough up blood. The monster wrapped his legs around Mahli and used them to prevent them from rising any higher.

Saudade triumphantly stated via their connected minds, "We're up where the oxygen is thin. It's fortunate that bodily injuries ultimately have no effect on me, no matter what state I'm in. Saudade sardonically sent the next thought, "Don't worry my dear Mahli, I believe in you." Mahli's eyes teared up and froze upon meeting the thin air. His oppressor had received the memories and feelings, as they pertained to Farrah.

"I know that you will return me to my former glory", Saudade reassured his incapacitated captive. He placed his hands on Mahli's head and before long, the monster's powers returned in full. Saudade placed himself on Mahli's back and steered him back towards the earth.

They shot towards a stunned Farrah. As they entered the portion of the atmosphere which contained more oxygen, Mahli coughed up the blood which he couldn't before. Unable to match their speed, Farrah got grabbed by Saudade. The monster brought Farrah up to the region, where he had regained his full abilities. Her thoughts warred against an oppression she had never experienced before.

She tried to lift her sword as she angrily stared at the monstrosity but physical strength now completely failed her. The blade fell from trembling fingers. Even if she was at her optimum health, she would be no match against Saudade's strength and speed now; even at this moment she knew this but she wasn't going to give up. There was more at stake here than herself.

Saudade's mind entered Mahli's, "Amazing, even as I'm holding on to her, she's resisting. All it took was one touch to shatter your previous loved ones' minds Mahli. You have truly done well in your attempts to protect her and the rest of this army. However, I will completely break them, starting with her. I can tell that she means the most to you. I've realized that pain is so much more effective when you can hope against the inevitable, only for that hope to be proven false within the moment.

That's why I've let your hope and the pain within your mind to remain. I want you to experience the ultimate torture."

He grabbed onto Farrah's head and caused her oppressive feelings to amplify. She fought against his attacks. She thought of her army down below and of Mahli. Hope miraculously blossomed within her freezing body as she felt failure's vulnerability and she resisted Saudade's onslaught. She gave Mahli a smile of reassurance.

An icy electric current, not having anything to do with the surrounding air, shocked Farrah from within. She tried to keep her smile for Mahli but it slowly faded as her mind fractured again. Saudade had allowed her to feel victory in order to snatch it away from her. A memory which Mahli had healed, an experience which took place when she was thirteen, became uncoupled within her mind from the healer's mending.

She could feel and see her widowed father's hands wrap over her throat as she saw him force his sexual frustrations upon her. She struggled to breathe as he continued to press himself further into her.

Farrah's painful emotions overflowed and

burst through the dams which she had erected within her mind. Her will to fight back died.

"The human mind can only take so much", Saudade proclaimed with a sadistic pleasure. The monster continued to flood Farrah's mind even when she went into a heart attack. In under a minute, she went limp and one last icy breath left her body. The murderer forced his captives and himself downwards, after he angled them away from the ongoing battle.

Saudade laid Mahli on the ground. He laughed as he set Farrah's corpse next to Mahli. "You failed her", the monster said with a feigned disappointment. Her glazed eyes stared back into Mahli's weeping ones. The creature continued, "Just like you will fail the rest of your friends." Mahli turned his eyes to see Saudade turn to the nearby battle. Just as he was about to leap from the ground to the air combatants, he froze. It was difficult for Mahli to look from this angle but it appeared as if his oppressor looked confused.

A small white bird flew over a stunned Saudade and his eyes followed it as it landed on Mahli's chest. An indescribably warm sensation filled Mahli and seemed to overflow from his pores.

He had never seen this creature before but as soon as it had alighted on him, he knew who it was. It appeared to have a small birthmark of a lion upon its chest and the bird seemed to be smiling at him with a loving approval. His eyes remained focused on that bird as victory was assured to him. He now knew that he was not truly paralyzed, the monster could only affect a person's thoughts and could not directly injure anyone. His belief in his injury was powerful yet it was not true.

The monster and he were of the same mind and he had matched his speed before; when he first grabbed onto him when his painful emotions were returned to him by the monster, on the day his family died. Mahli remembered Farrah's assurances that he could defeat Saudade, he could match his strength, no she assured him that he, being his nemesis's originator, could surpass it. He could hear her voice through his memory, "I believe in you."

This moment of healing lasted a couple of moments, yet it seemed to last an hour. The bird flew away before Saudade could advance upon it. Another unfamiliar experience froze Saudade. An explosion erupted from the ground about two miles ahead of the battle. Saudade turned his face again. "Impossible", whispered the murderer in horror.

Sentient flames rose from the earth and into the sky. Incorrupt ones still existed. Mahli had never seen phoenixes like these. Their scarlet and flaxen flames were especially vibrant and these phoenixes appeared to be much larger than the ones he had seen. They were so numerous. They approached the combatants who had ceased fighting because of their shock. Some of the healthy phoenixes unthreateningly grabbed the humans to take them to safety, while others simultaneously attacked Saudade's soldiers. Mahli tenderly closed his dear friend's eyes.

Breaking from his stupor, Saudade narrowly missed Mahli's grasp. Instinctively, he ran forward, with Mahli keeping pace, just a few steps behind. "No!", Saudade screamed.

As they approached the canopy of air combatants, it appeared that the phoenixes were flying in slow motion to Mahli. He was almost at the speed of thought's doorstep. An additional burst of confidence erupted within him. The combatants of the air froze in the healer's vision when he and his assailant arrived beneath it.

Mahli grabbed onto Saudade's head as he transferred copies of his uplifting emotions and the attached memories into the monster. The monster fell to his knees as he whimpered. Saudade's strength of resistance was disappearing fast. He tried to turn his head but it was held firmly in place. The phoenixes slowly started to move again. He swiveled his vision sideways and was frightened when he couldn't see his enemy within his peripheral vision. The battle had remained stationary over Mahli as light started to shine forth from the monster.

"Who was that creature?", Saudade cried as he thought of that peculiar white bird and as warmth continued to flood his soul.

"The messenger of a king from the other side of the world", answered Mahli as he continued his work. "And these magnificent creatures are a faction of his army. Farrah's army will win."

As the last bit of night escaped from Saudade's soul, he exploded into a luminous being. It was as if day had arrived, yet only the diseased phoenixes shielded their vision.

As Mahli let go and fell to his knees, his speed returned to normal. The transformed entity spoke, "I know that I cannot exist. It would be selfish of me to stay alive. Thanks to the logic which you left me with, I know that as a being of unadulterated uplifting feelings, I would ultimately do harm rather than good. To feel compassion, one must know pain, because it is through hurt that one has the ability to feel sympathy towards another. To truly love outside of one's self, one must have the choice whether to esteem another in one's own heart or not. In this world, as it is in its present state, the absence of pain doesn't equate happiness, rather it gives only a mirror image, a corrupted version that has no essence because it is through pain that one knows the value of joy. Take care Mahli and continue your work." The entity turned his head to face Mahli. He kindly smiled before he instantly vanished. The entity had sacrificed its life for everyone. It was over. Mahli sobbed as he smiled.

Mahli looked above and realized that the king's phoenixes were keeping the diseased ones at bay. Mahli knew what to do next. He entered the speed of thought again as he propelled himself from the ground. He didn't need his wings to lift himself into the air anymore, yet he used this invention of Farrah's as he soared from diseased phoenix to diseased phoenix. After a corrupted phoenix received a touch from the unseen rescuer, the creature burst into flame, evidence of its returned health. After Mahli finished his healing in the sky, he sped towards Farrah. He knew that he couldn't heal physical injuries nor could he resurrect the dead, not even the diseased phoenixes who had lost their lives. Yet he wanted to hold his dear friend.

As he held Farrah's cold still body in his embrace, his back to everyone else, he whispered, "Even with a relationship as strong as ours was, I never told you 'I love you'. I know you knew it but one of the things I regret is that I never got to directly tell you. I love you, I love you so much Farrah, I wish you were here with me, I'm so sorry, I should have tried harder, maybe you could still be alive." He paused a few moments as his body continued to shake and as his tears continued to freely flow. He gently rubbed her rahki bracelet, intact around her right wrist, and kissed the top of her head gingerly. "Saudade is gone Farrah, he's finally gone. You would've loved to know of the beautiful creature that helped me and of the magnificent phoenixes." Mahli held his dead friend for a minute more before a blinding electrical blue light pierced his vision and soul.

As his vision swam, he saw the image of an exceptionally large ebony lion. He had an unshakeable sense that this winged lion was incredibly kind and full of love. Suddenly he had an awareness of who this was: the king from the other side of the world. His name appeared within his mind. As Mahli's vision adjusted, Farrah gasped.

* Side Note

Out of respect for the fallen, the Mohabbat tribe had designated the fallen city of Khushee as, 'Viraag.' However, it was a superstitious tribe, the Dara Hua tribe, which had staked the skeletons as a monument for what they deemed a cursed place. This clan had arrived at this place soon after it and its inhabitants had burned.

<u>REUNION</u>

Remembrance

&

Inspiration

About *Reunion*

Out of all my stories in *Sanity's War*, this one is ultimately the most tragic. However, it contains doses of humor and this story is arguably the most inspirational. Welcome to *Reunion: Remembrance and Inspiration.*

"Do you remember that time when you took me on a canoe ride through Alvice? We were the only ones on the water then. It was in the summer, yet the temperature was delicate. No cloud appeared within our vicinity and the constellations were like twinkling neon lights in the jet-black sky. You knew how to navigate through the channel yet you pretended to be an amateur, in order to lift my spirits even further."

As his friend relayed the shared memory, Ray found himself in the city of Alvice with her. *Crystal's raven hued hair had not yet adopted a premature white streak and graceful lines had not yet formed upon her richly brown skin. Tears flowed from her eyes yet they accompanied laughter, unlike an hour before that moment.*

A white collared shirt and ebony shorts clung to his drenched frame as warm saltwater dripped from them.

"I fell", Ray spoke with feigned shock and embarrassment.

"You think?", Crystal gently teased.

Ray grinned at her and looked past the bow, to look at the place that he had landed upon faking his loss in balance. Ripples travelled through the crystal clear ocean's surface. He raised his eyes and observed the people on each side of the waterway. Most of them displayed various expressions of displeasure over Ray's shenanigans. Yet one person, who appeared to be around 60 years old, held the jester's attention. After a few moments of contemplation, Ray opened his delicate smile into a wide grin and dove into the water.

Ray kept his eyes on Crystal as he pulled the canoe and its occupant towards a destination, which was only about 20 feet away. Crystal and her friend tied the boat to the dock and made their way to the gentleman. The man with neatly trimmed gray hair and a well-groomed pencil thin mustache wiped his eyes, as hearty laughter leapt from his mouth with lessening frequency.

"Bonsoir," chimed the amused spectator as pleasant laughter still shone forth from his eyes. "We are delighted that you have decided to join us." All those within earshot gave expressions which begged to differ with his statement. Most onlookers there still looked on with varying degrees of disapproval at the duo who traversed through the water, as if the boy and girl were headlines of breaking catastrophic news. Ray kindly chuckled at the guests' expressions as Crystal continued to beam, neither would let their spirits fall from on high. The tuxedoed man ignored the grimaces, agape mouths, and cold stares which surrounded him as he spoke, "This way please."

The balding man decked in lavender led the young adults in between extravagantly adorned customers, and to a scarlet clothed table that stood only a few paces ahead. One of the few smiling gentleman within the vicinity winked at Ray and Crystal as they passed. After the man in lavender sat the friends down, he took two intricately woven scarlet napkins from the table. He unwound them, flourished them in the air, and neatly placed one upon each of their laps. He continued to speak, after he swiftly lit the candle at the center of their table.

"I will promptly be back with towels for you, monsieur, and menus for you both. I will personally serve you. My name is Lafayette."

Crystal and Ray watched in amazement as the kind man walked with gusto and disappeared into the indoor section of the restaurant. Ray and

Crystal's focus travelled to the banner which hung over the rear door, just to make doubly sure. Gold letters stitched into the cloth spelled Lafayette's. A smiling man adorned in a black tuxedo speedily exited to take the order of a woman seated closest to the door.

Crystal pushed her empty dessert plate away. Ray deftly brought a piece of his chocolate chip embedded cannoli to his mouth as he signed their check with his other hand. Her torso, adorned by a canary-yellow t-shirt, leaned forwards as she brought her elbows to the tabletop. Crystal laid her chin within her cupped palms and she rested her eyes upon Ray's. A cozy breeze twirled the few stray curly strands of Crystal's shoulder length hair. The gentle breeze rustled the split ends which appeared to stand, at attention, upon Ray's headful of red-orange hair. Her gesture of admiration caught his attention. Ray gently placed the fork and pen down as he aligned his pupils with Crystal's. The orange flame, which danced on top

of the deep blue candle's head, reflected in their eyes.

"Thank you for spending time with me tonight," Crystal uttered with an endearing smile. She looked towards the check and tip, "Thank you again for paying for this..." she looked towards the canoe, "...and that", she finished.

Ray responded, "Spending time with you far outweighs any material costs".

Crystal's goldenrod crucifix hung in the air as she leaned towards her friend and tenderly kissed his cheek. The ends of his mustache rose higher as his grin widened. With his baritone voice, he verbalized a phrase which he had given to her twice before during that night, "Happy Birthday, Crystal."

After they shook hands with Lafayette, they traveled at a leisurely pace towards their college campus. The canoe's gentle traverse through the water lulled Crystal to sleep. After they docked, Ray offered to carry her since she looked exhausted. He gingerly assured her that the task wouldn't be too much for him. She smiled and gratefully nodded. She positioned herself at his back as she wrapped her arms around his *shoulders and her legs around his torso. He carried her through the short trip that lay between the campus's marina and her dorm, not caring what looks he received from passerby. She dozed off sometime during that brief journey.*

When he arrived at the door to her dorm room he gently intoned, "We're here sleepyhead." They embraced each other before they wished each other a peaceful night's sleep.

"Ray?" Crystal's question, gently spoken, retuned Ray from that memory. He allowed his vision to focus on Crystal's as he returned her smile. He looked at the rest of his friends, all of them were here. Six sat upon the six chairs surrounding his table while the rest stood within his dining room. Josia and Francesca (childhood sweethearts and the first to get married within the group), were the only ones who wore matching hats for this occasion.

Ray's closed lip smile split into a grin as his friends sang a tune in unison. Crystal set each note free with utter grace. Josia and Francesca hit all the notes...except the correct ones at the precise moments. The others sang somewhere in between those two spectrums. Everyone sang with unhinged joy and palpable love.

When Ray's friends finished singing, the woman who sat closest to him raised her glass of sparkling cider and shouted the chorus of the song. "Happy Birthday, Ray!" His other friends raised their glasses at this toast. George, who had been quite thirsty, sheepishly smiled at Ray as the rest drank down the golden and carbonated liquid. Ray jokingly shook his head in disappointment as he beamed at his friend with the bushy hazel beard.

Music blared from the connecting living room with such suddenness that Ray and a couple others jumped, as if they had woken from a dream in which they had been falling. George was the only one to have actually jumped out of his seat, yet he landed upon his feet with finesse. He twirled away from the table and slid one of his cowboy booted feet away from himself. As they all laughed, Carlito stepped away from the record player, which he had switched on, and he started to dance alongside George.

"You always had the best taste in music, Ray," Carlito yelled over the music. "Well, almost always...I mean sometimes. My musical tastes are usually better but this song is rockin'!" Carlito winked as Ray and the rest laughed at his good-natured jests.

Crystal tenderly took Ray's hand into hers and she led him towards the dancing comedians. As Ray, Crystal, George, and Carlito jubilantly danced alongside each other, the rest walked towards the unofficial dance floor. They continued to dance as the next soul song played. This time, the friends paired off in couples. Since there was an uneven number, George volunteered to continue solo. He danced with the air in such an elegant way that it seemed as if he had been dancing alongside an individual who just happened to be invisible.

About midway through the song, Ray's eyes began to fill with tears. His dancing partner's smile wavered as she too began to cry. The lemon colored wallpaper lost its luster. The wooden floorboards appeared more worn than before. The lights flickered and returned with less power. Ray embraced Crystal as her silent cry escalated into a sob. Their friends continued to dance, yet he saw that they were weeping as well. They and the music began to fade as he whispered, "Please don't go." He looked down at Crystal as he softly entreated, "Just one minute more".

Crystal met Ray's gaze as she let loose a phrase which burst with anguish, "You left us."

Ray muttered, "I caused you all so much pain. I am not going to hurt any of you again."

Crystal softly expressed, "Stop doing this to yourself."

He let Crystal go and smiled despite his pain. He assured her, "Most likely, you've all but forgotten me anyways. This is for the best." A translucent Crystal shook her head in denial and disappointment, yet not with malice. Their friends rapidly slowed their dance and froze. She wiped her eyes, which still streamed, and instantly vanished with the rest of Ray's friends.

Ray shook the corrupted memory away as he came back to the time at hand. He focused again upon the photo in front of him. The photograph featured eleven people in their forties, brimming with joy and looking directly at the camera. They were clustered on either side of Ray, except for Crystal. She had stood behind him with her arms wrapped around his chest. It was a photograph which became a decade old on this day. So much had changed since his last birthday party.

After a few minutes transpired into history,

Ray flipped the page and saw a thirteen year old in the fore-ground. His daughter had an open-mouthed smile and teary eyes. Her complexion was a mixture of Scottish and Indian. Ray's memory traveled to the point right before his daughter captured this photo.

"Hey, look at this", Isabelle shouted to her parents in the rear seats. Ray and Jiyah, in the midst of their laughter, turned to the camera which their eighteen year old daughter had stretched out before them. Not a moment later, she snapped the photograph. Her parents continued to laugh as they wiped their eyes.

Isabelle turned to the smiling driver and questioned with pretended disappointment, "Miss Rebecca, you really don't think my stories are funny?"

"They are...amusing," the navigator teased.

Isabelle melodramatically set her mouth agape and comically widened her eyes in feigned shock. She stared at the woman with raven hued dreadlocks.

Rebecca kept her eyes ahead as she grinned and revealed her pearly white teeth. She tenderly spoke, "Dear, you're missing the scenery."

"Well, I deliberately saved my funniest story for last and this one is true," Isabelle assured them. She puffed out her back and with the theatricality of a movie trailer announcer, she stated, "It is a grand tale, an account of an event which took place many moons ago." She resumed talking in her normal voice, "Truth be told, this narrative is brief and it happened this morning."

Isabelle spoke again with a dramatic voice, "As you know, before the sun rose, I made coffee. What I neglected to tell all of you is that I was feeling particularly adventurous. So I allowed not quite one, not two, nor three, but four heaping spoonfuls of sugar slide into my delightful beverage. As I was sipping heartily, I couldn't help but notice how startlingly salty my coffee was."

Ray, Jiyah, and Rebecca howled with laughter. Isabelle burst out laughing from their contagious guffaws as she deftly aimed her camera lens at the driver.

"Got you!", Isabelle cheerfully uttered as she clicked the shutter button.

Rebecca's laughter persisted as she stated, "Now I remember what I forgot to do. I knew that I should have labelled those twin jars as soon as I filled them."

It took some time for their laughter to dial down. As their laughter subsided, Rebecca whispered as she decelerated the vehicle, "Do you all see that? Face front Isabelle."

Isabelle, who had angled herself so she could see her parents and Rebecca at the same time, turned her head to face the plains ahead. She uncrossed her legs as she turned and placed her feet on the floor. "Wow", she whispered.

Isabelle pushed her heels off the soil as she stood on the tips of her toes, to hasten the time between contact. She had never been so close to her favorite creature. The giraffe kept bending her neck until her nose connected to Isabelle's.

The three people there reacted in various ways to this very moment. The trainer had her hands clasped together in appreciation. Jiyah had placed her hand above her heart as she teared up with an overwhelming sense of awe. Ray, who had made sure the sound and flash were off before they embarked on this journey (as to not startle any creatures that they may have come across within the preserve), snapped a photo of the moment.

"Here you go, you slender necked beauty", Isabelle gingerly whispered as she slowly raised a hand full of giraffe treats to the animal's mouth. The giraffe happily scooped the kibbles with her tongue. Afterwards, the animal strolled to rejoin the other giraffes that were heading to feast on foliage.

Ray turned the page to see the photo that he took eleven years ago. The setting sun illuminated Isabelle and the giraffe, with golden and crimson hues. As weariness continued to eat its way through Ray's opposition for sleep, he brought his photo album to a close.

As he walked from his living room, he recognized the similarity of the flames' shadows to dancing individuals. Light burst from the overhanging chandelier as Ray crossed into his dining room. "Surprise", the crowd shouted. "You didn't think that we'd forget your birthday, did you?", questioned Carlito. "No way, Raymond!", chimed Francesca.

Ray saw himself and Crystal enter the dining

room, shivering from the winter air that they had just escaped. Ray witnessed his agape mouth transform into a grand grin as his tears of joy replaced tears of sorrow. Crystal rubbed his shoulder as her eyes moistened upon witnessing gratefulness overwhelm him. "Sit down Ray, your cake is almost ready" proclaimed Josia as he pulled a chair out for his friend.

It was custom for them to have one blow out the candles for the first event of any birthday party. The tradition was supposed to grant the individual's wishes so they could be enjoyed throughout the party and the rest of the year. This was all done for fun.

As the memory jumped ahead a few minutes, Ray watched the younger versions of his friends and himself laugh. For a moment he forgot what they were laughing about but when a decorated cake materialized onto the table, he remembered. They were guffawing over the forty candles which Greg had placed into Ray's birthday cake and the fact that those candles had relit after each time that Ray had blown them out.

Ray slowly walked towards the vivid scene to tenderly place a hand on Crystal's shoulder, yet his hand passed through her. The vision vanished as he returned from his memory. He looked beyond his dining room window and acknowledged that his scrawny bended tree looked like a giraffe bending its neck. He witnessed someone run towards his home as the sun set.

The individual stopped next to his tree. The bundled figure doubled over and gasped from the run. When the person rose, gloved hands still upon knees, the person's mahogany hued irises stared into Ray's emerald ones. The individual who stood outside pulled down the ebony collar and scarlet scarf that covered her mouth, as she displayed a brilliant smile. In one breath, she proclaimed, "It's me, Isabelle, I'm here Dad!"

Ray turned his head from the fabricated vision. When he looked ahead again, Isabelle stood indoors and before him. Her jacket was open to reveal a blood soaked shirt and an open wound, which went through her heart. "You couldn't save me, you failed all of us", Isabelle shouted through her sobs. Ray shut his eyes and shook his head as he unsuccessfully held back tears. When he re-opened his eyes, Isabelle was gone. He departed his dimly lit and dusty dining room to collapse onto his double sized bed.

Though his body was exhausted, Ray's mind kept him from sleep and agony continued to consume him from within. Pain's power lessened when he thought back to a night when an extraordinarily attractive woman stood beneath the frame of their bedroom door.

He switched his bedroom light on to see her more clearly. The ends of her sienna pigmented hair laid across the center of her back. Intricate henna designs decorated her arms, hands, and bare feet. Ray felt his heart grow light and jump as his dimpled cheeks grew hot. He arose and approached his wife.

As love, excitement, and nervousness twirled within her soul, Jiyah brought a trembling hand to brush a strand off of Ray's forehead. She stared into the emerald rimmed windows of his soul as she whispered with an immense smile, "I love you, Raymond, Ailbe O'Sullivan."

"I love you too Jiyah, Ravati O'Sullivan", Ray responded.

Jiyah tenderly pressed her lips onto Ray's. They continued to kiss each other as they held each other in an embrace. After some moments had passed, they parted so that she could remove his tuxedo and he would be able to help her slip out of her wedding dress.

When every article of clothing had been removed, they took a few steps back to admire each other's bodies. It was their first time seeing each other like this. "You are so beautiful", Ray whispered, his voice affected by a medley of elated emotions.

"And you are exceptionally attractive", Jiyah declared with a voice that trembled from a plethora of euphoric sentiments.

As they spent a minute within an embrace, they felt the rhythm of their breaths, the warmth emanate from each other, and the beats of one another's hearts. They brushed their lips together and against each other's necks. Ray gently ran his hands over her arms, chest, stomach and back while Jiyah did the same for him. When they laid intertwined in their bed, they tenderly rubbed one another's feet, legs, their torsos, and the areas in between. They sporadically broke from kissing to spend many moments looking into each other's eyes, to survey one another's bodies, and to speak words of affirmation to each other.

Before they progressed further in their passionate yet tender lovemaking, Ray grabbed a transparent rubber contraceptive from the side table. He and Jiyah had agreed to wait at least one year to bring a child into this world.

After they brought each other to ecstasy's peak, Ray switched off the light. In moments, they fell asleep within each other's caress.

Ray blinked the approximately twenty-five year old memory away as sleep finally overtook him.

Three hours later, he awoke in shivers and sweat, despite the tepid air. He clutched his sheets, curled into a fetal position and gasped as pain crippled his spirit. He attempted to hold his grip onto favorable memories, yet they began to slip through his fingers, like the details of a dream when one awakens.

A couple minutes later, he stood before his bathroom mirror and held his reflection's gaze. Ray whispered, "If you could overcome these urges time after time, you will be able to triumph again. Fight against this, come on!"

He clutched the edges of his sink counter as his hope and joy continued to drain from his soul.

With instinct, he landed a punch upon the counter as he tried to focus on his fleeing heartwarming memories. Yet death, who had left him alone for a year, continued to amplify its desire for him. He released a weary exhale, "Help".

Ray removed his undershirt and looked down upon the marks that weaved across his torso. Upon his freckled shoulders, arms, and pecs, were scarlet scars and prominent bruises. His floodgates of cerebral resistance gave in to the deluge of sorrow.

His mind became overcome with instinct as he
brought his fists to his body with a ferocity unlike any time before.

Three minutes later, he spit out blood for the fourth time as he collapsed to the floor. He saw the vision of his dying daughter again. "You failed us all", she shouted. It was an imagined moment, fueled by guilt. Yet Ray's shattered mind accepted the vision's representation of fallacy as truth. He pulled the cabinet's bottom drawer to retrieve a pair of scissors.

With great difficulty and a suppressed cry of pain, he heaved himself off the floor. "Look at yourself," Ray hissed through his blood smeared teeth. He wiped his tear streaked eyes and cheeks. "You are pathetic", he jeered to himself.

His shortcomings cycled through his mind as he pressed the edge of a scissor blade to his skin. He looked into the mirror as he etched lines and when he finished, he dropped his scissors. His blood flowed from the inscribed message, to his stomach, down his legs, and onto the tiles. The words across his chest spelt, "Failure". Ray sardonically laughed as he resumed to weep.

He trekked through the snow that the blizzard from last week had left in its wake. He still ached from the assault which he enacted five minutes ago yet he was determined. Ray stumbled countless times in the snow covered countryside but he marched on. He clutched his jacket and hood tighter as snowflakes twirled towards him, since he didn't want to die by winter's caress. As he approached his destination that laid approximately fifteen minutes away, Ray recalled a twelve year old event which took place in the city of Aayush.

He traced her beautiful brown arms as he locked his lips with hers. Ray ignored the unease which gnawed at his gut and heart as he undid his lover's ruby red sari. They collapsed onto a mattress as they helped each other out of the rest of their garments. Ray paused to remove a rubber protector from its wrapper.

As he continued to make love to her, a hollow sensation escalated along with his guilt. Yet, he proceeded and his fondles brought her to the peak. After he reached the summit, he noticed how truly meaningless making love felt when it was purely physical. Nausea inflicted Ray as he fully felt the shattered sacred bond between him and his wife.

Ray quickly got up and put his clothes on as he apologized profusely to the woman whom he just met. The thirty year old woman didn't reply to her customer as she got dressed. Not long after Ray stepped outside the room, screams ensnared his attention.

He rushed to the end of the shanty building's corridor. He hesitated a few seconds while he stood beside the entrance of the room which he ran to. Yet his debilitating fear was overthrown when the girl shrieked again. Ray threw open the curtain that served as the room's door.

A middle-aged man had his pants down around his ankles and his hands around the throat of a partially undressed underage girl. The abuser rapidly threw his head around and Ray kicked his skull. After the man stumbled onto his back, Ray sent his foot into the abuser's jaw, which rendered the abuser unconscious. Ray grabbed the pre-teen's shirt and quickly helped her into it. The weeping girl wrapped her arms around Ray's neck as he took her into his arms.

As Ray ran past the open office door, he ignored the manager's vehement protests that accompanied his threats for violence. When Ray entered the night, he continued to sprint as fast as he could through the congested streets and he dodged the few men who tried to grab him or the feverish girl.

When he arrived at the nearest emergency room, two miles away, he collapsed to his knees. He still clutched onto her as he fell onto his back and blacked out.

Ray awoke to a doctor who looked down at him. The doctor stated that Ray had been out for a couple of hours but other than some minor bruises, from his fall, and dehydration, he was fine. The doctor handed him a water bottle which Ray emptied without taking a breath.

"I'm afraid that there's no gentle way of saying this", Doctor Khan stated. "The little girl you brought in doesn't have a lot of time left. She's asked to see you when you're ready."

Ray shot up and sped to the young girl's hospital room. Ray could feel her dangerously high temperature and shivers as she clutched onto him. "What's your name", Ray inquired as he grasped onto a hope which defied reality.

"Neha", the little girl responded.

He listened to her weakening voice as she revealed that she was an orphan, sold off two years ago by her uncle and aunt who lived in poverty. Her tears soaked Ray's shirt as she told him that her hope and her prayers died long ago until he arrived to rescue her. Ray failed to fight back tears when she called him an angel, the only true family she had left, and asked if it was okay if she called him Dad. He assured her that it was okay and he called her his daughter.

Ray assured her that he would take care of her and help her become whoever she wanted to be. "What would you like to do when you grow up", Ray asked her.

"I want to save every child, just like you

saved me", Neha replied. Ray noticed that throughout their conversation, he could feel her fever increase, despite the pills and cooling pads that the nurse had given her.

Ray let the girl go as he stated, "Here, I notice that you're sleepy and cold, let me tuck you in." The little girl whose immune system was compromised continued to shiver but she smiled as Ray pulled the covers around her. He sat in the chair next to the bed as he held her hand and he noticed that her temperature was deadly hot. "Neha, what is an activity you enjoy?'

"Dancing", she replied through quivering lips.

"You may not believe this but I love dancing too, Neha. Since we're both tired, we can dance together within our imaginations, that is, if you would like to dance with me".

Neha nodded as she beamed up at him.

"Okay, Neha, let's close our eyes and set the scene. What do you see?"

"Look, Dad. I see my favorite creatures, fireflies. Do you see them too?", Neha slowly whispered.

"I see them too, Neha. There are so many

beautiful fireflies flying around in this cool night, a night lit with magnificent multicolored stars and a brilliant full moon." He imagined a plethora of twinkling lights gracefully moving around and above them. It was as if they had found themselves in the land of infant stars; stars which awaited to ascend to the night's ceiling. Neha's caramel colored eyes reflected the blinking gold lights.

Ray saw a breeze rustle the leaves and limbs of evergreen trees as he felt its warmth secure him. In this place, he held out his hand to Neha and he vocalized instructions as he led her in a simplified waltz. Not long into the dance within their minds, she fell asleep. Ray attempted to ignore Neha's labored breaths and swelling fever as exhaustion carried him into sleep.

An insistent siren awoke him about three hours later. Ray sat up in shock as he saw someone approaching him and Neha. His heartbeat quickened as he looked at Neha's heart monitor. Ray embraced Neha. Despite Doctor Khan's gentle pleas for Ray to let her go, he held on to her as he felt her body turn cold.

Ray's soul was numb as a five feet and three inch by two feet casket descended into the earth. His ears were deaf to the pastor who gave a eulogy for a girl whose life he never experienced. Ray tried to feel grateful for those that were here. His family, friends, and a few of the strangers who helped fundraise Neha's funeral, accompanied him. Yet, only sorrow interrupted his numbness since all he could continue to recognize was that, besides him, those who attended this funeral were all strangers to Neha. Guilt collided into his heart as he realized the stranger he had slept with might have been trafficked in her youth, just like Neha. Perhaps she had a similar personality full of hope, before it was shattered by decades of strangers' desires.

Ray turned to his wife and though he tried to look into her eyes, his shame compelled him to look down. "Jiyah, when we get home, I need to tell you the truth", he stuttered.

Ray's surroundings focused in his awareness as he came back to his present time. Ray pulled out his stopwatch and noted that about five more minutes were going to pass before he heard the whistle of whom he wanted to meet. He looked down at the path he had kneeled at approximately fifteen minutes ago. His mind returned to the day of the funeral.

He witnessed his wife as she sat at the edge of their bed. Compassion and apprehension emanated from Jiyah as she awaited to hear her husband give a true account of what happened during his business trip. He was apprehensive about being the cause of his wife's grief and he was terrified of the fatal repercussions, yet he knew he had to speak the truth. Time skipped ahead and Ray's wife wept as Ray finished his account. Unspoken words separated them for what seemed like an eternity during those moments.

A whistle reached Ray's ears. A memory of separation plunged into his mind:

A judge turned the divorce papers towards him. He stared at Jiyah's signature as he yearned to wake from this reality. Though Ray felt regret, he knew pleading even once more would be no use. He barely steadied his hand enough to sign the papers. After Jiyah and Ray left the office, they never saw each other again.

The whistles became louder and more frequent. His mind retuned to the day he told her the truth, a month before the divorce:

Ray acted upon instinct as he moved in to hug his wife goodbye. Jiyah took a couple steps back as she shook her head. "I'm sorry, I can't touch you", she stammered apologetically.

"Goodbye", Ray whispered as he failed to restrain the tears he had reigned in moments ago.

"This isn't easy for me either, you know", Jiyah stated with more anger than she had wanted to display. She turned her head in time to hide her face as she burst into tears.

"Goodbye, Ray," Jiyah spoke through her disintegrating composure. She picked her suitcase up and walked through the open door, to meet the taxi which awaited her and Isabelle.

Isabelle walked towards her Dad and gave him an embrace. Ray could feel despair, fury, and disappointment emanate from her. She quickly followed her Mom without saying anything. It was the last time he saw his daughter.

Ray rested his head upon the path. "I'm sorry Jiyah", he whispered. He yearned for the moment of decapitation and the moment his head would crush. By the time the train rounded the bend, it would be too late for the conductor to brake.

Ray recalled calling Crystal the day after Jiyah and he cut their bond. He didn't tell her everything then yet he did reveal that he had divorced his wife and that it was his fault. He asked if it was okay to meet.

A week later, Crystal and Ray sat on his back porch steps. The air was crisp and the breeze was light. As he told her all the details, he realized she didn't display any negative emotions towards him. Yet, his voice increasingly shook with a plethora of pain as he went on. Crystal placed a gloved hand into her friend's, to let him know that her love for him was unbreakable.

When Ray finished telling what led to his divorce, Crystal spoke. "I can't imagine the pain you're going through Ray. You making love to someone other than your wife was completely wrong yet you know that and you feel regret for what you did. Learn from your past wrong but do not dwell in the pain that it brings. I know it's easier said than done but do not give up on yourself because I won't give up on you.

You said that Jiyah and Isabelle won't contact you but try again after some more time has passed. Respect their space. You already know that they are going through immense pain as well.

Maybe you can become friends again with Jiyah, sometime down the road. And Isabelle is still your daughter, nothing will change that and I have faith that she will come around.

It's important to remember that you did something amazing in the district of Aayush as well. You took a dying girl and you gave her hope when she had none. You provided her with love when she felt cruelty. You are not a failure Ray, you are amazing. My dear friend, I love you and nothing will change that."

He initiated a hug and the friends held on to each other for a long time. Despite his tears, he smiled broadly. Warmth had returned to reside with the pain in Ray's soul.

Crystal's phone buzzed. She briefly prayed for Ray before she let him go and inquired, "One more thing. Tell me the truth, are you suicidal right now?"

"No.", Ray said with assurance.

Crystal kissed Ray's forehead, stood up and helped her friend to his feet. She looked at her new text, a message which announced that the last person had recently sneaked through the front door and that everyone was ready. "Let's go inside, I'm feeling a bit chilly", Crystal stated as she masked her excitement. It was Ray's fortieth birthday.

Almost three years from that day, Ray and Crystal spoke for the final time. Crystal's voice reached forth from the receiver, "What will this accomplish, Ray? Please don't do this."

Ray replied, "It's too late, I already moved."

Crystal responded, "Please tell me where you moved. Don't you dare cut yourself from the people who love you."

"This will be better for you and the rest of our friends, Ray replied. "I can no longer feel joy, Crystal, I can't even fake happiness anymore". It's been a year and I've felt pain during almost every waking moment. I'm getting worse, despite everyone who has viscously fought for me. I refuse to allow my pain to hurt any one of you anymore. This will cause pain to those whom still love me the same, like you, but eventually everyone will all but forget me. You will know peace again."

Crystal raised her voice, "Ray, pain is a hallmark of true love. The basis of real friendship is not the happiness one can bring to another. The foundation of authentic friendship is love for each other, no matter how intense or frequent the pain a friend may be experiencing. I love you, please..."

Ray interrupted her, "I'm sorry Crystal. You will understand that what I'm doing is for the best. Goodb..."

Crystal cut in, "Wait Ray! Did you forget the poem that you wrote for me?" Before Ray could respond, Crystal gracefully sang, despite her tears:

'There is sadness in your eyes and in mine
but allow the love that I have for you to outshine
the demon within your
mind,
as your words and embraces have pushed back
against mine.
A new beginning is born every day, begun at the
moment when the sun
trickles
and then pours its light into the sky.
Truth be told, every moment is a miracle,
an opportunity for honest renewal.'

Crystal pleaded "Don't give up Ray, I know this is difficult but you will be able to cope again. Let me and our friends continue to help you. You need..."

Ray had bit his lip, in an unsuccessful attempt at preventing himself from sobbing. A moment after his friend finished her reply, Ray took a deep breath to state, "I'm sorry, Crystal. Goodbye." He hung up.

The conductor hit the brakes as soon as it was safe to do so. When the train slowed to a crawl, he leapt off. The conductor ran towards the bend, where Ray's figure lay. A few minutes later, he halted in front of Ray and stammered, "What is wrong with you?"

With every ounce of willpower he could muster, Ray had raised his torso and head, right when the engine had rounded the bend. The train had sped past, not even a second later.

The elderly man knelt beside Ray, placed a hand on his shoulder and asked, "Are you okay?"

"No," replied Ray. "It's been seven years since I last contacted them. I haven't formed meaningful relationships with anyone in this place.

I'm so tired."

The conductor looked at him quizzically, yet Ray ignored his expression as he asked for a favor. He was going to do something he had not done since seven years ago.

A few months after her parents divorced, Isabelle had applied for a job so she could live on her own. She was supposed to be a fashion model, yet her employers incrementally manipulated her into succumbing to their mistreatment. She remained since it paid her bills and she had grown to hate herself.

A few hours ago, she got off work, and she received the highest paycheck yet. However, it was also her worst workday. The cameras recorded

Isabelle as her coworkers had cursed her out and smiled. She laughed in return, just as the director had instructed. Two men removed their pants and periodically gagged her as she pretended to enjoy the torture.

The cameraman paused the recording when she ran to the sink and vomited. He told her not to worry, he would just edit that part out. Isabelle came out smiling, just like the unconditionally happy, aroused, and submissive girl that her manager had taught her to be. She reminded herself that she would be rewarded mightily for her performance if she continued to comply.

Isabelle pretended to reach ecstatic release, multiple times, as the inhumane strangers took turns forcing themselves upon her. A semblance of relief sparked within Isabelle as they got ready to coerce her into swallowing a product of their rage, because that was the sign that the abuse was almost over.

She now sat at the edge of her cheap apartment bed. Isabelle's entire body screamed in agony. Her tears splashed upon the words she had just finished writing. She looked at the title of her poem, *Romance vs Objectification*. She crumpled the paper and threw it across the room.

Isabelle grabbed the pistol that laid beside her and removed the safety. She looked up at her ceiling and prayed, "Please, help me". Isabelle felt abandoned as she placed the muzzle in her mouth, pointed the barrel upwards, and placed her finger on the trigger. Her phone rang.

With immense effort, Isabelle placed the gun aside and reached into her pocket. She gasped as she looked at the caller ID. The person who she had attempted to contact was finally reaching out for her. Solace tumbled within her as she answered his call with a whisper, "Dad?"

Jiyah clutched her sheets as she stared at the pillow beside her. Her mind travelled out of her condo and to the night that she and Ray committed to creating a child. She focused on the moment when they had just finished making love.

"What do you think our child will be like", an undercurrent of excitement crackled within her voice.

Ray looked into Jiyah's dilated pupils as his grin reached epic proportions, "A glorious troublemaker."

Compelled by the bliss that lingered from their lovemaking, Jiyah snorted with laughter. Her husband joined her as he tenderly held her close to his chest. When she finished, she draped an arm across him and stared deeply into his eyes.

He laid a hand on her stomach and whispered, "I'm not sure exactly what our child will be like but I know that she or he will carry some of us within their soul."

Jiyah replied, "Our child will be the greatest gift that we receive."

"Absolutely, Jiyah", Ray warmly responded.

Jiyah drifted out of the memory as she laid a hand on the cold section of mattress beside her. It would have been the morning of their anniversary. She wondered where Ray had disappeared to. Jiyah desperately wished that he was okay. On the day they divorced, she made him re-commit to his promise of not harming himself. Jiyah knew of his mental ailments and she pleaded with him to continue his therapy. Though she felt that divorce was the right option because of Ray's struggles with commitment, she carried a deep regret for having completely cutting him out of her life.

It was a month after their marriage when Jiyah walked in on Ray as he watched an erotic video. She caught him in three similar situations, even after marital therapy. She could live with him after his repeated apologies and assurances that he would fight harder. She believed him even after the third time. Yet, when he had sex with another person, it broke her resolve to remain his wife. She also felt guilt pierce her since she and Ray hadn't made love in five years, no matter that external circumstances had all but prevented them from doing so. She thought their love would not be weakened by a lapse in their sex life, true love would have confirmed this.

Yet, ever since she left, pain gnawed at her heart. Jiyah missed Ray terribly. She tried contacting him four years after she vowed never to do so. She knew her attempt should have arrived far sooner, she desperately wished she could turn back time. Perhaps then, she reasoned, he wouldn't be too despondent to respond. She assured herself that he was still alive. Her tears trickled down as her phone rang.

She turned over and picked up her phone from the bedside table. Her heart skipped as she rapidly sat up and wiped her eyes. Her vision hadn't deceived her. Her caller-ID read, "Ray."

★   ★   ★

For the first time in years, Ray smiled as he cried. He handed the phone back to the conductor, thanked him and apologized. He wasn't able to contact Crystal, yet his spirits remained buoyant. He would just try again later.

He laughed joyously as he ran back to his house. His daughter and Jiyah were going to reunite with him.

Ray cleaned his house to the best of his ability. A house he had modeled almost exactly like his previous
house.

He showered, cut off most of his shoulder length hair, and trimmed his coarse beard. He stood on his front porch, though approximately thirty minutes remained between his daughter and ex-wife.

Forty-nine minutes later, when the sun began to rise, Ray paced the porch and placed his trembling hands within the pockets of his jeans.

Fifty-three minutes later, he sat at the top of his front steps and he attempted to lift the sinking sensation within his gut.

Three minutes later, his heart fluttered. He squinted into the distance as he took notice of an approaching sable sedan. He stood up and beamed when he could make out the faces of his daughter and Jiyah. Isabelle got out before the car arrived at a complete stop. She ran towards her Dad and embraced him. They held on to each other as Jiyah walked towards them. Ray's ex-wife noticed his stoop and busted lips as he and his daughter parted. Jiyah saw Ray instinctively glanced at his chest, navel, and his sleeve covered arms when he looked down. He gave a barely audible yet heartfelt apology to his family.

Jiyah slowly closed the distance between them and gingerly wrapped her arms around him as she placed her head over his heart. No words needed to be said within that moment as a tidal wave of relief cascaded upon his soul. He gratefully retuned Jiyah's embrace. Father, Mother, and Daughter held each other close as their elated tears fell upon one another.

That day, Isabelle cooked for the family, with the groceries she and her Mother had bought. Ray's family began to catch up with one another as they sat in a circle near the fireplace. They sipped hot cocoa as Ray relayed that though he had greatly isolated himself, even cutting himself from the internet, phone, television, and radio, he had continued to write countless stories. He explained that he used a pseudonym when Jiyah asked why she had never seen any of these works. He would mail each manuscript to his editor. When a manuscript passed the test, he would send it to his publisher, so it could be mass produced and sold. He mailed checks to give away most of the money made from his sales. He gave the majority of his profits to organizations which gave relief to the victims of human trafficking.

Jiyah told Ray that she had remained a

dentist yet became a motivational speaker for those who struggled with loving unconditionally. She would conclude every speech with the importance of forgiveness.

Isabelle stated that she, like her Father, wrote stories, though she didn't have the confidence to have them sold. She adopted this hobby when she was twenty-seven years old. She faltered over her words when she said that she was also a first grade teacher, a job which she acquired a year after her parents' divorce.

Isabelle pulled her knees up to her chin and hugged her legs as she confessed that she actually quit teaching three months after she got it. Not even her mother knew that her daughter left her job, a job which Isabelle quit because it barely paid the bills and because she felt inadequate.

Anxiety and embarrassment caused her to tremble as she prepared to reveal what she had been doing after she quit. However, the miraculous comfort that this family reunion bought compelled her to speak the truth about her situation. Isabelle's Mother immediately embraced her as her Father knelt before her and held onto her hands.

She divulged how she had been scammed by

a supposed modeling agency, which promised to pay her a hefty salary. They ended up paying her more than what she received as a teacher, yet it was only a portion of the pay that they had promised. She relayed the mental and physical abuse she began to experience the week after she was hired. Isabelle's eyeliner streaked down her cheeks as she wept and recounted the torture she most recently endured. She trembled when she revealed her suicidal attempt from several hours ago.

Ray divulged that he too attempted to end his life hours earlier. He stated that the knowledge of her, Jiyah's, Crystal's and the rest of his friends' steadfast love, is what ultimately saved him; despite what his condition compelled him to feel.

Ray noticed that at the moment he mentioned Crystal's name, Isabelle and his wife winced. Yet he decided not to inquire about their peculiar reactions as they sat on the floor, held on to each other, and prayed.

Soon after dinner, Isabelle fell asleep on Ray's sofa. Her Father gently carried her to his bed as Jiyah walked beside them. After they tucked her in, Ray checked to make sure their daughter was still sound asleep. When he and Jiyah went to the living room, he inquired about Crystal.

When Jiyah looked down, Ray pleaded with empathy. "It's okay, you can tell me Jiyah. She was your friend and Isabelle's too. What happened?"

Jiyah loved Ray too much to deceive him. She held Ray in an embrace as she revealed, "She died Ray."

As Ray collapsed, Jiyah stumbled. She helped him to the sofa and as they sat down, she continued to hold onto him.

"When did she die?", Ray gasped.

"Six years ago," replied Jiyah as she attempted not to cry.

It hit Ray that Crystal died a year after she and he last spoke. With a foreboding guess at the truth, he inquired, "How did she die?"

Jiyah didn't know how much time passed before she was finally able to answer, yet each second seemed excruciating. Her weakening composure broke down as she replied, "She killed herself."

A flood of agony drowned Ray as he sobbed and screamed. Guilt assaulted him along with the torture of loss. He thought to himself, if he remained in contact with Crystal, she may still be alive. She promised that she hadn't been suicidal since Ray rescued her. Therefore, he felt responsible for the suicidal urges which compelled Crystal to take her life.

Ray remembered the evening he first became Crystal's friend.

Thirty years ago, in the city of Alvice, he heard her weep in an empty classroom. They were just classmates at that moment, yet Ray walked in and that's when he saw her sitting on the ledge of an open window. Her feet dangled fifty feet above the garden floor. He quietly made his presence known and sat with her.

After she sensed Ray's authentic empathy and knowing that her pain was too much to bear alone, she revealed that she had struggled with adjusting to this new place. She was never adopted and struggled with suicidal urges in various points within her life, she confessed. She told Ray that her urges had been especially powerful lately since, for the first time in her life, she was all alone. The pain had also been strengthened on this particular night since it was her birthday.

Ray held her hands, wished her a Happy Birthday and assured her that she was no longer alone. Crystal wiped away her tears and smiled as warmth numbed her pain. They spent a few minutes sitting like this while Ray created a poem within his mind.

Ray looked into Crystal's eyes as the sun disappeared below the horizon. He gently spoke:

"There is sadness in your eyes and in mine
but allow the love that I have for you to outshine
the demon within your
mind,
as your words and embraces have pushed back
against mine.
A new beginning is born every day, begun at the
moment when the sun
trickles
and then pours its light into the sky.
Truth be told, every moment is a miracle,
an opportunity for honest renewal."

Crystal sobbed as she held on to her friend. After a while, Ray gently pulled away and emphatically stated, "Come with me, we're going to celebrate your birthday."

A year later, Ray's emotional mask, one which he wore since childhood, began to fall apart. When this happened, Crystal was there for him. She, emphatically yet gently asked her friend to reveal what he was going through. One night, he wrote a story and gave it to her.

*Though **Nayati** was a fictional story, Crystal knew Ray well enough that it represented what he went through and she realized that he had the same struggles as her. She could see Ray and herself in his story's main characters.*

She encouraged Ray to publish this story and to keep on writing. She could anticipate that writing would be a powerful coping mechanism for Ray and she was confident that his writing would inspire others.

It had been seven weeks since Ray's practically ongoing family reunion began. Ray looked over his new story, which he dedicated to Crystal. His tale was inspired by the damage his mental oppressions wrought yet it also displayed a gratefulness for a healthy level of sadness. He now fully realized that one could not have empathy if one couldn't feel heartbreak. Ray also implied that community was essential in coping with hardship.

Farrah, one of his main characters, was inspired by Crystal. Farrah had died near the end of this story, yet with the last two words, he had written her resurrection. Ray wiped his eyes as he closed his manuscript. The title, **A War for a Dream**, stood upon the front page of his approved document.

Ray turned his eyes to **Toska's War**, the manuscript which lay next to his, an account which was approved by editors, three days ago. He assured his daughter that though her writing style was different, it was no less powerful. He smiled proudly at his daughter's story as he placed the documents into separate envelopes. He would mail them to his publisher, on his way out.

As Ray grabbed his coat, he brought out his phone to look again at the photo which Isabelle sent her parents, three hours ago. There she was, looking at the camera and beaming brilliantly with young children, as she shook Lynn Riverdell's hand. Lynn was the CEO of *A Refuge for Sacred Souls*, a local non-profit organization for the sexually abused.

As Ray drove to his destination, he reflected on some of the time which followed the end of his self-isolation. *Ray and his family spent time with each other every day and they spent much of that time supporting each other through their grief. Isabelle's parents stood by her side as she quit the job which exploited her and applied as a teacher for the young children at **A Refuge for Sacred Souls**. Her parents danced enthusiastically with her when she was awarded the job.*

*Three weeks since the start of the reunion, when Isabelle began her work at the organization, Ray found the strength and inspiration to begin his work on **A War for a Dream**. In turn, with the* *gentle coaxing of her parents, Isabelle wrote* ***Toska's War****.*

Gratefulness soared within Ray as he walked up to the podium. Jiyah had used her influence as a renowned motivational speaker for Ray. It was because of her that he would now be able to give a speech to a full convention center. Ray looked at the front row and he saw Jiyah proudly beam at him as she used her hands to form a heart. She had told him that though she had forgiven him, she didn't know yet if marrying him again would be the right option. However, she would remain by his side as his best friend. Ray was thankful to hear her say this since he felt that this was more than he could ever ask for.

Ray looked at Isabelle, who sat next to Jiyah, and she excitedly waved at him as she snapped a photo. He chuckled warmly as he returned his daughter's wave. He smiled at his friends who sat with his wife and daughter. He turned his affectionate gaze towards the crowd, a large portion made up of those who dealt with or knew someone who had to struggle with self-downing mentalities. Ray looked towards one of the nearby doors and imagined Crystal standing there, grinning wildly at him. He visualized her mouth these words, "I love you, my dear friend." With tears in his eyes and a contagious grin, Ray gave his speech:

"Anxiety is a panic from the future, reaching down into the present. Depression is an unbearable pain, living in the present, reaching down into the past. When anxiety and depression combine, it is a deadly mixture. Having depression and anxiety can corrupt one's perspective on life.

In the grand scheme of life, good memories can may be no more than fleeting entities. Good moments can be like dreams that one can barely remember as time passes on, just as the details of a dream fade away upon one's awakening.

For those with chronic anxiety and chronic depression, fear and regret are mainstays in one's life and they arrive regardless of surrounding circumstances. The pain brought on by this mental illness is like none other. Physical pain pales in comparison.

Depression and anxiety can be so powerful that suicide becomes an instinct. I know this because I have chronic depression and chronic anxiety and I've struggled with suicidal urges. Suicidal urges can get so intense that for the victim, it can be like holding in one's breath and refusing to breathe in oxygen because if one breathed in, it would be the equivalent of committing suicide. That's how intense fighting against suicidal urges can be. However, I want to remind everyone that no matter how intense suicidal urges may get, it is always possible not to give in.

Yet, I also want to be clear that I do not feel hatred or disappointment for anyone who has committed suicide since I know how difficult it is to overcome. I feel an aching loss for those who are no longer with us.

Though depression and anxiety may never completely go away, you are not alone. Grab on to those who you love and who love you back. Don't forget that you are loved and that love goes beyond a feeling. Love doesn't require happiness. Love is the recognition of an individual's amazing worth and steadfast support for that individual, no matter what he or she may be going through.

You may fall many times, as I have, but never give up on life. I made a promise to always choose life no matter how difficult it gets and I will stand by that promise. I too, want you to stand by that promise, no matter how difficult your struggles may get and I do promise that though depression and anxiety may still be with you, you will feel happiness again.

Don't give into your doubts because they are not true! Victory is yours! If you struggle with self-worth like I do, look through the eyes of those who love you because you are amazing. Despite what you may feel right now, the constant truth is that you are a beautiful soul. This world would be so much worse if even one of us were to disappear from it.

So rise! If you fall into the pit of oppression, rise! If you fall again, rise! If you struggle to rise for yourself, then rise for the people you've enriched with your life! As long as you have life, it is never impossible to get up again, no matter how many times one falls or how dramatic the fall is. You will rise!"

Isabelle O'Sullivan's Story

TOSKA'S WAR

A Selection of Moments from Before & During the War

Dedicated to all who feel overwhelmed and alone in their struggles, regardless of what those struggles are.

"No single word in English renders all the shades of toska. At its deepest and most painful, it is a sensation of great spiritual anguish, often without any specific cause. At less morbid levels it is a dull ache of the soul, a longing with nothing to long for, a sick pining, a vague restlessness, mental throes, yearning."

-Vladimir Nabokov

The Warrior's Poem
(The Morning before the War)

Warrior: Some of the greatest dreams have given birth to the strongest nightmares. Often, when I approach the heavens, I give into the lies from Hope's Terror, believing that I don't have enough hope to fight against the gravity of Toska's frequented prison. As I witness the saints' children vomit into mouths which expel hope into dreamers' ears, I struggle to find the key that will unlock Freedom's gates. I wish to permanently reside within the land of reality, where the deceptively overpowering feeling of negativity dies within the arms of Recognition, Logic, and the acceptance of Love; a state of mind where I will forever feel the love that others have continually let embrace me.

Breaking Point
(The Afternoon before the War)

Warrior: Our innocence isn't supposed to pass away until we reach adulthood but I remember the day when knowledge murdered my innocence.

Toska: I know how to make the pain end, there is only one way. If you take this path, joy will no longer give you comfort but this oppression will be absent from you. You are in so much pain now, don't you want that freedom? Won't it be better to feel nothing, for your afflictive thoughts to cease? Don't you want peace?

Warrior: Even my life is precious. I won't entertain your desire for me. I will never give up.

Toska: Shhhh...It's okay. I will never leave you. I will always be there to remind you that you are worthless. Do you really think that anyone truly loves you? Which one of those whom you love has remained faithful, no matter what? That's why it's best to keep our relationship a secret.

Warrior: Shut up!

Toska: You know that you are powerless to resist me. They don't know your secrets. And now, the pain that you feel will increase so it will be near unbearable and you will experience it during most of your days.

Oh, you could have saved them from disappointment all those years ago. Allow yourself to feel devastated for them but you better not cry, not in public anyways. Be strong, and trap your sadness for them and your self-hatred within your soul. Emotional distance has separated you from everyone except me, I'm the only one who truly loves you.

Warrior: You're right. I am so damaged. To all who believe that I am a hero, know that I am far from one. I need to tell you about my abuse by someone named Toska...

Toska: You've made a mistake by telling them about me, now you will really be alone. Now, you will easily succumb to the advice that I gave you long ago.

Warrior: To those whom I love, I swear that I won't give up, no matter what happens. If you distance yourselves from me, I understand, either way, I promise you that I will never give up.

Toska: You have a greater desire than the one which I've presented to you?

Warrior: Absolutely. You see, I've learned something valuable through my experience with you. Now I am usually tuned into others' pain, even when they don't say anything about it and I desperately want to help them in any way that I can, that is my passion. And guess what makes me happy? When I see joy light up their faces because it is then that I know that you have lost your battle with them. You think that you are invincible but I know who you are terrified of. Love and hope. Though you will win battles against me you will not win the imminent war, love and hope will. And my past mistakes? I have been forgiven.

Toska: You really think your hope will be realized? The people closest to you are going to leave you. They only stuck with you out of a sense of necessity. When you told them about me, they only comforted you out of moral obligation. No one will be able to withstand the contagious horror which you will endure. As our war approaches its end, you will truly be alone.

The Night
(Toska's War: Part 1)

Warrior: Please don't leave me. I thrust my hands into my soul, searching, pleading, crying for a strength which I already know is running towards Death's embrace. Hope thrashes within Pain's clasp, trying to at least inhale one more gasp of air.

Hope's blood breaks through the floodgates and streams past the windows of my soul.

Toska, wrapped in Invisibility's cloak, laughs as he leans in and screams, "If you truly love them, you'll protect them from the agony still beating against your chest, it's time to silence the truth about my present presence. Here they come, I've made a new mask for you, place it over your vulnerability. You see that border? Cross it and meet peace, it is the only way that I can be transformed, please trust me. It's okay if you say no once again, I will be patient."

After my oppressor has spoken, Hope speaks the truth but finds only enough breath for fragmented whispers, and he says, "Don't forget that your love for them is mutual. Don't be afraid to keep the truth free, untainted by Fear's edits, you are not alone in your struggles."

Suddenly my surroundings transform Hope shrieks as my knees hit the border. I am now at the edge of the plain, in front of a deceptively beautiful yet truly sinister canyon. My warden's patience is expiring. I attempt to stand but I crumple back to the ground. The chasm's drafts caress my face, it'd be so easy to lean just a little more forward. My screams joins with Hope's as I rip off my fractured mask. My strength of resistance is approaching its end but I do not want to succumb to the strength of the crevice's desire.

That's when I feel your arms wrap around me and I see terror reign on my captor's confidence. You continue to hold me in an embrace as you pull me away from the edge, towards safety. Your words of kindness snatches my dying Hope from the depths of Pain. You heard my plea and you arrived for me.

Salvation:
(Toska's War: Part 2)

Warrior: My feet pound the ivory tears, spilt from the gray firmament above, as my every inhale grips onto reluctant life. I can barely see you but I can feel your hand, clenching onto mine, as we run from the heat that is transporting my oppressor's home into nonexistence; Winter's fever rapidly intensifies as you and I continue to run into the distance, away from the flames' embrace.

I feared that you wouldn't love me enough to rescue me, when you found out where I lived and who I lived with. "You are alone"; this was the phrase that Toska repeatedly screamed into my soul, until my resistance turned into belief but my Hope was resurrected when you kicked in the door and pulled me from the unseen captor's clasp. Warmth blossoms within me as my hand grows limp within your palm, as my legs crumple towards the snow covered earth, and as darkness completely overtakes my vision, how can this be?

As consciousness gently awakens my mind, I slowly open my eyes. Your worried features hover above mine, a friendly face framed by the ebony blanket draped across the sky. Your eyes mirror the stars, stars that are like places where moths have eaten through, holes which allow the daylight to trickle through. The night is oppressive yet it is vulnerable.

Your compassion rekindles the hope that had flickered away from my heart. Your embrace anchors me against the waves of exhaustion and I feel safe again. I know that no matter how many times I fall, you will always be there for me and you will always help me rise again. You are full of unconditional love and patience. For this, I am so grateful.

A Conversation
(Toska's War: Part 3)

Warrior: Miracles do exist. The world is full of people who have not the love to rescue those who have been drugged by a desire to inflict harm upon one's own wellbeing. So how blessed is the one who has been led by Fate, to the presence of those who don't restrain their love with conditions. Undeserving am I to have found them, yet gratefulness twirls its warmth within my heart. Redemption has been resurrected and it is shining its light on the horizon. My dear friends, my family, you've pulled me from the depths of an oceanic grave and you have guided my ship back on the right course, I can see the light.

Toska: Hope is beautiful. Without it, the torture that I bring would not be as intense. How many times have you believed that Hope's noose lay across my neck, only for you to feel my rope constrict yours as the floor suddenly fell beneath your feet? I am patient as I allow Hope to cast its light on the walls of your heart before I eventually, without warning, snuff it out. It's only a matter of time before you won't be able to heal again, your heart can only take so much, why don't you just give up? When you least expect it, I will bring my child to you again, you aren't invincible to Finality's desires.

Warrior: I WON'T GIVE UP! You will always fall beneath my loved ones' feet. I am not going to lie to myself...I won't deny your power but neither will I deny your vulnerability. I dare you to look into my eyes, feel the injury that my desire for life brings to you. Denial of my battle has caused my downfall too many times in the past so I will know history, not to dwell in it, but to remind myself the importance of being honest and knowing that Love will calm the tempest in my mind.

I battle you every day but your temptations for me to end it all, no matter how many times they occur, will never find victory. Though I've had my head pounded by you almost every day, and your torture may increase, Finality's urges will be swept away by Hope's currents. You will always be disappointed because I will never give up.

Toska's Imminent Triumph
(Toska's War: Part 4)

The Warrior: I am running, running out of energy again but never inspiration. I hate myself, no, yes, it's a cycle. At the highest of my good days, Toska dies within the land of the forgotten. On the worst of my days, Agony strangles me, leading my moments of triumph into the abyss, where I can no longer remember the feeling of peace. How did I get to this point? Much of it is from my own doing (that's what Toska tells me), much of it born with me.

Help? No I don't need help, yes I need help. I hate myself, no, I hate my helplessness. Yes that's what I hate. I hate it whenever I fail others, I'm sorry. I hate Toska, I hate that I can't rescue those who receive injuries because they are fighting for me.

The urges to completely give up are arriving

again from that land far away, they are getting closer, but I will stare defiantly, I will stay invincible. Am I invulnerable? No, but if I was able to overcome those nightmarish urges before, with help, it will happen again.

You know, do you know, yes you know that I am not perfect, not a hero, but a broken soul trapped in a cycle of oppressive illness. I escaped before, only with your help, but I am back at the border, approaching it that is.

Toska, Toska, why won't you leave those whom I love alone. I'll continue to bear my soul, thrusting Hope's blade into my heart and using the blood to relay the pain within. I hope that my inspiration inspires you.

To those whom I love, words cannot describe how sorry I am if you are becoming a victim like me. Never doubt how much I love all of you. I would fly to the moon just for you if it would make you happy, yes it's cliché, I know. Sometimes my smiles don't reach my soul, I am an actor but when I receive your kindness and your sweet words, I know Hope is not gone.

I'll stand again, I'll stand again, it's a process, I may take a little while, forgive me. You keep telling me that my war is not a burden for you and there's nothing to be sorry for, I'm sorry...there I go messing up again.

Even though I am currently losing the war, I know Toska's victories will not last. Your love shocks my doubts into submission.

The Warrior's Panicked Plea
(Toska's War: Part 5)

The Warrior: To those whom I love, please turn your face, hide your eyes, and close the pathway that leads to your perception of sound; do it when I'm around. I don't want you to feel anguish, please let your smile remain, my pain I have lost to over and over again and I don't have the heart to tell you that it increases when I least expect it. My victories are relegated to moments, moments farther and farther from abundance.

I don't want you to be overwhelmed by my struggles so please turn away, I give you my blessing. You have done so much for me. I am sorry that I'm falling, fighting is becoming more difficult, many times it is nigh on impossible.

"Don't fight me anymore", the monster says to me as he compels me to do the deed but Hope is worth fighting for. But I assure you that I can't give up, no, I won't give up.

It must be tiring to love me, with my unwanted struggles seeping past my skin, pouring forth from my soul, but I have love too, that is why I am trying to protect you.

I said to leave me but it's only because I don't want you to be overtaken by Toska's War, I love you and I love seeing you smile. You see, my love for you and your love for me keeps me going. However, if you don't have the desire to stay with me because of Hope's death giving birth, within my mind, to reality, I understand. Before you go, may you please hug me one last time?

Shattering a Fractured Mind
(Toska's War: Part 6)

Warrior: Here I am, a prisoner trapped within failure, just a ghost passing by in the world of Triumph. The people whom I love seem like fleeting dreams, I am drunk from pain and the demon who assaults my consciousness feels far more real. Why is Toska so cruel, why can't I feel the happiness which used to rule?

Please stay just one extra moment, just hold me a little while longer. When you lock your arms around my back, your warm torso pressed up against mine, my consciousness is snapped back into the physical world around me and I can feel your soul, brimming with love, overflow into mine. You shouldn't stay any longer, I see Toska as I try to rise from the ground. You must have ran and I am relieved. I only notice the presence of the creature and I now. His red irises border empty, bottomless pools and I see my reflection lunging from the windows of his soul. He smiles at me as he wraps a scarlet wing around my shoulders, his fur only appears red because of my blood which drips from it. Tears pour from my eyes and I shriek inwardly as he possesses my body. He puppeteers me and I appear triumphant, despite my wounds, to many passerby. When he leaves, I gasp for air as the monster grips my throat and resumes punching my bloodied head.

The creature has finally reached satisfaction from his assault and I see him leave to work at his station. He is rewrapping the gift that I refused those months ago, he knows it'll be easier for me to give in now that he's completely broken me.

But what is this? It dawns on me that Toska had blocked my senses to everything that he didn't want me to experience, well, his endeavor isn't completely successful because I miraculously feel your heartbeat next to mine. You never left me. My tears continue to flow but they are now expressions of relief, intermingled with the pain. Did you get hurt too? Why do you love me so much? You still haven't given up on me, your love truly knows no bounds.

You're coming into focus, your words are healing me. I know that I can defeat the monster again, I could not have regained this hope without you. I will not give up, even if Toska's ultimate temptation arrives again after that time long ago.

I will stumble and I will fall, I'm still broken, this I know, but redemption is still here. I am staring at the monster in front of me, I'm waiting to subdue Toska again in his war against me. Yes, he will rise afterwards and he may completely break me time and time again but I will also eventually overthrow him in each battle, no matter how intense it gets. Love is ultimately more powerful than the demon in my mind, you have shown me this.

I have to keep my loved ones in my mind in order to not stay down. It may take time but I will rise again, no matter how many times I fall and even if falling is a lifetime occurrence, I will get to the place where rising is a lifetime occurrence too.

The End
(Toska's War: The Finale)

Warrior: Toska's clawed hand collides with my head as mine rams into his diaphragm, coated from the crimson rivers coursing within my veins. My body can no longer contain my swiftly churning sea of anguish, so the floodgates burst and my scream is unleashed. Now granted with greater speed than ever before, I hammer my knuckles into the cage of bones protecting his heart as I feel the pain, that he alone should be receiving, damage me too.

The monster heaves as he tries to parry my attacks and connect his punches with my head but he is not fast enough for my explosion of desperation, or so it appears. I'm too lost within the moment to remember that he could easily escape, if he truly was in danger. I continue advancing my assault as my fear converts into hope and as triumph focuses within my mind, for the first time. Toska's back inches towards the cliff, at the edge of the plain.

A previously unnoticed escalation of exhaustion and horrific pain reaches the point of detonation within me, paralyzing my attack. We are only about two feet from the canyon's ledge. I collapse to my knees and my hope falls towards the abyss of my mind. As I see Toska slowly remove his mask of pained grimace, the soul of my hope escapes its carcass, and reincarnates into a body of resignation. This is what the creature wanted, I no longer have energy to fight back. Toska smiles, straightens his back and widens his shoulders with ease, revealing that he didn't feel any pain from my attack.

My captor puts voice to his current thoughts, "Hope is a miraculous entity. If you hadn't realized that it is a traitor, loyal to me, only after you had climbed the mountain and snatched it from the peak, your pain wouldn't be so deep."

I turn my head and I see you running towards us but it is too late, there is no redemption for me. At least you won't have to worry about me anymore. Toska hearing the crescendo of your footsteps, turns his scarlet eyes towards you with a grin full of menace. His foot collides into my chest as he grabs me and sends us off the cliff, into the Canyon of Isolation.

A kaleidoscope, of flickering stars, the

mahogany cliff, small jagged rocks down below, and my relentless oppressor, twirl within my vision as the monster and I tumble through the sky.

As soon as the creature and I reach our destination, the ground shatters my bones and I try to scream but the bones puncturing my torso renders me incapable. Toska laughs with sadistic pleasure. The fall inflicted no damage to that monster who is impervious to pain.

He grabs my skull as he begins to show me his motivational visions, no, they are my thoughts, manipulated by him. Why am I still attempting to resist him? I've become too weak and there is no one to rescue me now, the monster and I are alone.

Traumatic experiences, now heightened by Toska, unravel within my mind. Good moments, within my life, are brought to the surface before they rapidly leave me. Now, only nightmares exist and they are a true reflection of reality.

The monster, now acting as a ventriloquist for my soul, screams a sequence of statements. These are the thoughts within my mind:

1) "Romance isn't meant for me, my broken soul will always be too much for someone else to

experience."

2) "I will always fail my loved ones. There will never be close relationships which last for me since all I am able to bring, ultimately, is disappointment."

3) "I should stop bringing pain to others and prevent it from reaching any people that I meet in the future. I should sacrifice my well-being for them."

4) "Fate, please don't let my traumatic pain touch anymore souls. If you don't step in, Fate, no matter. I have a desire for Toska to lead me to Finality's door. I'm too tired to fight anymore."

Suddenly, a previously forgotten symphony of voices breaks my hypnotization. It's from all of you, from those who love me. Toska will not take these voices from me! I love you all so much, I won't give in to death.

My strength renews as I cycle through your loving words. The warmth from your long embraces erupt in the forefront of my mind. Toska lets go, as he becomes paralyzed by Horror. Nausea courses through his bones, as he witnesses my body heal by the miraculous re-blossoming of Hope's healing power.

I know that you, those who share my love, love me too. I see your beautiful smiles and I can't resist joining you. Your joy envelops me as you share your laughter with me and as you call my name. No! I won't let the monster take these memories from me too!

I leap up, grab Toska's head and he resumes his assault by grabbing onto mine. I fiercely hold onto my loving memories as I force copies of them into the demon's mind. I can't attack fire with fire, I've been fighting wrong this whole time. As Toska forces me to re-live my negative moments, I readily accept them. I hold onto them tightly but I uncouple these train of memories from guilt and I let that part fly, no longer harmful, into the sky.

I uncouple regret from my traumatic moments because it is through painful experiences that I can better relate to and help others. I no longer flood Toska's mind with negativity, only positivity.

My oppressor shrieks and a blinding light floods my senses as he explodes into a seemingly new entity. Unconsciousness blankets me.

I'm gently awoken by a luminous being and as my awareness comes into focus, I realize that Toska has transformed from an agent of my destruction into a powerful force for Hope. An unforeseen miracle has manifested. The night still churns within him but it no longer controls him.

I look to the horizon and witness the sunrise. Unable to contain myself, I dance, laugh, and cry with joy, because of my newfound freedom.

Bonus: A Letter (The Afternoon before the War)

Warrior: My dear peers, can I tell you the truth, untainted by Fear's edits? The truth is a difficult thing to utter, especially when one doesn't want those whom they love to be hurt by one's own personal Hell. The truth? The truth is I've masked my struggles with delicate words, delicate when compared to the reality which relays my recent abuse.

My oppression, like a cancer coursing through my blood, causes me to vomit the good which I receive, the peace that I intake is temporary. My body and my mind eventually reject the cure. I feel as if my illness is terminal. No one's fault, only my oppressor's, Toska.

I hope that the love that I have for you outshines the demon within your mind, as your words and embraces pushes back against mine. I am so grateful for all of you.

Toska is drugging my mind and I'm hallucinating, it seems that the nightmares in my mind are stronger than the reality which surrounds me, almost dreamlike in comparison. The peaceful moments fade away as the hours go by, as Toska refocuses my mind.

One day I will feel the reality that I want for most of my days, and Toska will be submissive, his negative effects relegated to a relatively distant dream instead. I will be farther than ever from that place now but I will get there eventually, I must believe it. I will one day cry from relief and happiness instead of reoccurring pain. One day, I will be able to give you some of that pure contentment.

Isabelle O'Sullivan's
Additional Literature

INSPIRATIONAL
MESSAGES
ABOUT
HOPE & LOVE

A Beautiful Freedom for Tears

What a beautiful experience that was, when laughter set free those tears once held captive within us. Those streams passed through the sparkling windows of our soul; they abandoned the outdoors, that vast place where we venture when alone, and they entered the intimacy of our glass home.

A Failure or a Fighter?

Does falling every time, after one rises, make an individual a failure? Or does rising every time, after one falls, make an individual a fighter?

For the afflicted, one's instinct inclines an individual towards the first perspective. It is an unwanted yet powerfully persuasive mentality. However, the first perspective isn't representative of reality. For to keep on rising, no matter how many or how drastically one falls, defines one as a fighter, not perfect, since no one is, but it certainly makes one a fighter. Many times, not only is assistance wanted to get up again, it is needed, so one shouldn't be ashamed to ask; help will arrive.

Now, to completely fail, one would have to stay down and refuse to ever get up again. Besides, no one should label another, himself, or herself as a failure, no matter what. Especially since there are oppressions which are highly impossible to overcome at times, not impossible, but nightmarishly difficult. So the second perspective is faulty in itself. No one is a failure, every single person has the capacity to triumph again.

A Message for Those Who Feel Overwhelmed

My message for all of you is this, no matter what your struggles are, never give up. If you are still lost within a nightmare don't hesitate to let others know because secrets don't murder pain, pain tortures those who guard them. Pain's power is weakened when we reveal our secrets to those whom we love and trust. If you don't know how to talk about your struggles in front of another, you can still voice them via the talents you are blessed with...

1) If drawing from the well of your heart to water your tongue is too difficult, then paint paper with the words or images residing within your soul, or...

2) Pair your thoughts with melody and let the listener be transported by your song as it dances with passion, or...

3) Unleash your emotions by moving your body through music, the people whom you've decided to open up to will feel your story.

There are talents too numerous to name but know that every person has them. Whatever your talents are, you are able to use them to entertain yes, but if you so need, they can be communicators for what you may desperately want to say, for anyone who thinks they are powerless to speak.

Remember that you are never alone. To any loved one you've decided to be vulnerable with, whether they be family by blood or family through friendship, or both, know that you won't fight your

battles alone. They will hold you in an embrace as they carry you away from the pain which attempts to continually connect its punches with your battered soul. Your rescuers will patiently help nurse you back to health as their love floods your soul with warmth. Even if your hope has died, their ever authentic love will be the heartbeat that beats next to yours, their kindness resurrecting from the ashes that which has died, giving
evidence to the phoenix within you.

Your mental oppressors may cause you to backslide numerous times in the days ahead, maybe even for those who have reached freedom but don't lose heart. If your doubts tell you it's not worth fighting your struggles again, remember that the absence of light will never be eternal, your escape into the light has already proven this.

Perhaps you'll even suddenly and frighteningly experience being brought to that border between a nightmare and nothingness but don't be ashamed, even if those unwanted visits are frequent. When this happens, immediately yell for help with everything you have left, and at least one person whom you've confided in will not hesitate to run and rescue you.

None of us are perfect, we are all in this together. So the person or people whom you've decided to be vulnerable with will need help in their struggles as well, no matter if they are similar or different. Your love for each other will keep hope alive as you stare your monsters down, and fight them.

Lean on each other, hold each other crying, laughing, and sharing your love with one another as you journey towards freedom together. Nightmares are vulnerable and love is eternal. You are not alone.

A Message for Those Who Have Lost Hope

Do not be afraid of being sad around others, you are not and you will never be a burden. When you're sad, it just gives your loved ones a desire to help you since they love you so much. Know that these negative feelings will pass, even if it doesn't feel like it within this moment. Know how much you mean to others and know that their lives are made better because of you, recognize the beauty that you, yes YOU, bring to others' lives. Life would be so much worse without you.

It is so easy to completely give up on oneself and give in. Oftentimes it is so difficult, it feels impossible, to keep on fighting because of exhaustion and it seems like failure will always win but I am here to tell you that you aren't alone. If you can't find the strength to continue because you are currently incapable of loving yourself, do not be afraid. The self-negative thoughts are not true. Others love you. You must continue fighting for the sake of those who already love you so much; find strength in their love for you. You will eventually push through, that is the truth, no matter what your self-negative thoughts constantly say.

A Message of Gratefulness

You want to know one of the most beautiful things that one has the fortune of experiencing? Others' desire to fight alongside one in their personal war, no matter how frequent the battles.

Generous ones' compassion for one another, knowing no wall between the literal and figurative meaning of family, they treat friends as one of their own. Others' assistance in nursing one towards strength, no matter the distance of time and how many times it takes to arrive at that destination for the wounded. The answer to the question that I posed is this: It is the gift of unconditional love.

A Message of Hope for the Addicted

If you allow yourself to constantly replay a moment of failure within your mind, only to constantly live in guilt, then your best case scenario would result in you frequently traveling through a cycle of temporary independence, losing hope, giving in...and then you would ultimately give up the fight. That's not the path that you want to take. Claw for confidence until you attain it, as you anticipate your future.

The journey may be fluid as you run towards your destination. However, every time you stumble, remember that triumph will meet you, as it has in the past. Eventually, you will triumphantly meet your record of independence again...and you will also attain victory as you surpass it. Fight for that belief, strive to cultivate that seed until it blossoms into a reality.

Also, know this: There's no shame in calling for help, to do so is actually courageous, an evidence of great strength but only confess to those whom you trust and care about you. The people who truly love you will not look upon you with disdain but with compassion as they help you get through your struggle.

Do Not Be Afraid of this Word

Help. Many times it is the hardest word to utter to another. Oftentimes this word is kept in the shadows since the afflicted sincerely wish not to be a burden. But the truth is that the loved ones of the downtrodden do not view them as an unbearable weight but as a beautiful soul who they desperately want to rescue, once they knew of the pain that crushed him or her. So if you are under duress, utter that word, and be not ashamed of it: Help.

Doubt's Vulnerability

Ever terrified of its own vulnerability and of others' love, Doubt wages war for its own unrightful triumph. Doubt desperately and viciously attacks because it is terrified of a truth that is beneficial only to his victims. Hope pleads patiently for us to always cling in its embrace, despite the severity of Melancholy's abuse. Intense struggles may be persistent but Pain underestimates the power of others' love for each other.

New Years' Resolutions

Remember that commitments to resolutions can certainly be gained at the gates of new years but also beyond as well. A new beginning is born every day, begun at the moment when the sun trickles and then pours its light into the sky. Every moment is a miracle, an opportunity for honest renewal.

No One is Without Family

We all come from the same ancestors. Their blood and your blood courses through my veins. Their blood and my blood lives within you.

Remember These Three Things

1) Not only do people need you, there are those who love you with a passion. They desperately want you in their lives. You are loved. Fiercely hold on to this truth.

2) Don't let your past faults distract you from the miracle of the present.

3) Everyone has their struggles. Be kind to others and yourself. Never give up.

Romance vs Objectification

When did love convert to selfishness? Why are you the subject of their objectification, constantly unclothed by ever starving animalistic urges, the prisoner of madmen? The cowards are blind to Truth's light.

You are royalty, you define beauty, your attractive appearance is a reflection of what blossoms within; you are a precious soul who ignites the wick of wise hearts, inspiring admirers to be the one who cultivates the fields of romance with you as you feed each other of its fruit.

Your oppressors' manifestations of hate expose your tormentors' own self-loathing, they alone are guilty of their evil deeds. You are innocent. Instead of feeding their emptiness with love, they gorge it with hatred that will never satisfy. The evidence of their cruelty mar your body but never your beauty, the experience of making love is no concern to them, they've corrupted it; the selfish abuse the innocent, making individuals endure a nightmare of pain and treating them as vessels to swallow a product of their rage. The oppressors display their conquests for the world to see, exploitation is sickening. No one deserves to experience violence or humiliation.

You deserve to be loved. An honorable partner is out there. You and your significant other will work to always uplift one another. After you both sign for lifelong commitment, gentle caresses, long embraces, and prolonged kisses will accompany intimate explorations of areas of beauty which were previously covered from each lover.

Together, you will reach the peak of ecstasy, far beyond a physical experience, it will be a powerfully emotional one as well. As you fall asleep in each other's arms, you will know what love, in all of its manifestations, is truly supposed to be.

Stumbling is Natural, Do Not Lose Heart

You may stumble many times and you may backslide, maybe the journey will last a lifetime but even so, many victories will be met along the way. Don't lose heart. Always remember that you are not alone. Unconditional love exists and others have wrapped it around you. Triumph is always attainable, no matter how many times you fall.

The Miracle of Love

Your smile can wipe away the tears hiding within someone. Your compassion is your hand entering the ocean, reaching out for those who feel alone.

You Are Not Alone

If failure is met after success, fight the impulse to completely let go and fight the urge to stay down. Strive to rise again and fight your way back to triumph. Remember, loneliness doesn't have to reappear. Always speak up if you want someone or a group to accompany you on the journey. You have people rooting for you. Victory will be yours again.

Afterword from the Author

Dear you, thank you so much for reading my book. I hope that the stories within have inspired you.

My book is particularly inspired by the unsung heroes who fight Anxiety/Depression every day, as well as the souls who lost their lives.

Though the characters and situations in this book are fictional, the unspoken war of Anxiety/Depression are not.

Anxiety is a panic for the future, reaching down into the present. Depression is an excruciating pain, living in the present, reaching down into the past. Fear and regret can arrive even when surrounding circumstances are good, while those past good moments can be like dreams that one can barely remember as time passes on; just as the details of a dream fade away upon one's awakening. It is at this point when all hope seems to be lost.

When depression and anxiety are at its strongest, self-harm and suicide can become an instinct. These urges can get so intense that it may feel as if one has to hold their breath in order not to give into those urges. However, to all with these struggles, I want to remind you that it is always possible to not give in.

Despite what you may feel right now, the constant truth is that you are a beautiful soul. Know that this world is made so much better because you exist. Don't forget that you are loved and that love goes beyond a feeling. So whenever you struggle with self-worth, look through the eyes of those who love you to recognize that you are amazing.

If you have fallen, then rise. When you fall again, rise again. Remember that struggling is an act of war. Therefore, every time you fight back, you are rising and therefore: victorious.

I promise you that you are not alone in your struggles so don't hesitate to reach out for help. Whenever you fall, be patient with yourself, yet determined in rising again. The people whose lives you've enriched and the lives you've yet to touch need you. As long as you have life, it always possible to get up again, no matter how many times one falls or how dramatic the fall is. You will rise. Dear you, victory is yours.

To summarize my message, I give you this poem:

Anxiety is a panic from the future, reaching down into the present. Depression is a painful sadness in the present, reaching down into the past. Self-harm and suicide are floodwaters that can threaten to burst through the barriers within the mind; though choice is not a slave to those urges. Love is a dedication to stay around for others because they do care, to inspire all, and it's a recognition of self-worth that goes beyond a feeling. To be human is to fall but determination is the ability to be patient and to rise every time. Comfort is the reality that you are wanted, needed, and that you never have to fight your demons alone.

- Charlie Avinash Nicholas

ABOUT THE AUTHOR

A Beverage of Surprise

One night, I let two grand spoonfuls of sugar slide into my tea. As I took a hearty sip, I couldn't help but notice how alarmingly salty my beverage tasted. This experience inspired me to include a similar incident in my fictional story, *Reunion: Remembrance and Inspiration*.

A Red Chili Pepper

That moment of revelation when one overestimates their ability to handle spice? Oh, how I am well acquainted with this experience. One fine Fall afternoon, I ate an entire red chili pepper, all by itself. The spiciness frolicked within me, with a steadily increasing enthusiasm; it felt as if the 4th of July arrived early, taking place within my belly.

A Startling Prankster

Wasabi is sneaky. Wasabi is a prankster amongst food. To those in the beginner stages, Wasabi is a leader, a guide who will lead one into a false sense of security as it trickles some spice onto an individual's senses, making it seem that its power may have gotten wimpy. A few moments will proceed to pass before Wasabi makes its ultimate effect known. Wasabi is a startling spice bomb.

Feeling like Columbus

Once upon a time, I had a Latin American Cultural Studies class. One day, I was running late and when I walked into the classroom, I noticed that everyone was taking a test. Mild panic and great confusion blossomed within me since I was unprepared, I had been sure that this class wouldn't have any tests! I looked around again and noticed that I didn't recognize anybody but our class was large so I thought, "This is strange but understandable. Maybe I'm just in shock after seeing people with tests in front of them." However, reality began to truly sink in. My teacher also wasn't there, but I assured myself with a runaway hope, "Oh, it must be a substitute." I received the test and saw questions about environmentalism. My realization was needlessly confirmed. I had taken a couple of extra steps, accidentally walking through the wrong classroom door.

Mistaken Identity

I uncertainly but joyfully waved at a friend whom I saw in the not so far distance, only to realize a moment too late, when our eyes met, that I was joyfully waving at a stranger.

The Day I Freed a Dolphin

At a young age, I was inspired to make a change and I decided to do so by freeing a dolphin. I took one of my toys, a miniature toy dolphin, and I flushed it down the toilet. I whispered, "Swim away dolphin, swim away."

The Day Where a Man Almost Became a Sandwich

Once upon a time, there was a man, in a rush, who tried to get onto an elevator. He almost wasn't fast enough to escape the clutches of the elevator doors...they almost made a sandwich out of him! However, he dramatically jumped past those closing doors just in time. Whew! Except...he jumped the wrong way, in his panic, he leapt backward instead of forward. This man now had to contend with standing on the wrong side of the soon to be transported crowd. He could see a mixture of pity and slight confusion on their faces before the elevator doors completely closed. Yep, that man was me.

<u>Two Very Different Things</u>

During a day, residing within the past, a general contractor came over to my family's house. Wanting to figure out why one of our ceiling lights refused to bring light, he requested a lighter. This confused me a bit. When I brought it out, the feeling of confusion became mutual; I know since, at that moment, the evidence was the foundation of his expression. The answer to the misunderstanding became apparent as he reiterated that word which played a trick on my ear. "Ladder", not "lighter".

Book II

Strange

And other Accounts from the Taboo War

Foreword

Dear reader,

There is a war that is not often talked about and rarely seen. Mere discussions on the Taboo War are still ironically unspoken by many of those who have given it that initially derogatory name. Indeed, I am here to bring awareness to the war between the Grim Reaper's strange sons, and to those whom my cousin Lexi calls the Unsung Heroes.

The Unsung Heroes have gained the courage to speak to me about the Taboo War, a title which they've proudly redeemed the name of. They've entrusted me to share their stories with you since they're an exceptionally humble team.

There is more information to gather but this compilation will do for now since time is of the essence. The reality is that lives are at stake and I have faith that their stories of heroism will inspire those who have lost hope in this war.

I believe that what I've compiled here will be enough to shatter the stigmas that have been launched at anyone who dares speak the truth.

The warriors have honored me by insisting that I am a part of their group and I guess that I am a fighter like them. I've told them that I don't feel much like a hero since I'm as flawed as Fool's Gold but they repeatedly remind me that they are flawed too. Though I've never met any of Death's descendants like they have, I am committed to the fight and putting this book together is one way that I'm fighting.

Without further ado, here are their experiences.

- Richard Frye

Strange

1

Into the Night

Jackson Rathbone: The windowpane shatters. I fly through the night's bone-chilling tears before the back of my head slams onto the fire escape's railing. My chin collides onto my collarbone and my teeth snap together. I black out momentarily only to awake to warm liquid trickling into my mouth. My pain ratchets up in intensity as I turn just my head to spit the blood out. I open my mouth and vomit bile tinged with blood.

I lay sprawled across the metal grating, my apartment window's jagged teeth piercing my back, my blood trickling past the glass, and my puke dripping onto the landing below. I turn my face to the heavens. Rain plummets into my eyes and within seconds, my own rain forms behind the windows of my soul. My scalding rain breaks through the surface of my eyes and courses down my cheeks as it intertwines with the goose-bump inducing tears from the clouds. Sobbing, I face my open window and see the light reaching forth as it begins to be eclipsed by something inside. Two clawed hands grip either side of the window frame. Since the creature threw me, I've only been outside for around a minute, though it's felt like an eternity.

My window frame widens as the lipless and eternally grinning monster pushes itself through. The noiseless creature's talons clasp the bottom frame and it leans its face towards mine. I squint from the glare and heat of the eternal fire dancing within its eyeless sockets. I know what it intends to do but my body is refusing to move now. The bloodied bat sets its eyes towards downtown and it flaps its semi-transparent wings. With everything that I have, I shake off the fear paralyzing me and I stand and grab what's still left for me to grasp of the flying monstrosity. Its foot slips from my sweaty and bloody grip but just when I think that I have nothing left, I scramble onto the top of the railing and I leap towards the fleeing creature. I soar towards the monster, my outstretched hands ready to latch onto him. My stomach sinks as mere inches from the creature, I plummet towards the ground.

2

Revelation

Like magma from a volcano, his breath erupted through his nostrils and mouth. Before pain could overtake his shock, darkness overtook him.

He regained consciousness about five minutes later. He was fortunate that the drop had only been twenty feet and that he hadn't landed onto his back, where tiny fragments of glass were embedded. He was blessed that an old mattress, pillows, and bags of clothes had been piled in front of the overflowing industrial trash can.

Shaking, he managed to stand before collapsing. Though he was feeling more pain than ever before, his desire to save his loved ones and the adrenaline from the trauma gave him the strength to move on. Like a gift from God, he saw a small harpoon lying next to the trash bin, up against the brick alley wall. It was rusted but he believed, perhaps out of desperation, that it would work. Doing what he could, he crawled towards the harpoon and grabbed it like a lifeline. Then, he dragged himself to the adjacent parking lot.

A wave of nausea washed over him and he hacked up blood as a coughing fit seized him.
Yet he crawled on. When his hacking ceased, his skinned elbows and forearms released red rivers.
Jackson Rathbone prayed that no one would see him since he didn't have time to deal with the police or the medics.

He reached his motorbike that was located in the center of the parking lot, between two cars. He heard faint yet crescendoing sirens and he dimly realized that many would have heard his window shattering from the recent fight. He stayed hidden between the vehicles and within their shadows as he continued to work.

He gritted from the effort, yet he was dexterous as he removed his bloody white T-shirt and undershirt: he used these to securely wrap the harpoon to his torso. He was careful to not place the crisscrossing bands over places where the glass jutted from his back. The cool harpoon was pressing lengthwise upon his heaving torso and its point was piercing the air. He saw the cop car round the corner and he froze in fright as it slowed down.

As soon as it reached the parking lot, it kept on going.

The cops pulled over to the apartment complex a block away. Jackson couldn't help but smile and chuckle. He felt no joy but he was amused and grateful for this latest miracle. He realized that whichever tenant had called had mistook the last number of his own apartment complex's address. Jackson shook off the creeping mania as he forced himself to focus. Cursing but otherwise ignoring the pain, Jackson clambered onto his motorbike and brought it roaring to life.

He raced past the cop duo as they went into the adjacent apartment's front lobby. He looked back and the younger policeman glanced at him with hazel eyes. The young officer didn't acknowledge Jackson beyond that glimpse. In fact, it seemed that he didn't see Mr. Rathbone or hear the roaring motorbike at all.

Ice seemed to rapidly blossom within Jackson's soul as realization dawned on him. Did he die from the fall, his body left behind in the alleyway? As he exited the lonely road and crossed onto the highway, he realized that he was very much alive. If he was a ghost, he wouldn't feel any pain, much less be able to commandeer physical items.

He flipped on the radio and tuned it to the downtown station to listen for any reports of unnatural activity. A scarlet sedan cut in front of Jackson and his instinct took over.

He swerved to the center lane but time wasn't on his side. He hit the blood-red sedan and passed right through as he exited onto the middle lane. As his heart pummeled his chest, he looked at the car but saw no damage nor acknowledgement from the driver or anyone else. He looked down and saw that his motorcycle, he, and everything on him was transparent with a ghostly white aura. Taking advantage of his new predicament, he barreled through the traffic in front of him.

3

The Invasion

He believed that he had done much good upon entering the heart of the city. He had only been there for about thirty minutes but he managed to murder seven people. Well, he didn't actually kill them since he couldn't lay a finger on any of his victims...well, he couldn't touch anyone except for one. But oh how he could and did corrupt their minds. Still, one may say that the monstrosity was about to sink his pus-streaked fangs into his eighth victim.

The silent and unseen creature strode through the second floor condo that had stretched to accommodate him. Jackson's best friend sat directly in front of him yet she didn't look up from her novel. The bat was invisible to everyone on this planet...except for one. He leaned towards her to whisper nightmares into her ear. His heart leapt in anticipation as he parted his fangs and a horrendous sequence of sounds pierced the air. Instinctively, he looked down at his chest.

Dumbfounded, he briefly thought that his chest had birthed rusty iron claws. Pain and realization overtook his three seconds of shock and exploded into his senses as his body dragged away from Megan.

He had been pierced before he could utter a whisper. Yet now he screamed with agony and fury but he was only able to emit strangled whispers. His compromised diaphragm was unable to carry his rage to his voice. He tried to pull forward and cut the harpoon's line but the majority of his strength had left him. He gasped for air which his lungs could no longer accept and he rapidly began to descend into death.

When Jackson finished reeling the monster in, he stared defiantly into his eyes. He had willed himself and his weapon into physical form right before he had pulled the trigger. He had heard a newscaster announce a suicide victim at Megan's condo complex and his heart had dropped upon the information. Though he naturally felt horror upon seeing the corpse, he felt immensely thankful that the victim was the guard in the lobby rather than his best friend.

As Jackson humorlessly smiled, he whispered

to the heaving monstrosity, "You're done." He raised his head to look at Megan, who hadn't paused in her reading. He hoped that he would become visible again after he buried this creature.

Gillith's tortured breathing ended and the fire vanished from his sockets. The creature's body ceased to give any sign of life but something was wrong. Jackson's affection for his best friend suddenly extinguished. Right before he could die, the monster had left his own failing body and, like a parasite, he had invaded Jackson's soul.

Jackson's eyes emanated ravenous hunger yet his stillness betrayed his resistance. He had an instinct to grab a knife from the adjacent kitchen to carve Megan. He sensed that he would be able to bring himself and the blade into the realm of humans with each hack of the knife; being able to vanish again, each time that he would withdraw the blade. He didn't need to worry about a struggle.

Oh, how his lust for carnage compelled him to slaughter the girl at the dining table. Megan was nothing to him but the closest prey. Yet, he did not move. Sweat trickled down his blood encrusted face as he remained where he was: in front of the inter-dimensional creature's corpse.

Within his mind, he saw the monstrosity as if Gillith hadn't sustained even the smallest of injuries.

However, the creature shrieked with horror and vehemence. The monster roared, "I drained your love and poured bloodlust into your heart, how the hell are you resisting!?"

Jackson snapped, "Love doesn't require an emotion you bastard!" He looked down and saw a lengthy chain piled beside his feet. He scooped it up and the monstrosity didn't move. Jackson knew that Gillith's soul wouldn't flee since his body was the lifeline for the creature. The monstrosity regained resolve and tried to grab the chain but his clawed fingers passed right through the links.

Jackson wept as Gillith slammed his fists into his head. His tears were of gratefulness since Jackson's bloodlust lessened its grip and affection trickled into his heart with each of the monster's punches. Yet he understood that he wouldn't be able to fully regain that which was stolen without help. He fervently whispered prayers and wisdom dominated his doubt. As the monstrosity continued to hail blows, Jackson fought with everything he had to wrap the chain around himself and the struggling creature. Finally, Jackson's deliberate measures and answered prayers caused the chain to secure the monster's soul to his.

"What have you done?", hissed the creature.

"There is only one remedy that will fully restore my soul which you've corrupted," retorted Jackson. He embraced the creature and once the monster understood, he willingly leapt into Jackson's innermost soul.

"You won't survive", Gillith chortled.

"You will never make me a psychopath," Jackson retorted as he trapped the monster inside.

Affection exploded like never before and so did the pain. Jackson screeched as his soul fractured in a raging fire. Flames shot from his eyes, nose and mouth to several miles into the sky. His head exploded and everything vanished.

Megan jumped from her chair when she noticed Jackson appear suddenly before her. She gasped as his bleeding form collapsed onto the floor. She ran towards him as she frantically withdrew her cell phone and dialed for the ambulance. Megan placed a hand over her best friend's heart as her tears fell upon him.

4

Nightmare

Jackson awoke next to his wife. "Hi sweety," Josie whispered groggily. "What's wrong? You look troubled." Concern emanated from his wife's features as she tenderly placed a hand on her husband's cheek.

"It was a nightmare but it seemed so real," Jackson replied as he wiped away his tears. "I'm sorry for waking you."

"You failed," Josie stated softly yet emphatically. She grinned as she reiterated the phrase.

Josie's eyes fell from her sockets and onto the bed. Jackson tried to scream and scamper away. However, his voice had been extinguished and he was completely paralyzed. Josie's face dripped like molten wax to reveal a jet-black and bottomless abyss.

"You failed me," he heard his wife whimper inside his head. "YOU FAILED ME!", she shrieked telepathically as she rapidly placed her husband's head within her faceless one. The smell of decaying flesh caused him to puke.

He felt Josie slowly push him past the bone frame of her face and he heard her skull fracture as it stretched. It barely widened enough for her to squeeze his torso through. Hours seemed to pass before he finally tumbled into that endless cavern.

Jackson's joyful memories with his friends and family flashed by. They were true until the moving pictures showed him slaughtering his loved ones. However, Jackson believed that these murders may as well be factual. He sensed that he had torn their souls apart by failing them.

Paralysis left Jackson and he shook uncontrollably as he vomited again. He heard his loved ones' voices repeating the mantra that he had failed them. Their voices crescendoed until he could barely hear his own thoughts. Gillith's voice matched the others in clarity though it was a whisper: "You failed them."

Jackson groaned to himself, "Please, give them peace."

The monstrosity solemnly replied, "You can save them."

5

The Jump

Blue jays twirled within the sunny summer sky as Jackson looked at the deserted street below. A delicate breeze playfully ruffled his flaxen hair as it brought him the scent of the sea.

Jackson heard the voice of the monstrosity and for the first time it sounded playful: "The final steps to everlasting peace are yours."

Jackson observed the skyline and enjoyed the warmth of the sun's rays. Yet, pain continued to detonate, endlessly within his soul, though his heart was quiet for the first time. In the back of his mind, he heard a sustained, shrill, and monotonous beep.

Peace. Jackson had faith that peace would embrace him 500 feet below. Yet, what compelled his heart the most was the instinct that his sacrifice would be able to save his loved ones. As he raised his left foot from the ledge, he heard something far more real than the voice of the creature or the nightmares he had experienced since imprisoning Gillith. It was the voice of Megan: "Please come back. Please don't leave us." The agony in his best friend's voice pierced his still heart but this pain was somehow a balm to his soul as well. It was empathy.

A young man arrived within Jackson's line of sight as he placed his hand in his. The stranger was a grotesque sight, his body, too immense, threatened to break the constraints of his skin. "That voice isn't real, my friend," the monstrosity whispered with feigned sympathy. Come, let's jump together."

Just then, Jackson heard a familiar psalm sung from the heavens. It was his mother's voice.

"You are a failure, Jackson," Gilleth proclaimed with malice. "A womanizer, a deceiver, an abandoner."

Jackson heard his best friend join in his mother's song. Their two voices sounded like a choir. As his family and strangers joined the medley, Jackson gained the courage to look directly into the now fearful eyes of his oppressor.

Warmth continued to blossom next to the ice of agony within Jackson's essence. To Gilleth, he proclaimed, "The past is my teacher for better days."

The monstrosity burst from his ill-constructed disguise as he hissed, "You..."

Jackson raised a hand and telekinetically shut his oppressor's mouth and he almost crumpled from the effort. A force which had been increasing by imperceptible amounts suddenly amped up in intensity; it threatened to pull Jackson to the street. Suddenly, he knew what to do though he prayed that he wasn't too late. With his remaining strength,

Jackson violently kicked off from the ledge and towards the sky.

A portal opened in the sky above Jackson and he tumbled towards it as Gillith thrashed on the roof below. As Jackson twirled towards the opening, he witnessed his first encounter and tussle with the beast: Gilleth had fled him out of fear; not knowing that a human would be able to see him.

As lighting repeatedly struck his chest Jackson saw Megan accompany the paramedics and his limp body from her condo.

He witnessed his mother, father, and siblings as they stood around him. He saw two of the four medics there as they attempted to shock his heart into life. Everyone except those operating the defibrillator were singing to him.

Jackson Rathbone: I am tortured and I always will be. Yet I am a warrior and I will never stop fighting. This is the war that I was chosen to fight. Morally, I am better than no one else. I've just been blessed with the abilities to do this job. We all have a place in the war and these are the battles that I was chosen to fight. I sense that there are more monstrosities for me to battle, more people to rescue. I choose to keep on fighting.

Jackson's heart pumped again and as he passed through the portal, he awoke from his coma.

Tris's Poem

The
Growing
Distance
between
Us

Dear Diary, miles travel between Donovan and I.

I stand at the edge of the still sea and portals of light ebb within the tranquil water. I step upon this sky, my eyes reflect the stars which shine so brilliantly. As I dive into the sea, I swim towards the closest star, I need to grasp it in order to feel it. Oh, Donovan, it is one of our blissful memories.

I am finally a few feet away from this star, one of the portals to the Sun which is hidden within the earth. I sob as a current drags me from the warmth and nearer to the shallows, where the water brings winter to the soul; it is the place where the bones begin to freeze and where the oxygen thins dramatically.

This whirlpool finally wrestles me back to the surface. It's only been a few hours yet I have lost count of how many times I've been brought back. It seems to matter not where I dive. My strength has sunk from its peak, yet there are many places my feet have not yet touched, so I will not grow too weak to travel this ocean vast. I know that I will find that place where knowledge holds my grieving soul. Though distance has driven us apart, I know that we haven't grown distant within each other's hearts.

One day, oh maybe one day, Donovan, you and I will be able to re-unite. I know that I will do my part. This winter, I will host a reunion.

A Winter Miracle

&

Isolation's

Sinister

Persuasions

1

Awaiting a Bus

Ivory tears fall in slow-motion upon me. A gust of icy wind slams the falling snow onto my meagerly dressed body as it cuts me to the bone. Mist steams forth from my nose and streams between my chattering teeth. Brilliant sunlight lands onto the approaching bus and extends its reach to pierce my watery eyes. The intense beam of light slides across the unpainted vehicle and disappears thereafter. As the mode of my escape approaches ever closer, someone speaks my name. I turn around to look at the source of the voice.

An elderly gentleman with shortly cropped snowy white hair, eyes ablaze with empathy, and a heartwarming smile, greets my vision. After a brief moment, I realize that I may recognize him though I can't place whom he might be. He addresses me again as he says, "Please don't make the same mistake that I did."

With my mind awhirl, I reply, "Who are

you...never mind, I'm sorry. I need to go now. I can't afford to stay out here any longer."

I turn around on the oak bench and gasp a mouthful of the sky's icy breath. The bus has stopped about 60 feet from my stop and the snowfall has halted. A few drops of snow are semi-shattered in mid-impact upon the bus, cars, buildings, bench, earth, and I. The flames of realization rapidly melts my shock into acceptance when I continue to study my surroundings. I gently push aside the few snow drops which hang directly in front of my eyes so that I can gain a better look.

The gentleman kneels in front of me and gingerly shakes my arm as he delicately inquires, "Do you recognize me?"

He peers into my eyes with hope, sympathy, and apprehension shining forth from his. I study his face and I touch my mine in amazement when it dawns on me who this individual is.

He sits beside me as he appeases with a quavering voice, "Don't run away. You've forgotten how much they love you."

He extends his right hand as he tenderly states, "I know you're in pain. Let me help you."

Somehow, I know what will happen if I put

my hand in his own. After a few seconds pass, I wipe the few tears which I failed to keep within and I place my right hand onto his. I'm instantly returned to my past:

2

Dancing with Her

"Take my hand, Donavan," Tris proclaimed with assurance.

Flaxen flames twirled and leapt within the marble fireplace behind my dear friend. The dregs which remained of my resistance washed away as I observed her beseeched emerald eyes, her comforting smile that was framed by rosewood lipstick, and her outstretched silky hand. As soon as I placed my palm up against hers, my imagination transformed our surroundings. The electric lamps dimmed and the Christmas tree's lights brightened until their rainbow hues overcame every shadow that the fire did not reach. Perfectly spherical drops of bath-warm snow fell upon us as she brought me a mere inch away from her bosom. The asphalt, steel, and pine roof of her home transitioned to smoke as a delicate breeze carried it away. We burst out laughing as we whirled amongst the flurries. I felt as if we were as light as the wind.

By the time I learned all the steps she carried me through, the sky was ablaze with the mighty rivers of Aurora, an invisible orchestra had played its ninth refrain of my favorite carol, and translucent periwinkle butterflies had begun to flutter about us.

"See, Donovan? You've underestimated yourself. You're a good dance partner, you needn't be overwhelmed by our friends," Tris spoke as she gingerly pinched and tenderly shook the end of my nose. "You rarely give yourself enough credit, my friend." She paused to give me a pensive stare as she inquired with mirth, "Where have you gone this time?"

Too late, I unlocked my eyes from hers as scarlet floodlights illuminated my tan cheeks. "I'm still here," I chuckled. Our surroundings returned to reality. A familiar sinister voice proceeded to whisper within the bowels of my mind but I managed to shut his mouth without much delay.

"Thank you," I reply as I swivel my sight from

the polished floorboards to Tris's face. "I am so grateful for you and," I choked suddenly as the menacing voice casually glanced a fist upon my bliss. I tried to continue my sentence but I faltered yet again as tears skimmed the surface of my eyes.

Tris interlaced her arms around my back as she pressed her torso against mine and she placed her head upon my shoulder. Time fled backwards as I felt her heart pulse alongside mine...

3

The First Time that She Held Me

...Rain cascaded upon us as Tris and I held each other in an embrace. I trembled violently, not from the chilly precipitation, but from the damage done internally. She barely knew me a minute prior to then since she had no knowledge of the parasite within me. A year ago, when she found me in the rain, it had been a month since we met. Yet there she was, treating me as a member of her soul, not for the first time. How could I have doubted her love? I pulled back to peer into her streaming eyes. With each beat of my virus's heart, my confidence

was assaulted. However, at this moment, her soul reached forth to melt my hidden nemesis's grip upon mine. Yet, why did my friend love me? Why do those whose blood doesn't course with mine care for me even after I got infected?

I mumble, "I still don't understand."

My future self's voice reaches forth from the present to address my recurring question that originated from the past, "It's time to see yourself through their eyes."

As an ebony cloud flexed his muscle, white-hot electric veins stood starkly upon the steely-gray sky. When the light illuminated the faces of my friend and I, time seemed to crawl. When the lightning vanished, time snapped back to its natural pace and I enter Tris's mind.

In this moment in time, I feel empathy continually surge from the generator of her heart where an unseen knife had continually plunged and withdrew. Her younger memories interlace with mine as I behold my own sapphire rimmed irises.

Her memory wound back to two years ago and lands upon the day when we first met...

4

Interlaced Souls

...I'm running through a sun ray streamed field of wheat. I feel her heart crescendo as she turns around to look at me advancing upon her, (I'm slowly adjusting to this weird sensation of seeing myself from someone else's eyes).

I feel her breath, throat, tongue and lips carry her words when she exclaims, "Slow down, you fiend!" Laughter courses through her as mild anxiety and mad exhilaration flow through her. Her head turns again so she can have a clear view of the field ahead.

"Pride goes before the fall so let me win and I shall bear the burden of victory! I shall sacrifice myself for you, if only you let me, oh person whom I met but an hour ago."

As she begins to swivel her entire body to face me again, she proclaims, "For you, I shall...oh sheesh, Speedy Gonzales!" I am but a couple feet away from her. I yelp within my mind as a cramp moves through her calf. She stumbles backward but I manage to turn our bodies so I can experience the brunt of the fall.

Fright for her predicament metamorphoses to worry for me when we land, I on the dirt and she on me. Her apprehension increases when she sees me wince. "Oh my gosh, are you okay?" I vigorously nod my head as she gets up and helps me to stand.

I burst into a smile as the videographer finally catches up to us. I rapidly clasp my hands behind my back as Tris massages her leg. I inquire of her, "Are you alright?" After she gives me a reassuring nod and tells me not to worry, it is but a cramp, I announce "Tag! You're out!" I pump my fist into the air as the cameraman cheers. Tris opens her mouth in astonishment, in our tumble and the aftermath, she had been so

focused on my well-being. Yet, she can't conceal her grin as her surprise gives way to joy. She blinks away the sweat pouring into her eyes as she exclaims, "Congratulations Donovan!"

Before I fully realize what I'm doing, I place my hand upon my heart as I bow for her and the camera. In my flourish, I unintentionally reveal one of my skinned elbows. Greg, the videographer, whistles and closes his camcorder when he sees the wound. The pain that blossoms within Tris when she notices my injury is more potent than my injuries. Reluctantly, I show her my other blood drenched elbow. I'm startled but pleased when she swiftly gives me a hug.

As Greg, Tris, and I walk ahead towards the finish line and towards our other college friends, I embarrassingly attempt to capture that which has fled from me: "I'm sorry, it usually takes me a while to remember names..."

"Tris," she answers without a hint of what my supremely sensitive self perceived: disappointment.

She gives me a heartwarming smile and I proclaim, "This may seem weird for me to say but I truly believe that we'll be the best of friends."

Tris replies, "I truly believe this too. I'm a good judge of character when it comes to choosing my friends, and I assure you that what you believe is already true."

I mask my insecurities with a joke, spoken in a melodramatically all-knowing manner, "Ah, but once you truly get to know me dear Trish, you shall run faster than I have today."

She suddenly adopts a serious demeanor though her love doesn't weaken as she places her hands upon my shoulders. She utters, "Tris." Perplexed for a second, she laughs heartily along with Greg and states, "You were close, you just added an 'h' to the name which my parents gave me."

I chuckle as I understand my mistake and she embraces me. After a little while into this embrace, I notice the understanding which had accompanied her emotions since the moment she peered into my eyes and introduced herself with a smile. It is now that I fully realize that her gift is that of perception. She knew my struggles at the moment she befriended me. Since we encountered each other, she knew that my unbridled joy was but a mask to my recently shattered soul and she loved me; a person with that type of love certainly cares for me still and always will. She never said so because she was willing to let me reveal my struggles at my own pace. Why did I let my illness influence me into thinking that only my love was steadfast? I reflect upon the rest of my friends and realize that their love is the same.

Our friends rush towards us when we come into the clearing. Jacob, my captain, yelled over the din, "I'm guessing from you three's gentle walk together that yous tagged Tris here before she could cross the finish line. Unless yous grew a soft spot for her and decided to tie the game together."

He chortled at his own joke and I joined him before I replied with a reassuring wink, "Have no fear Jacob, I've given our team victory." Though he joined the cheers of our team, my contented heart couldn't possibly soar any higher. I glanced at Tris as her teammates took turns cajoling her, massaging her strained leg, and rubbing her shoulders. Before I could turn my eyes and join in the celebration, Tris caught my gaze and gave me a brilliant smile as she gave me a thumbs up. It was from that moment that the impossible happened: my heart flew ever higher. As Jacob hoisted me upon his shoulders, my mind gained an additional connection with his and our friends below.

In rapid, non-linear succession, I experience the impact that I had in my friends' lives as I witnessed what I meant to them from their perspectives:

Their hearts melted as my words of affirmation leapt from my letters and into their hearts. I always wondered whether my words were *ever adequate in expressing my affections. Some sob with gratitude and I cry along with them as I feel my impact upon their hearts.*

Eruptions of laughter, cheers, and applause take place when I dressed up as Tarzan during one Halloween celebration. Short of money, I arrived with nothing but a torn piece of tablecloth around my underpants and nary a shirt. I always felt self-conscious about this night yet there was no reproach within my friend's hearts as they witnessed a brand of my humor.

Guffaws ensued at our reserved tables when a chicken strip seemingly had enough of my assaults when I attempted, for the eleventh time, to pick it up with a pair of chopsticks. Apparently wanting to be done with it already, my chicken flew and landed quite spectacularly upon a stranger's

yet-to-be-filled plate. The elderly gentleman who had looked a bit sour ever since he was seated looked at me and said, in all seriousness, "Perhaps it's because your chicken watched me eating and noticed that I'm an expert with chopsticks." He burst into a toothy grin as he ate my chicken and my friends laughed harder. Our tears flowed when he proceeded to tell us humorous stories.

That summer night when my illness first reached its peak. It was then that the parasite finally drained all of my hope. Trapped alone in a lightless night, I collapsed and writhed. As my unseen oppressor thrust his hand through my soul and twisted it, I screamed at the top of my lungs yet my shrieks were without sound. As my tears mixed with the luminous pearly blood of my soul, my oppressor materialized. My bruised heart hammered faster due to horror. Part of his bloody skull was exposed since half of his rotting face hung off. Train tracks materialized in front of me and a brilliant golden light proceeded to calm me.

The soil shakes as the train on fire rounds the bend about a mile away. I was so tired, I just wanted to go to sleep and I thought that this would be the only way. As I heaved myself onto the tracks, my parasite tenderly held my hand. "I'm not going to fight anymore," I whispered as I turned to my oppressor and smiled. The burning locomotive was about nine feet from me when I felt her arms wrap around me and yank me from pulverization. Tris had found me just in time.

My friends' looks of weariness from the past year were not exhaustion of being with me for they did not think of me as a burden. Their looks were of sorrow at my pain as they witnessed me grow weaker each day. From my perspective, I am like a time lapse of a withering rose, yet to them I am a soul no less precious from the hardships that I endure, no matter how many or intense my oppressions are. Some of them believe that

laughter is the best way to heal a loved one's wounds, others an open ear, while some make draughts of inspiring words; all attempt to help because of a passionate love.

My memories even interlace with my family. Though I have no doubt of their utmost love for me, the messages of the journey I'm on are reinforced in their memory unfolding within

me. I know I'm reaching the end as my parents, their hearts singing in jubilation, cradled me, not even a day old. My life is not just my own. It belongs to all the souls whom I am connected to and have yet to touch.

With an exhale and a close of my eyes, I feel myself returning to the present.

5

The Decision

I open my eyes and wipe my streaming eyes. Even though I do not doubt my friends' love anymore, I shake my head as my tears flow, "Staying with them would be..."

"Selfish?", the gentleman seated next to me finishes my sentence. "Take it from me, what you've set out to do is selfish. Do not isolate yourself from them. You'll cut a piece of their heart out if you do and they'll never be able to fill the hole that you would have left by deliberately abandoning them. Right now, you feel as if with each triumph you make against your mental oppression, you fall and you doubt that there is anything that you can do about this predicament. You feel increasingly weak with what seems like a cycle of sinking in the sea and swimming past the surface only for a moment's reprieve of air.

"However, you must not give up like me. You

now know how much others love you and I implore you to not give up on yourself for their sake since you love them dearly too. Don't fear the pain that comes to you for pain is not a stranger to others. You feel empathy for your loved ones and they feel the same way about you. Yes, empathy can be quite painful but empathy without pain is a farce and without empathy, love cannot be selfless. From the smile on your face and the twinkle in your eyes, I can tell that you understand," my future self expresses with a radiant smile.

I nod and pronounce, "I'm not leaving my loved ones anywhere. Thank you for helping me."

He wraps me in a bear hug and I return his embrace. I close my eyes to enjoy this moment. He whispers, "Don't worry, I will be alive, though I will no longer be here. We cannot change our past but we can change our future, based upon the decisions we make now. I'm going to be with our friends and family. Those who have died in your future will die without doubting our love."

My arms collapse onto me when air replaces the place where my future self sat. I open my eyes as I feel snow alighting upon my face. I shiver, not having realized that the weather was temperate here when time appeared to freeze. I jump up and run back to Tris's home as the bus halts upon reaching my bench. I laugh in appreciation as I've learned to love myself by viewing myself through others' eyes. I let out a yell of triumph as I realize that I've been given a chance to turn from a grave mistake. I leap off the ground when I relive my memories which intermingled with my loved ones. Pain still churns through me yet I no longer fear this pain.

A mile later, I knock upon Tris's apartment door. Tris opens the door and brings me inside as she exclaims, "Donovan! Merry Christmas! I'm so happy to see you! You're super early, but the rest will be here soon, you can help me finish putting the party decorations up..." she pauses when I wrap my arms around her. My friend quickly returns my embrace. "Aw, I love you so much," she declares. "What's on your mind?" she inquires as we continue to hold onto each other.

I answer, "I have so much to say. Yet, I want to wait until the rest arrive to tell my story. For now, know that I'm so grateful and that I love you dearly too. Merry Christmas, Tris."

A Conversation of Four

The aroma of cheap beer, along with a hint of sweat and urine pervades this dimly lit-hole-in-the-wall bar. There are only four occupants in here, myself included. All of us are sitting at a round, roughly hewn table.

The owner of this watering hole sits across from me, my psychotic oppressor, you may know him well. His name is Agony.

The person whom I've labelled my sociopathic abuser sits to my left and his skin is gently glowing. His name is Hope.

The person, who's rescued me countless times, is a person who appears normal yet her power is awe inspiring. She sits at my right and her name is Love.

As for me, Karen's my name if you truly want to know. However, you can call me Soul since your experiences may align with mine.

I invite you to listen in on our conversation:

Love: Dear Karen, where does you oppressor hurt you? What does the pain feel like?

What does Agony tell you? What is it like when those urges to stay down blind you? Answering these questions will help get the weight off your mind.

Karen: My oppressor has injured my spirit, it has shattered upon his touch. His assault is so intense that it is the greatest pain that I have ever known. I hurt the most within the center of my bosom, therein a force violently pushes inwards.

Agony has hijacked my mind and now I believe that my broken nature has become a burden to all I know. Guilt courses through my veins like never before. I fear that I am beyond redemption's door.

Hope: You are not, nor will you ever be, a burden to those whose hearts beat for yours. The affection you have for them will always be mutual, this I know.

Karen: Why should I believe you? Every time that I am able to find and spend time with you, you allow me to get snatched away by Agony. The fall from your supposed grace makes my pain so much more nightmarish. I feel as if you are an agent for Agony.

Dear Love, Agony steals many of my comforting memories, only you, an agent of my companions, and that deceptive Hope, are able to retrieve them. As for when I receive those urges to stay down, I feel no presence of Hope or joy. It is then that I forget that I was a source for some of their heartwarming smiles, a subject of their compassionate words, and a partaker of those anchoring embraces.

Agony jumps over the table with lightning speed and begins to strangle me from behind. Before Love and Hope can stop him, he moves with inhuman speed to un-holster his weapon as he removes its safety. He places the cold, heavy metal over my heart and he brings my finger to the trigger. He overlays his hands over mine, trapping them there. His chest is pressed up against my back and the base of my skull. His proximity allows my fractured mind to shatter.

Agony: My captive, how many times will it be that I surprise you with these urges to remain down, before you commit to give in, once and for all? You are worthless. Hope and Love are figments of your imagination. Only you and I are here. If you really love others, you will cut your fractured soul from them as you finally embrace eternal defeat. After you've separated yourself from them, they will have peace since there won't be any more obligatory and tiresome work to endlessly lift you up. Most of them have lost the desire to be with you, those that still do soon won't. So sacrifice yourself for them, won't you give them that peace? Let's not delay time, I can feel you slipping away now.

Love: No! Don't listen to his lies, Karen. I know those urges to remain down feel like the best option right now but don't give in! I can feel your torment but my admiration for you has not waned.

I know it's difficult but strive to think of the good memories. Remember their sweet words, the empathy in their eyes, and their warm embraces. They truly care about you, through thick and thin. Obligation would not result in such a response, only Love is capable. I am how others view you, I am their affection. They know your pain and through me, they are fighting for you, so don't you give in.

Hope: Agony has great control over your mind dear Karen, but the choice to stay down is only up to you. If Agony had complete control over you, he alone would have murdered your resolve a long time ago. He would not have wasted his time in trying to convince you to give up the fight.

And I am not Agony's accomplice. If I was, then I would have helped him in convincing you to never rise again. All I've ever done is help rescue you. I am an accomplice of Love and I represent Truth.

You are capable of overcoming this, I believe in you.

The truth, spoken by Love and Hope, has taken me by force and it touches the spirit of Agony. I remove my finger from the trigger and wrestle from my oppressor's grasp. Able to break free, I throw the weapon across the room. I collapse as I shiver and sob. Agony regains his composure as he reaches out for me. Hope punches him in the gut and Love delivers the knockout blow.

My rescuers allow me to wrap my arms around their shoulders. They help carry me through the doorway and into the sunlit outdoors.

I know my urges to stay down will return. I know that Agony will always have some type of presence in my life...well, that's how it seems. I still feel him in my spirit, I can't seem to get rid of his presence.

Love: Now, let it be known: To struggle doesn't mean that one hasn't attained victory. Rather, victory is refusing to stay down. Struggle is a definition of victory. So truly, Agony is terrified of you because you have already won.

No matter what comes your way and no matter how many times you fall, the beautiful thing is that you are not alone in your fight.

Hope: And you will never be alone.

Love: And others love you, just as you love them.

Hope: And no matter what, you will always be loved.

The Mind of Lucian Frye

Sorrow's Rhythm

Lucian Frye: *Frigid freshwater rises with each inhale for oxygen. From this depth, I still see the Sun rays*

pierce through my intended grave. Hope is reaching out for me. I thrash against Death's tow as I begin to swim to the surface. I'm just an arm's length from contacting the air when my lungs give out. I see you above the water line and my vision fails just as you break the surface. I awake, violently coughing the substance which my oppressor left me in. I begin to see you more clearly as my vision comes into focus. Still gasping, I push against the sturdy shore and reach out for you, my companion, my rescuer. Right before our hands can connect, I'm pulled under again.

I am falling through a tunnel, whose walls are the shade of a moonless and starless night. My distance from the luminous light is rapidly increasing. The walls are too far apart for me to stop my plight. The speed from my soundless journey continues until Hope's light completely disappears. That's when I stop, weightless in the air.

Crimson eyes break the darkness. Slowly, I

see the rest of my torturer as my vision adjusts. What is Sorrow like? He is about two feet taller than me. My oppressor's wingspan is about twice my height. He looks like a giant bat, skeletally thin, yet impossibly strong. In a few spots, his fur is caked dry with my blood. Otherwise his coat is the shade of these tunnel walls. His breath smells of decaying bodies.

My demon is right. How many more times do I have to fall from Hope to realize that it's temporary. I don't want to fight Sorrow anymore. The monster smiles as he unleashes his assault on me. Fists collide into my head, my diaphragm, and my stomach. He erupts into laughter as his punches continue to destroy my soul. I join him in laughter as I team up with him by injuring myself. Yes, pain is what I deserve. The creature touches my head and we are transported to another place.

I collapse on to all fours but my limbs give way. I vomit bile and blood. Some of it seeps through cracks in the desert floor. Ahead of me, there are two diverging paths. Sorrow tells me that if I were to take the one on the right, he would carry me to its destination. At the end of this path, there lay a place where I could rest my head. I *would soon experience an eternal and dreamless sleep at those train tracks. It would be there that I would finally attain peace. He reminds me how I've arrived at Death's door many times in the past. He says that it is inevitable that I will eventually give in.*

Sorrow says that if I choose the path on the left, then I would have to travel without assistance, despite my severe injuries. He would only injure me further there. At the end of that path, if I were to make it, there lay Triumph. However, Sorrow reminds me that I would experience another inevitable fall.

Suddenly, I see your words, full of love, within my mind. Our love is immune to my horrors. I close my eyes and despite my injured mind, I focus, with great difficulty, on your words. Eventually, I find myself back in a sequence of memories. I see your smiles, I hear your voices, I feel some of your embraces. I love you all and you love me too. I have to continue fighting. You've given me strength and I know which path to take. I crawl towards it. I wake up within frigid freshwater...

...but I choose not to escape by an endless

sleep since this would rip the souls of my companions. My life is not my own. Therefore, I also will choose to no longer abuse myself, no matter how long my Oppressor and I live within this sequence of Hope's death and resurrection.

The Soul of Scott Wendall

Melancholy
Has a Son

"Everyone has a breaking point", my oppressor assures me as I fall to my knees. My body burns from the assault of the Arctic wind, aches from the punches thrown, and is feverish from flames that threaten to consume me. I raise my vision to look at the demon who is crouched down in front of me, the one who spoke through our connected minds. Scarlet-flaxen fire leaps from the places where his eyes should have been and the flames flood the sight of my eyes. His fire is sharply contrasted with the snow that is twirling about us. The frozen rainfall compliments his fanged ivory smile.

He gestures with a claw that is sprinkled with my blood as he whispers through my mind, "My son is on his way, once again. This time, will you dare refuse his pleas"? He lifts me up with startling speed as he stands yet again. Nausea churns within me and my vision swings as my feet dangle 5,550 feet above the blizzard blanketed earth. The 5,000 foot tall monster drops me into his cavernous mouth to prepare me for Suicide's arrival.

I fall through a fleshy and light starved tunnel for what seems an eternity. However, I soon see a brilliant emerald light which expands as I descend closer to it. The fall concludes when I crash through this bright ocean of acid and reach the bottom that is littered with skeletons. My skin is all but gone now but I force myself to rise. Halfway through my swim to the surface of this quicksand thick liquid, my strength gives way. I've held my breath since I crashed but I can't hold it any longer. Fire disintegrates my lungs as I ingest acid. The pain paralyzes my desire to fight on. All my failures, fears, and self-hatred consume my mind as this cursed ocean rises into my skull.

My oppressor has primed me for Suicide's welcome. Yet, all is not lost. Your love finds a way to overcome the barriers of my agony and I begin to remember how important it is to hope again. I see your smiles that warm my heart, I hear your compassionate words that rescue me from myself, and I feel your embraces that anchored me against waves of oppression. I can't love myself now so I look at myself through your eyes and I have a desire to cry as I feel your love.

I have to take my own advice and know that it's okay to directly ask for help when I need it and that it is always possible to rise after a fall.

I shake my head and I am outside again in the Winter, laying on the ground; I have returned to reality. I see the demon again as he really is, just a little taller than me. He has been corrupting my mind by persuading me to believe that all was lost and that I had better isolate myself from you. I yank his clawed hands from my head and kick him back. He steadies himself in front of me.

As he gets ready to assault me again, he snarls, "Even if you rise, you will fall again. Everyone has a breaking point from which they will never be able to

return." He smiles as he looks behind me, "Suicide will return soon to persuade you."

I grit my teeth as I whisper, "Come what may, I will never give in. My soul would be torn apart if any of my loved ones committed suicide. I will not have them experience that pain by taking my life! And though I've hurt myself and have urges to hurt myself like never before, I don't have to give in. There is always a choice, no matter how difficult it may be. I don't have to hurt myself anymore."

I turn my fists away from myself and aim them for my oppressor. Though Suicide may arrive to tempt me by surprise, I won't give in to his temptations. Staying alert as I can for his possible return, I angle myself so I can have an easy lookout for Death's path behind me and the demon in front of me.

"Do you really think you'll be able to taste victory again?", the Demon questions me as he readies his fists.

I notice his fear as he sees me rise from the ground. I see his terror as I play those happy memories of you and I. Even thinking about your love is an act powerful enough to burn my oppressor's ego.

I answer, as I cry, "Victory is always a community effort so I see why you hate it when I am surrounded by loved ones, I know why you want me to separate myself from them. However, comfort is the truth that I never have to fight my demons alone.

By the way, here's a surprise for you. I've won a long time ago because victory is refusing to stay down, despite the pain. Truly, struggle is a sign of victory."

My Dear Malvinia

My dear Malvinia,

Can I tell you the truth, untainted by fear's edits? My dear friend, the truth is a difficult thing to utter, especially when one doesn't want those whom they love to be hurt by one's own personal Hell. The truth? The truth is I've masked one of my struggles with delicate words, delicate when compared to that one word which describes my recent agony.

My melancholy, like a cancer coursing through my blood, causes me to vomit the good which I receive, the happiness that I intake is temporary, my body, my mind eventually rejects the cure, I feel as if my illness, my agony, is terminal. No one's fault, but my wounded mentality.

Six months ago, as you held me in your embrace, you asked me if I was doing better. I assured you that I was but I could tell that you knew better. The truth is that I was indeed battling something which I did not want you to feel burdened by.

Now we have arrived to that word which I have been dancing around, the symptom, a symptom of my dejection. My urges to commit myself to an early grave had been quite frequent, these impulses I did not want but they came nonetheless. Thankfully, I am not getting them at this moment of my writing. These urges had arrived as a result of the intense torture that I felt from my snapped mentality and I desperately wanted the pain to end.

However, your encouragements to keep on fighting my illness, and the kindness and love from you, my dear Malvinia, helped me to overcome those episodes and I have never gone as far as attempting to follow through with my powerful inclinations.

As I continue on this trek of honesty, I reassure you that 171 nights ago was the last time that the Grim Reaper whispered into my ear. However, my pain has remained steady in its macabre intensity. The virus in my mind assaults my memories, making the good ones seem distant, even taking some of them and distorting them into nightmares and I have more nightmares than not.

How do I get back to that time when happy days greatly outnumbered the bad, when the virus was but an infant in my mind and had yet to attack me during most seconds of my life? I am aware of my insanity. I know that my ill thoughts towards myself are illogical, but this knowledge doesn't change how powerful the pain is.

Now, I have another temptation that I haven't yet told you about. I'm devastated to tell you that I've been avoiding you since our last meeting because the marks of my failure lay across my arms. I am ashamed that I gave in to my inclinations for injuring myself. I'm distressed when I imagine your grief once you know what I have done, yet you deserve the truth. Truth is, my temptations have not yet ceased...at least not while I compose this letter.

One day, I hope to fully be able to live in the now and not go through my surroundings as if it were a dream. Yet, Melancholy's projections are currently a more dominant reality within my mind, almost like I'm hallucinating. It seems the nightmares in my mind are stronger than the joy that surrounds me, which are almost dreamlike in comparison; dreams which fade away as the hours go by, as my evolving virus refocuses my mind.

Though I now hide myself from shame and to keep the marks upon my arms concealed, know that I will run and help you if you should ever ask of it, regardless of my own predicament.

I acknowledge that every one of us has struggles, no matter if they're different or similar, they are no less intense. Yes, in my heart, my faith has been shaken. However, in my mind, I realize that the truth is that our struggles shall not overcome us as long as we keep on fighting, no matter how we feel.

The love that I have received from you, my amazing friend, has been a major inspiration and, truthfully, you are a miracle in my life. Time and time again, you've proven that your love for me is true, despite, forgive me, my Melancholy's contradictions.

One day we will feel the reality that we want for most of our days. I am far from that place now but I will get there eventually, I must believe it. I will one day cry from relief and happiness instead of sorrow, even if it is just for one day.

One day, perhaps, I will be able to once again give you and our friends some of the pure joy that I've always wanted to give. I will make it into the light and maybe find that place again where I will no longer lack in the ability of making others and myself smile, laugh, and cry tears of joy.

Either way, I finally accept that I am loved dearly and please know, if ever you have doubted, that I love you so much too and that is the only thing which is truly important. Thank you Malvinia.

Ever since that night when we first met, you have ultimately helped save my life and my heart aches whenever I think back upon your messages that I too had a positive impact within your life, a truth which I had trouble believing. In my stupor, I hadn't realized that I may be shredding your soul by distancing myself from you. I'm so sorry.

I wrongly believed that I was protecting you from my pain. However, like the abused who finally realize that they are worthy of love, I realized that all I've done is hurt you by believing the abuser in my mind, instead of you. I inadvertently increased your own pain much more than my presence would ever have done. I'm sorry for forgetting that true friendship is unconditional, no matter what trials arrive.

I had forgotten that friendship isn't based upon the joy one brings to another, that would be selfish. As you said, true love of all types is based upon a desire to be with another because each recognizes the beauty of one another's souls, and there is a desire to do the best for one another, regardless of any other feelings. I am so sorry.

I accept your invitation, contained within your last letter. Happy Birthday, Malvinia. I'm coming back.

With lots of love,

Scott Wendall

Ms. Rosaline's Dream

With a satellite view, I look as magma erupts from the earth and freezes within space. As the exposed core slows its rotations, my heart changes its pace to a crawl. Hours ago, the world thrived as our beautiful souls regaled inspiring tales.

"You thought you were on victory's path", the monster snarled as he punches through my heart. My soul flies from my body but before it can completely leave, Hope tethers it with a few wisps of fraying resistance. As my soul hangs from my body, certain desires re-birth within me; those inclinations about the supposed peace that I would obtain upon ceasing my resistance against cynicism.

An aged massive humanoid bat envelops me in his wings as I fear not knowing how much longer I'll be able to keep Hope from the Grim Reaper's pleas. Yet your wave of love overtakes my mind, causing the monster's eyes to shine as the Sun.

Your message plays through my heart as I begin to awake:

Our struggles, whatever they may be, are a part of who we are, yet let's not allow this truth to paralyze our existence. Through our afflictions, we can unearth inspiration. Prone to give up, though we may be, our love for one another shall never leave. Now repeat this mantra alongside me.

My Dear, Scott Wendall

Dear friend, once again, thank you so much. I am ecstatic to have seen you, to have heard your voice, and to have held you close to myself again. Do not give in to your fancies of doubt which insist that you soured my birthday party with your presence. Please do not be ashamed of feeling sorrow.

You've been utterly honest with me, baring it all in your last letter. Yet I haven't been fully honest with you about what I've perceived of you nor what I struggle with. My time for confiding in you had arrived at the moment you fully opened yourself to me yet I didn't want you to feel burdened by me because of that which you struggle with.

I must also confess that I had a guess about your oppression, even before you fully confided in me a year ago, yet I said nothing then because I did not want to portray myself as presumptuous, since I had a fear of coming across as rude. I took notice as a bit of the battle between hope and sorrow peered forth from your eyes, even as you smiled. Yet your agony did not, it does not, nor will it ever, give me the desire to end my deep friendship with you.

Now, the pain that speaks to you, the

depression that steals too many of your good memories, the urges for self-inflicted injuries, I am familiar with them. Just because I smile and laugh often, doesn't mean that my pain is minimal, far from it; we all have an exceptional talent and I've used mine to mask my pain.

I realize that by withholding this information about my demons has caused you harm, though I thought that I was protecting you with a marathon of bliss. The knowledge that it was at turns tainted and fabricated were only privy to me.

I should have spoken up when you confided in me, to let you know that we share these demons, therefore we have the unique ability to truly understand one another's troubles, in addition to nourishing each other with our steadfast love. However, past decisions cannot be undone yet the present is here for better tomorrows.

Where do you want to meet again? Let's see each other as soon as possible.

Love you always,

Malvinia Rosaline.

<u>Dear Beautiful Soul</u>

(From Karen
to Gideon)

There was a time when
I witnessed your beautiful soul rays,
shine through your eyes.
We were still young when your childhood died.
I did nothing to comfort you as the days passed,
though I did feel a portion of your sorrow.
I remember more than one day where
I had ample opportunity to save you.
One day, you waited alone in a crowd.
That light had gone from your eyes
but I preferred spending time with those
who still had joy.
I assured myself that you would be okay.
Yet, not long after,
you helped me, despite your
broken soul and my selfish inaction.

With your tender hands,
you spun stories as you rescued hope,
from doubt,
only to give hope to me.
I assured myself that you would get better.
As the years passed, we grew distant,
and you became Oppression's favorite captive.
However, you still managed to openly smile and

laugh

even when your injuries became interlaced with the

physical realm.

I tried my best to be there for you

when I realized how damaging your pain became,

but it was too late to heal the bond we had

when we were young.

I struggled to stop myself from crying

when I saw your tears freely

flow for the first time.

Though I yearned to hug you,

I never found the

"right moment".

At least, I got to hold your hand.

Your hand

that wrote inspiring messages for me, all those

years ago.

Your hand

A member of your injured soul.

Your hand,

that now held

the hand of the soul

who left you to fend for yourself all those years

ago.

I think that day was the last that I saw you.
Since then, you told me that you've courageously
embarked on a journey to start anew.

Dear friend,
I am so proud of you.
If ever there is anything I can do, please don't
hesitate
to let me know.

Gideon Leaves a Note

I truly realized that I'm no longer meant to rise, I need to go, I hope that I was wholly successful in inspiring you but I can't follow my own advice anymore. I am beyond any lasting redemption.

Please remember me for all the good moments I shared with you, my loved ones. I look back on the moments when laughter was shared amongst us, when adventures thrilled us, when hope was alive within us. However, the Present shows me that I will never be the source of joy that the Past presents. Truly, Happiness has divorced himself from the pain within me and I will never be whole again.

So please, I know I've lifted you up but now you know why I must go. You are so courageous for all the times which you've fought for me but I will no longer allow you to be hurt by my oppression. I cannot feel joy and I don't want my pain to corrupt your souls. You won't have to worry anymore.

I picture your beautiful smiles and I love you too much to keep your souls interlaced with mine. Staying with you would be selfish of me.

Please Death, come quickly, I yearn to save them and I cannot fight for them anymore. Death, please take me.

An Ancient Warrior Responds

Death, stay away from him! Gideon, focus on my voice! My name is Love and I never left you. I want you to realize that you're doing right by fighting the best you can. So don't you feel ashamed. Every ounce of your courage is a tidal wave of triumph.

Do not give into guilt for what you go through and do not believe that your pain will drive others away. I am reality. Sometimes intense battles will occur with such frequency that you will be tempted to give it all up. However, there will always be a way out into the light, no matter how difficult the fight may get.

Every effort which you carry out is an act of war, so do not feel guilt. Keep speaking about your struggles since it will help those that relate to your pain; they will remember that they are not alone. And keep on infusing your speech with hope, since this can rescue those who struggle towards finding it.

Re-discover the knowledge that though the

war will continue, happiness will break through your soul again.

Do not believe that Death is the answer, all it will do is destroy the souls of your loved ones. So continue your fight, open your mind's eye to realize that despite your pain, I will never abandon you because I am more than a feeling.

Is This the Finale?

"Goodbye," whispered Gideon. "There isn't much time, you need to let me go. This is the end".

Crimson and sapphire flames roared around them as he looked into her eyes and forced a smile. He continued to wipe away her tears and he turned his vision onto the cocooning inferno.

Karen placed a hand on each of her friend's cheeks as she forced him to look into her indigo eyes. "Who are you to give up? Who are you to abandon us, the ones whose souls are interlaced with yours? Damn it, I'm not giving up on you so don't you dare give up on yourself. I love you..." Karen wrapped her arms around Gideon's torso as he fell and they both collapsed to the scorched earth. She let go and gritted her teeth as blood seeped from her knees. She knew
that only seconds separated them from the fire. Yet she gently and firmly spoke, "I'm not going to leave you. I'm here with you, and from now on I always will be, come what may."

She clutched onto her friend as he coughed crimson drops and shivered violently. Karen closed her eyes and sang to him as the flames enveloped them.

The mystical inferno plunged her soul into arctic waters as it connected her mind with her friend's. Tortured shrieks for help entered her ears and they sliced through her soul. Rot pierced her nostrils and mouth before it proceeded to churn her gut into unnatural motions. She opened her eyes and saw an unidentifiable individual thrashing as amber flames consumed him or her, just a few paces ahead of them. Those flames were the only source of light within this moonless and starless night.

Shock paralyzed her as the individual continued to scream for help. A delicate breath across Karen's cheek unchained her as Gideon intoned, "It's okay. Remember that this isn't real, no matter how tangible it seems".

"Who is that?" Karen stuttered before she was interrupted by a crowd of burning and screaming individuals whom materialized around them.

"The first person who you saw burning was you," sobbed Gideon. "All who are burning are the souls which I have failed or am bound to fail. I failed you by letting you in here with me."

Karen grasped her friend's arms as she

fought to realize that the horrors she was seeing were a product of Gideon's infected mind. She screamed over the furor as sweat formed upon her brow, "Look into my eyes. You did not fail me. Don't look away, come back. Focus on me Gideon. You. Did. Not. Fail. Me. Love doesn't abandon you because of pain, no matter how intense it is. Love endures, it comforts, and it rescues. I love you Gideon."

The image of her burning corpse disappeared. Staying courageous, despite the remaining horror which encircled them, Karen proclaimed, "That's right, I'm right here, I'm here for you. You haven't failed anyone, Gideon. You also underestimate yourself. Don't forget how you've rescued me and everyone else. I assure you, that I, you, and the rest of our loved ones are in this together. We all make mistakes but that's a condition of our humanity. And if anyone belittles you, the problem with them is their attitude and it has nothing to do with you, my dear friend."

Karen wrapped her arms around her friend's torso and she kissed his cheek. They held onto each other and her heat poured into his thawing soul as his thawed hers. As one, the screams, thrashing souls, and flames gradually transformed into individuals who smiled in approval as they glowed with a golden aura.

The naked night sky slowly became clothed with stars as Karen sang her gentle tune again. Eventually a sliver of the moon materialized and within a few minutes, it became whole. Gideon and Karen remained within each other's arms during this transformation, yet they turned to look into each other's eyes as affection and catharsis caused them to laugh fervently. Gideon was ripped from Karen's arms and she crashed onto her back. The moon fractured as the stars imploded and gravity reversed. Karen's friend was held by his captor as everyone plummeted towards the sky. Gideon knew who this creature was, though he had not seen this wingless and humanoid bat before. Karen's friend punched through the chest of the newborn from within the earth and grabbed onto his heart. Everyone's free fall halted as the destruction paused its work upon the galaxy. The embodiment of Gideon's oppression shrieked as Gideon flooded the creature's soul with hope and love. Yet Tante screamed out not in pain but frustration as Gideon's now dominant emotions brought tears to the creature's crimson eyes. The celestial bodies began to heal. The earth's gravity slowly bought them back to the ground as it gradually began to mend itself.

The speed of descent began to rapidly increase as gravity became close to its original state. Before Gideon could withdraw his hand and heal Tante's wound, the creature used his rapidly draining strength to kick him away. Gravity regained its normality when everyone was about seven feet from the ground. When Tante crashed, his spirit fled harmlessly towards the restored night sky.

As the sun rose, Karen interlaced her fingers around her friend's. Gideon's grin grew ever wider as he said, "Karen, thank you again for encouraging me to confront my pain head on and for being here with me, through it all."

"I'll always be here for you," replied Karen as she returned his smile. "You and I, we're in this together. As are the rest of our loved ones. Pain and distance shall have no effect upon any of our connected hearts.

Are you ready to continue on the journey?"

They turned their eyes from each other and looked ahead to the sun-kissed crimson, amber, and sapphire horizon. Gideon turned to look at the mirages which represented all those whose lives he touched. The images smiled and some waved. While his heart continued to warm and as his spirit soared ever higher, he met Karen's gaze and nodded.

Strange: And Other Accounts From the Taboo War

Written by Crystal Rosario

Book 3

Kaya: Where Have You Gone?

Dedicated to sexually assaulted children, misunderstood melancholic beings, and the vanished souls.

1

A Mother and Her Daughter

Location: The neighborhood of Miyajimaguchi in Hatsukaichi, Japan

Yu-Ri raised her slender hand to brush away a runaway tear. The problem, she thought bitterly, is that once a tear slips from its restraints, then it's nearly impossible to contain the others.

Her tears splashed onto the shallow sink and upon her white knuckled fists which clutched the edge of the indigo counter. She bit her ruby lipsticked lips to trap the scream which erupted from the depths of her breaking heart. Yu-Ri raised her head and looked into the golden framed bathroom mirror and she suppressed a groan as she rubbed the running mascara from her fair cheeks.

"*Ohayo Gozaimasu*, good morning!" Kaya announced, from behind her, with pure delight.

Yu-Ri steeled herself and whipped around as she intermingled laughter with her sobs. The transition was magnificent. Seeing her daughter always gave her courage when she needed it the most. "*Ohayo Gozaimasu*, my love," she proclaimed.

Kaya's grin fluttered before it settled into a frown. "Why are you crying Mama?" she asked.

Yu-Ri knelt down in front of Kaya as she brought one hand to stifle her laughter and another to, ever so gently, bop her nine year old daughter's nose. She ebbed her laughter but kept her smile as she reminded the prodigy, "You, dear daughter, know best that when one laughs so freely, then the floodgates of their tears are raised."

"So melon-dramatic but as true as cows go 'moo'," Kaya assured her mother with a delicate grin before she let out a sonorous and elongated "moooooo!"

Yu-Ri burst into laughter but her guffaws were authentic this time. "I never heard of that phrase," she stated between her gales of laughter. "Neither did I know that...

"...that you gave birth to a cow?" Kaya interjected as she chuckled. "Surprise!"

Like twin waterfalls, Yu-Ri's tears fell from her eyes and cascaded down her dimpled cheeks.

Yu-Ri mused that sometimes laughter was like her Kaya running away from a bath. At times, laughter could be so potent that it was nearly impossible for one to subdue it before it grew exhausted from its own run.

"I was going to say..." Yu-Ri managed to get out those words before laughter wagged a finger and proceeded to run at full speed again.

"...that you never heard of one accidentally say melon-dramatic instead of melodramatic?" Kaya suggested amidst her heartwarming giggles and tears which flowed past her own dimpled cheeks.

"You sly daughter of mine," laughed Yu-

Ri. "Your are correct."

After what seemed several minutes later, but was really under sixty seconds, Yu-Ri reigned in her laughter. Compassion emanated from Kaya's bright eyes as she placed a delicate hand upon her mother's cheek. Yu-Ri placed her own hand on top of her daughter's as she closed her eyes.

"I know when you are pretending that everything is okay mama," Kaya tenderly whispered. Yu-Ri opened her eyes and saw that her daughter was giving her an encouraging smile. "You can tell me what's wrong. I always tell you, Daddy, and Daichi when I'm having a bad day."

"I can't let Kaya know the truth, it would ruin her," Yu-Ri intoned.

She assured her daughter, "I was just feeling one of my random downs but as always, seeing you, Daddy, and your brother brightens my spirits. Where are daddy and Daichi anyway? Are they still sleeping?"

"They're up," Kaya replied. "Daddy is

preparing breakfast and he sent me to check up on you. Maybe if we go now, we can still help Daddy. The more help he gets, the faster we can go and the better that will be because I'm on a tight schedule."

Yu-Ri found realization as she laid her sight upon Kaya's lavender backpack and she tilted her chin towards the indigo ceiling while she closed her eyes. "I'm so sorry Kaya, I can't believe that I forgot that you're going to a faraway school! I don't know where my head is this morning." She groaned as awareness chided her. "Oh no, that came out rude, didn't it?",

"No worries Mommy!" Kaya piped. "By the way, I have great news!"

Kaya tenderly placed her palms upon her mother's cheeks as she continued, "I've made an extraordinary find, a treasure which will warm your heart."

Kaya's nibbled fingernails became overlaid with her Mother's calloused palms as Yu-Ri questioned with a heart melting smile,

"And what have you discovered?"

Kaya whispered as if she were letting her Mother in on a secret: "Well, it's kinda like when Daddy once forgot where his glasses were, only to discover that they were on top of his head. Mommy, I've found your head."

Yu-Ri was frozen in honest confusion for a moment before she rapidly placed an ivory hued hand over her lips. Laughter erupted forth from her soul as she embraced her daughter with her free arm. Yu-Ri brought her daughter to her bosom as they tumbled into a controlled fall. They remained like that, amidst their symphony of guffaws, for fifteen seconds that seemed as if they were a lifetime.

Tears streamed past Yu-Ri's cheeks again as she rocked upon the linoleum floor and she continued to cry as she allowed reality to reassert itself: her memory of her daughter when she was five years old ebbed away from the forefront of her focus. She clutched herself as her dying laughter resurrected into moans while her husband and son rushed into the restroom. They held one another as they grieved together. Kaya was eight years old when she vanished three weeks ago.

2

Four Months Ago: The First Day of Third Grade

Kaya glided into the kitchen as if they were ice skaters who were too joyous to worry about a graceful presentation when they proclaimed, "We're here!" Kaya's heart enthusiastically applauded before pretending to dive into her belly as her momentum continued. She turned her head to the left and witnessed what could have been Humpty Dumpty's relative slip from her brother's mouth to resignedly have a great fall.

The world kept on flying toward and around Kaya as her father whipped around from the stove to face the missile of joy. Riku caught his daughter, brought the hazel windows of her soul to his eye level, securely embraced her, and spun her around as they partook in each other's laughter. Yu-Ri remained splay-legged at the kitchen's doorway as she attempted to look on disapprovingly at her husband and Kaya yet their hysterics tickled her defenses into submission yet again since her daughter and Riku's morning routine commenced three days ago. Daito remained open-mouthed but he turned his attention from the clowning duo towards the soft boiled egg that lay broken upon the floor. He mournfully shouted, "That's not funny Kaya, Dad could have missed you this time and then I would have been sobbing over your broken body instead of just..."

"...Humpy Dumpty's?", Kaya interjected.

"I should never have read that story to you," replied Daito as he grabbed a rag to free the tile from the victim and his entrails.

Riku knew that it was inappropriate to keep on laughing yet it was nigh impossible to cease since he had caught the case of the giggles. However, it was not unfeasible and he managed to rapidly sober up when he caught sight of his wife's recomposed expression of sternness and his daughter's doe-eyed frown. He looked at Daito again and noticed that his son's lower lip quivered as he further broke the egg in his attempts to pick it up.

"Go ahead and relax at the table Daito," Riku stated as his daughter walked towards her ten year old brother, wrapped her arms around him, and tenderly wiped his teary eyes.

"I'll wipe away the mess," Riku asserted. "I just need to stir the soup for a couple more minutes," he proceeded as Yu-Ri knelt in front of her children, smiled, and rubbed her nose with Daito's while she rubbed his back.

Riku went on, "Breakfast is otherwise ready. Yu-Ri and Kaya, dears, would you mind bringing the eggs to the dining room when you're ready? There's more than enough for everybody."

***

"*Daito, Honto ni gomen ne*, I'm so sorry," Kaya murmured as Yu-Ri and Riku washed away their breakfast residue in the adjacent room. "It's not just Father this time and neither is it my strange advancement to that new school is it?" she whispered. "Is it your friends too?"

Daito's cheeks alighted like neon roses as he brought his third cup of miso broth to his lips. Kaya silently procured one of the tuna chunks that her sibling discarded into her emptied bowl as his zealous slurps complimented the sound of porcelain being submerged into the soapy rapids of the kitchen sink.

Kaya studied the boy who sat across from her at the foot high oak table as the Pacific fish (saturated with the stock of soybeans, seaweed, and noodles) delighted her taste buds as ever but her spirit refused to be warmed by it at that time. She rose ever so slightly and her suspicions that Daito was slurping while drinking nothing were confirmed.

So preoccupied was he with his lengthy act that he didn't even notice his sister's new location until she gently pretended to cough beside him. Daito's blush blushed as he sheepishly raised his eyes from the bowl to his sibling's eyes. He gave up half of his seat upon her gentle command to do so and she gracefully sat upon the freed section of his velvet cushion. Kaya picked up the last piece of tuna from her dish with her trusty bamboo chopsticks and cheerily ordered Daito to "Open wide, here comes the cho-cho train!"

"Come on Kaya, I'm not a baby!" he tersely murmured through a suppressed giggle.

"I know but I am, so indulge me," his sister merrily retorted. "Plus, I know there's still vacancy in your belly."

Daito opened his mouth with the mock sorrow of a plumber walking towards his nineteenth clogged latrine.

"Chugga, chugga, choo choo!" Kaya proclaimed as she mimed a locomotive inching its way towards a tunnel. When Daito closed his mouth upon the imaginary train, his sister exclaimed "Hey conductor, it moves!" in what was meant to be a terrified senior lady's voice. However, it sounded like the voice of a frightened squeaky mouse.

Daito exploded into laughter and the tuna in his mouth gained the gift of flight. The chunk of fish enthusiastically escaped the unstable toothed tunnel only to collide upon Kaya's face.

"Come here you," Kaya demanded in playful indignation as she wiped her face with one hand while she grabbed her brother around the shoulders with her unoccupied arm. They fell over laughing as she mildly rubbed her knuckles into the top of his head.

"Hey, what's all the commotion about?", Riku inquired with amusement as he entered the dining room while toweling a pot. "Your dishes are the only ones that need washing now. Hurry, hurry, my lovely goofballs. Kaya, you and Mother need to leave in nine minutes if you hope to make it on time."

***

"Since when has Father called me 'lovely'?", Daito asked his sister.

Kaya and Daito stood at the edge of their front garden of cherry blossoms as their parents engaged in their own conversation at an opposite corner. Crimson and golden light began to slide its way through the ebony sky and the distant stars started to conceal their faces for it was the arising Sun's turn to shine. The siblings turned to admire the brilliant transition after Kaya slipped her right hand into Daito's left one. Kaya looked into her brother's face as his face displayed the steadily brightening morning.

"Daddy's trying," Kaya whispered as she stroked Daito's hand. "I have no problem reminding you that he loves you Daito and that he was merely disappointed by your low marks from the last school year, especially since..."

"...Father is the headmaster and a

substitute teacher," Daito finished. "I know, I know."

Kaya proceeded, "He just wants you to put in good work again. By the way, you never answered my question about your friends."

Daito sighed in exasperation as the Sunrise became too bright to look upon. As he let his vision fall towards the ground, he defeatedly replied, "Look at me Kaya, in case you haven't gotten a good look during the years that we've spent together. Take a good look. Do you think anyone would truly befriend a fat person?" He suddenly adopted a jester's tone as he continued with a laugh, "Who, outside of our family, ever wants to be seen with me, the town's only hippo, the lone whale, the exclusive panda, the..."

Kaya's fierce embrace of Daito silenced him. Her warmth melted away the last layer of his composure; thus he broke down into tears. *"What am I doing? I'm supposed to be a pillar of strength for my little sister,"* Daito silently scolded himself. He mentally slapped himself as confessions proceeded to tumble out of his mouth, "I pretended to make friends during the past summer so you wouldn't worry about my friendships once you started going to a different school than me. I would normally just hide out at the docks during my free time as I created my imaginary friends. Additionally, my grades suffered last year because I was suffering at the thought of suddenly not spending as much time with you. I know that's selfish of me.

Anyway, I did try to make friends on my way to the pier every afternoon but I'm just so disgusted by how I look so my voice stopped working and I got super nervous and I accidentally bumped into people and I tripped into potholes and....and...and it doesn't help that some kids on the street run away from me in terror because they must mistake my frustrated face as rage towards them, while others laugh at my size."

"Dear brother," Kaya tenderly chided her brother as he caught his breath and she suppressed a cry. She looked up at him with shining eyes. "I'm going to miss you too buddy but never forget that although I'll be gone for the majority of most days, I'll never be gone for entire ones. Also, sure, there are bullies out there, especially at this time as more people try to comfort themselves by putting others down, but you can't believe that the whole world is against you. Isn't it likely that many of the people who ran were frightened by something else or merely playing some imagined game that had nothing to do with you? Isn't it reasonable that most of the people who seemed to be laughing at you weren't making fun of anything about you but were actually laughing at something else entirely?"

"That does seem logical," Daito admitted after a moment as his tears slowed their pace.

Kaya continued, "Plus, my friends are forever yours too. Eimi, Chiya and Kaede always want to spend more time with you. They don't care that you're a guy if it doesn't bother you that they're girls. Who cares if culture tells us that girls are meant to only have friendships with girls and guys are only supposed to be friends with other guys? Boys and girls look different on the outside, no doubt, but we have the same hearts and our souls are made of the same substance. So the parts of us that matter are really the same."

"I'm supposed to be your role model," her brother apologized. "What did I do to deserve such a wise and loving sister?", Daito inquired in embarrassment and gratitude.

"You do inspire me," Kaya tenderly admonished. "Did you already forget my first day at school when Fumi the Meanie publicly made fun of my first story that I was so proud of? I thought that sharing it with her and other classmates would win me friends but when she did that and her two friends laughed, I believed that maybe my story was garbage and that everyone in that school, except you, was cruel like them. But you calmed me down after you finally persuaded me to give you an answer for my sadness by reasoning that they couldn't possibly hate the content of my story because they dismissed it before they even got a chance to experience it. Besides, you stated that what really matters is that I gain enjoyment from my stories no matter what others feel about them.

If it weren't for you, then I wouldn't have understood that maybe they were jealous of my ability to brilliantly write or perhaps they just wanted to lash out because they had a rough home life or because of the rising distress in this nation. Quite possibly, it could have been all three.

So I went back to them a couple days later because I felt sorry for them, yes, yet I also felt drawn to them because they appeared as if they didn't need anyone since they always separated themselves from the group whenever they could. I wanted to be able to stand on my own like you seemed to but I didn't go to you since I didn't want any help from family and before you apologize Daito, I also learned through your consolations that standing on one's own feet doesn't mean to create distance between everyone else; it is recognizing one's own amazing worth.

Regardless, I didn't consider the irony of thinking that Fumi and her associates didn't need anyone when there were the three of them,; seemingly unable to escape from one another's presence.

When one of her henchwomen gave me a black eye, you taught me, in your own way, that compassion is a beautiful thing but to never let my heart lead me into abuse. The people who are insistently cruel are beyond help unless it comes from divine guidance. Papa and Mama taught this to me too but you were the one who got through to me by letting me throw a temper tantrum in front of you, which Father wouldn't allow, and by comforting me, which Mother tried her best to do.

You also helped me befriend those who have an abundance of love, people who are my friends to this day and, I remind you, your friends as well. So the question is what did I do to deserve the best brother in the world?"

"*Doumo Arigatou* Kaya, thank you so much," Daito stumbled in his reply, almost at a loss for words.

"Listen to me Daito," she continued as she noticed their parents' conversation nearing its conclusion. "When I get back later today, you and I are going to work on getting you to see how wonderful and handsome you are. We'll also find time between our homework and chores to spend time with our friends.

By the way, you told me that you wanted to be a sumo wrestler when you grow up so you could, in your words, 'prove that I'm not a cuddly teddy bear.' What do you really want to be Daito?"

"A brilliant teacher like Father," Daito answered.

Yu-Ri peered over at her children who still held one another in an embrace. "I'm sure that Kaya and I will be fine Riku. Really, just because we're women...anyways that's my final, say in the matter dear. You need to fix the bond between yourself and our son. You can see that he's in pain."

Riku gave a great heave as he reluctantly nodded. "Just be careful, okay?" he replied.

"Don't worry, I think our daughter and I will prance through the streets while we shout curses at anyone who carries a weapon," Yu-Ri merrily told her husband. "Honestly, you're acting like we had that in mind. Of course we'll be careful Riku." She kissed his cheek as she glanced at her stainless steel watch. "Come on, she and I are running late."

Riku and Yu-Ri quickly walked towards the roadway as Daito and Kaya did the same from the other end of the estate. The men quickly yet tightly took turns hugging the women (they embraced Kaya a bit more tightly) as they pecked their cheeks (Riku gave an extra kiss upon Kaya's forehead) and bid their goodbyes. As mother and daughter walked hand in hand towards the street, Kaya turned her face towards her brother and yelled, "Don't forget Daito! You're the best brother that I could have ever had. I'll see you later today."

"Hey, what about me, am I the best Daddy?", Riku asked in mock irritation.

"Yeah, I guess so," Kaya responded as she shrugged her shoulders in pretended indifference.

As the family laughed, Kaya vaulted over a presiding cultural aspect shared by not merely Japan by directly verbalizing her affection and even shouting it for nearby strangers to hear; she was eager to proclaim to her family members that holy phrase which so often was ever implied: "I love you!" she yelled to her father and brother.

Daito and Riku watched their female family members until they disappeared around the block and father and son beamed all the while.

"Come on Daito, we have about an hour before we have to head out," Riku told his son. "What do you want to do?"

"How about we begin with a game of

Menko?", suggested Daito.

"You're on," Riku declared as he genuinely beamed.

3

Four Months Ago: What Do You Know About Fumi?

Location: The neighborhood of Hasu in Ōno, Japan (Approximately 2.5 miles from Kaya's home)

Fumi's teeth chattered as a ghostly icicle plummeted from her throat to her gut. She used a sleeve of her kamino to wipe chilly beads of sweat from her forehead while she used her free hand to unsteadily pour the man in the coffee-colored coat a cup of Genmaicha tea. His richly blue sight rocketed from the little girl's trembling hands and sloshing green tea to rest upon her downturned face. "Careful dear," the man affectionately whispered to his niece as he peered at her reddening heart shaped face from over the rims of his ice blue shades. Fumi's twin reflections upon her Uncle's wide pupils, golden irises, and custom tinted glasses revealed that the ten year old girl continued to tremble as she tried her best to set the teacup down without splashing any more of its content.

Gen rested a manicured and lightly lavender scented hand upon his niece's sweaty one as she set the teapot down upon the frilly snow colored tablecloth. Fumi managed to grasp onto a miraculous bloom of resistance which was revealed by her victory over the urge to jerk her hand away from the monster's. Gen gently circulated his thumb over the back of the young girl's hand as he deftly removed his shades with his other hand, stared into her eyes, and hummed her a lullaby.

Fumi wrenched her hand away and fled out the door. She heard her Uncle's chasing footsteps and his scream for her to come back but she rapidly increased the distance between her pursuer and blended in with the town's throng. A sense of blissful weightlessness spread from Fumi's heart to the rest of her body as she realized that she was finally free.

Fumi continued to allow a part of her mind to soak in the imagination of her escape as she kept another aspect of her awareness in reality. She observed her two eleven year old sisters who were obliviously sipping their tea of roasted brown rice and green tea leaves as they laughed with one another while looking upon her anxious condition with a confused concern that was tinged with irritation. Uncle Gen always treated the twins with kindness and he intensified his affection for them once he adopted them upon their parents' deaths a year ago so they held nothing in their hearts except loving gratitude for their relative. He doted upon their younger sister too as far as they could tell.

"If only they knew that their bodies and sanity remain intact because of me," thought Fumi. She internally shuddered as an unbidden image of her white haired elderly Uncle with the pearly white teeth and bright eyes slept with Arisa and Hana as he did with her.

Interlude

At least since her earliest memory at the age of four, Fumi remembered that he discreetly touched her in a way that she imagined was only acceptable for adult romantic companions like her Father and Mother. During most instances, it was brief yet for the times when he somehow got her alone it was prolonged, such as her first memory of his evil touch after he washed her diaper when her parents were out (she wasn't potty trained until the start of second grad and his abuse was the main reason for this). Fumi felt her soul violently collapse inward at the first stimulating touch and she was stunned into a state of shock and shame which lasted several weeks; which her Uncle blamed upon merely feeling sick from a germ or virus. Her anguish which was so immense that it took a physical toll upon her which helped give weight to Gen's lie. The trauma from the event, along with her Uncle's threat that he would abuse her sisters if she ever told the truth to anyone, compelled Fumi to keep his first and subsequent abuses a secret as her soul shattered at every inappropriate touch.

***

Fumi even kept her Uncle's evil hidden as he quietly snuck into her room upon the first night that he adopted her and slept with her for the first time; She was nine years old on that initial night.

Her Uncle tenderly wiped away her tears as he continued his atrocious act and that made her feel more helpless than if he had displayed annoyance. She remained silent about the nightly visits which followed as her visible tears during those sleepless nightmares lessened and her sisters remained safe ever since she upheld her part of the unspoken agreement...yet Arisa and Hana unknowingly arrived at the brink of sharing some of Fumi's horror last night. That was the night when Uncle Gen laid with her in a new way which brought startling torment and a full forced punch to the gut from Fumi. She rapidly apologized in her panic as her Uncle doubled over while dryly heaving. She closed her eyes and unconsciously hugged her chest as she readied herself for him to strike her for the first time or to more cruelly lay into her. As Fumi listened to her Uncle catch his breath, she heard her bedsprings quietly squeak and she felt her mattress rise which obliged her to open her eyes. She saw Gen silently stumble to her bedroom door before he turned the handle. Still hunched over, her Uncle turned his head as he gave a brilliant smile and Fumi burst into tears while she bit into her bedsheets to prevent her sisters from hearing her tormented screams. She shook her head at Uncle Gen as she silently apologized and pleaded for him to not touch her sisters. She could see his mind rapidly turn for an alternate yet still cruel solution as his grin remained in place. He let go of the doorknob as he walked back to his youngest niece and knelt before her. He placed a wrinkled hand upon her cheek as he whispered in a deceivingly warmhearted tone,

"Oh, sweetheart. There's no need for these tears, haven't I proven that my devotion to you is real? I forgive you my dear sweet Fumi. However, there needs to be a consequence to ensure that you never lash out again. Nothing that I do to you will be enough. I need to discipline someone you love. So if not at least one of your sisters then who? Perhaps one of your friends will suffice?"

Fumi attempted to shake her head as her Uncle tilted his head and inched his face a millimeter away from hers. If she moved her head anyplace than backwards, her lips would have hit his. Fumi barely managed to keep her bile within her as an inner wound and dread massaged her with agony. She bit her tongue as the persistent waves of nausea brought both an inner heat which scorched her face and a sense of weightlessness that expanded from within her diaphragm. The tickle of her Uncle's breath upon her cheeks, nose, and lips as he spoke did nothing to help her effort in the battle.

"Do you know what's strange my dear Fumi? Many young girls keep diaries, even your sisters do, yet never in my life have I seen you with one. Is it possible that such a girlish custom just doesn't fancy you? No, practically unnoticeable though they were, I've sometimes noticed the fresh ink smudges on your hands after you've left your room...what's the matter? Thought you were clever, did you?

Fumi, where is your diary?"

Fumi hyperventilated as her uncle tenderly implored her to look into his eyes. She obliged and for the first time, she witnessed in his eyes a rage intermingled with pleasure despite his grandfatherly tone and persistent smile. What was terrifying was that the flames of anger which shone from the windows to his *soul were overtaken by floodlights of convincing remorse merely a second later.*

Silence passed between Gen and Fumi. She gasped as pain exploded from her neck and her vision dimmed. She attempted to gasp but the air refused to relieve her incrementally burning lungs. Uncle Gen slammed his niece's knees onto the oaken floorboards and he dragged her towards the door as he maintained his tight grip upon her throat.

"We're going to have fun with your sisters Fumi," her Uncle whispered.

Fumi's eyes instinctively flashed towards the space beneath her bed as she struggled to maintain her consciousness.

She gulped air and tried to push herself from the floor after her Uncle let go of her. She collapsed and vomited as her Uncle flipped on the light and crawled underneath the bed. He wheezed and suppressed coughs as he lifted a few loose floorboards and discovered not a journal but stacks of sealed and opened letters. He brought a few out as he came back up to sift through them in better light. They were a one way correspondence between Fumi and Kaya.

Uncle Gen's confidence solidified beyond his prior assumption as he speedily read through the unsealed letters which were addressed to Fumi yet his analysis brought upon him a tidal wave of shock when he opened Fumi's unsent letters to Kaya. The secret which startled him rapidly abated as his fantasy of vengeance became fed by it.

"Oh, Fumi sweetheart," Gen delicately addressed his niece while he placed her calloused fingers into his soft palms. With great ease, he led her around her bile since her mind had entered a doorless and windowless hall with no end in sight. Her Uncle sat her on the foot of her twin bed before he entered her bathroom across from it to gather the necessary materials to clean up the yellow entity upon the floor.

Fumi stared ahead unseeingly into her restroom as her Uncle wiped and sanitized the gnarled planks. Her mind gradually slipped away from the imperceptible maze with the single lane to arrive in her physical surroundings before she remembered her situation as well as new potential ones. She violently shivered as she swallowed back a new wave of nausea which was partly drawn by pain's belated and panicked arrival into her recently bruised and skinned knees yet her gulp plunged a dagger of pain down her throat.

Fumi's blurry vision into her minuscule bathroom was cut off by her Uncle's deeply lined navel. He bent down to her eye level as he whispered "Those letters have provided me with better proof than any diary ever could Fumi. Oh, you sad lost soul, are those fresh tears in your eyes?

Yes, I will take care of your friend and I know that I needn't remind you what will happen if you spoil the inevitable. Yet I am not without mercy. I see now that I may not have been gentle enough with you, though lords know that I never meant to be cruel to you whom I dearly adore."

Gen lowered his head to below his niece's navel as he told her "Lay back. It's okay."

Fumi attempted to escape into her favorite fantasy which masked her revulsions during her habitual abuse: It was an imagination of herself as a crimson butterfly following a galloping sable Kai Ken puppy in an endless rainbow floral garden.

Yet she lost track of her frolicking friend that time as the imagined Sun blinded her. She fought back the tentacles of the emotionless euphoria which suddenly spread through her body yet she was comforted by thoughts of her Uncle burning alive. That thought caused her to grin and her Uncle mistook the cause of her smile.

"See? You enjoyed that didn't you little girl? Not so confused now are you? I certainly enjoyed it; You're succulent dear niece."

He moved his face to Fumi's, gave her a peck, and guiltily told her "I won't have you do to me what I just did for you. Your mouth is filthy."

Uncle Gen stroked his niece's body as disgust drilled into every pore of her soul. Ants seemed to crawl underneath the skin of her limbs and ribcage as the distance between each of her Uncle's breaths shrank.

Fumi shut her eyes as her Uncle aligned his loins with hers yet she briefly slammed her eyelids open and sharply inhaled when he fiercely plunged into the place which had hurt her only an hour ago. She whimpered in agony as he tore into her. She quickly craned upwards to see if Gen had any guilt but all she witnessed was ravenous desire.

Fumi daydreamed about that sweet snow colored puppy in the luminous garden but the vegetation rotted as the Sun became scarlet and the graceful creature halted his run. The dog looked up at Fumi and he seemed to grin as the flesh over his teeth shrank into oblivion. He shrilly whined as his hazel eyes fell inwards while his skin tightened over his emaciating *frame until his organs and skeleton could easily be discerned. The puppy keeled over with no strength left to stand and none to vocalize his agony.*

Brown and black dust was all that was left of the plants which fell upon the animal by way of frequent multidirectional breezes. The discolored puppy's chest irregularly rose and fell as he irregularly succeeded in gasping for what remained of the breathable air. Fumi fluttered to the ground as strength vacated her wings before Fate landed her in front of the dog's seemingly eyeless sockets and surreal smile. He gave an immense, reeking, and feverish sigh before he became still.

Fumi struggled to resurrect her fantasy of life yet death infected her creations again: flames slowly skinned the puppy until he was a scorched blood blackened skeleton that time. She gave up her effort at the third as fatigue dragged her to the bottom of his ocean.

Fumi ached to wipe away the sweat which began to drip from Gen's rocking chest and onto her trembling face yet his hands pinned her wrists to the bed. Her eyes stung as her and Uncle Gen's perspiration slid through her clenched eyelids. She tasted salt as slivers of their sweat slithered past her clenched mouth.

She soundlessly pleaded for it to end while she internally whispered her sisters' names to keep herself from giving voice to the damage being done to the place below her womb.

Nine minutes later she was alone in her room again. She gingerly rose from her crumpled sheets which were soaked with their sweat as well as tinged with her tears, her blood, and his discharge. She stood only to immediately collapse onto the floor upon her side. She drew fresh blood as she bit her lower lip to prevent herself from shrieking. She haltingly dragged herself to her restroom with her fingertips. Flickers of hope intermittently materialized within her subconscious mind as she made way to clean her Uncle's filth from *her.*

***

Gen was going to hire an international trafficking ring to take Kaya. He made sure to let Fumi know this as he washed her sheets the morning after he discovered the letters and she had no doubt about his frightening yet outlandish statement because she knew that he had the resources to carry it out.

Uncle Gen had also called Fumi's school that dawn to let them know that she was abysmally sick and he convincingly faked a cough to emphasize his words "...I believe that it's highly contagious too."

Gen assured the headmaster that Arisa and Hana would go to Fumi's professors and gather her homework. He too confirmed that he would help Fumi complete her assignments.

***

On the second morning of her school absence (which was during the second to last week of classes) Fumi pulled her covers to her chin as Gen entered her room and sat across from her.

"I'm so sorry for hurting you the other night," Gen haltingly relayed. I..."

He broke off as he took out a checkered handkerchief and patted behind his hairy ears and his smooth upper lip. He sighed mournfully before he resumed.

"I was molested by my Grandmother when I was a little boy. I'm not sure why she did it but I wouldn't be surprised if she was touched in a certain way when she was a little girl by some relative."

Fumi burned with fury as she imagined herself shrieking "And you think that absolves you of your sins?"

Gen noticed the flames leaping within Fumi's eyes and he hurriedly continued, "What I'm trying to say is that I think that if it weren't for her then you would have never been moles...taken advantage of by me. Yet where my Grandmother was cruel, I've always only given you pleasure...discounting two nights ago. Aren't I right?

I didn't intend to hurt you when I...I merely became blinded by my temper when you hurt me so that's why I was so rough with you that night. If you would have told me that it hurt the first time that I moved down there instead of retaliating in anger by punching me then I would have stopped that act. I'm not saying that to shame you but so you know that I didn't want to hurt you."

Gen noticed that the fire within his niece's eyes burned brighter as a pause was born between them. He bent his head and grimaced as he grabbed his left arm yet the affliction which bore his impulses quickly subsided.

He nervously looked to his niece yet he noticed no recognition of his moment of weakness from her.

"Stupid cramp," Fumi's Uncle grumbled.

"I've been overworking in the garden.

Please Fumi, please know how shameful I am for what I did to you on Sunday...and...and the prior days. Please say something, can't you see that this guilt is consuming me cherished niece? You're a smart girl so tell me, would I have any regret if I did not truly care about you my Fumi?"

"MY Fumi," Fumi repeated the phrase within her head, with emphasis on the possessive word. She wasn't going to give in to the temptations of hope calling her towards trust yet her Uncle's last phrase strengthened her resolve. She could see by his eyes that her Uncle truly felt guilt yet she saw a persistent hunger as well. She foresaw that her Uncle's desire for her would soon supersede his regret like her parents' lust for alcohol won them over from the sorrow which they felt at how their drunkenness made them unavailable for their children. However, Fumi's heart overcoming herself was evidenced by her inquiry and by her voice which mournfully wavered upon the *last word,*

"What about Kaya?"

"There still has to be a consequence Fumi," Gen replied. "I need to make sure that you never disrespect me again while I need to guarantee that you don't grow up to be a violent woman. You'll eventually get married Fumi and who knows if your husband will be rough with you at nights? You need to realize the value of demure words because they may grant you grace and thus save you while brutality will only escalate your misery.

I also need to make an example of that cunning demonic girl especially since she is infecting you."

"Kaya is innocent so please don't corrupt your soul by harming a girl who committed no crime," Fumi pleaded. "You know the tone of her letters and you know how it is constant and how it differs from that of mine. I welcome you to reread them Uncle and then we can burn them. Please. The corruption is purely my fault but I am not fully swayed, so I can easily be

cured. I feel ashamed for my blossoming inclinations but I too felt terrified of seeking out help. I beg of your grace dear Uncle Gen."

Shame along with determination betrayed their presence within Fumi's uncle when his shoulders ever so slightly drooped, a coat of tears spread across his semi-downcast eyes, and his jaw firmed without strain when Fumi made her appeal; The manifestations his shame and determination became especially prominent when she spoke the last sentence. Thus the child's heart eased as she continued to erase a potential future where Kaya was abused by countless strangers.

"Kaya and I will never talk again," Fumi promised. "We're on different educational routes now since she's been selected to advance to that pretentious school as her last letter revealed and you can keep an eye on me as much as you want to make sure that we won't even cross paths with one another.

I have a confession to make too. I felt a fearful uncertainty when you first touched me *and that confusion has carried through the years but I cannot deny that, with exception to that specific act you did twice on Sunday, I've felt an increasing pleasure each time that you caressed me and slept with me. Not even my face could conceal my delight when you placed your lips there; you saw that.*

My heart was cold too during the times you were intimate with me because I believed that you only did it to use me as a thing to serve your desires but I see now that it isn't true. You've always did it for me. I won't lie and say that I'm over my anger but I want to be. I forgive you for being rough with me the other night...I'll learn to get over my fear from that and I'm so sorry for my greater error of hurting you then instead of talking to you. I'm also deeply sorry for Grandma's viciousness towards you. You didn't deserve her cruelty. The man I know is so kind; you've always nurtured my sisters and I: you were there for us when our parents wouldn't be.

Uncle Gen released his pent up anxiety

with a sigh as he wiped his eyes. "I think that's the most you've ever talked to me in one go," he told his niece. "You are wonderfully eloquent."

Fumi kept the praise directed towards her Uncle as she resumed, "I believe that your brave confession is changing my attitude. I also know that you would have never touched Arisa and Hana," Fumi lied. "You were just ashamed of being intimate with me and you needed to scare me so I wouldn't betray you to a closed minded society" (Fumi rushed on as she witnessed the predicted naked confusion and defensive fury coalescing in the depths of her Uncle's features) "but it doesn't matter. I need help. You can make me better. There's no need to feel shame for loving me. Why should we follow society's demands?

Please love me Uncle Gen," Fumi begged as she slowly bared herself. "And please be patient as I learn to love you with the same level of passion as your affection is for me."

Fumi inwardly shrieked and weeped as

she forced a brilliant smile for her beaming uncle. He affectionately stroked her cheek before he tenderly moved his hand downwards and leaned his face towards hers.

"You don't have long Chikushou," Fumi mentally cursed as she realized that her uncle's heart attack symptoms had manifested themselves to her before this day. She had witnessed subtler manifestations two nights ago while he was underneath her bed.

3.5

Four Months Ago: Fumi Initiates Her Plan

Fumi rapidly brought an arm up and barely managed to cover her sneeze. "Of course I have to still be sick on this day," Fumi furiously brooded. She caught the cold two weeks ago.

"It's okay if you stay home today," Arisa proclaimed to her younger sister who was within the kitchen. "Please do," she added underneath her breath.

"I don't know why she insisted on serving us tea," Hana whispered to her twin but she refrained from further complaints when she noticed the scolding look of her uncle.

Fumi dried the last dish as an epiphany alighted in her mind. She realized that her illness could be a miracle.

Fumi entered the dining room by slowly limping because of her deliberate injury from two days ago. She firmly proclaimed, "There's no need to fear Arisa and don't think that I haven't seen your annoyed glance either Hana. But Uncle Gen has already told you two, twice I might add, that I am no longer contagious. So please don't make me feel guilt for not wanting to miss my first day back at..." Fumi was interrupted by a detonation within her nose and she barely managed to catch the snot shrapnel with the left sleeve of her crimson kamino: "Achoo!" A trickle of elation twirled within her heart at her successful execution of a deliberate sneeze. Fumi just had to resist sneezing until that opportune moment which was actually quite difficult since she had sneaked a couple of ground black pepper spheres into her nostrils right before she left the kitchen.

She lowered her left arm from her nose and wiped her sleeve on the back of her dress as she discreetly removed the snotty pepper with her right hand.

"Maybe you should rest dear," Gen told Fumi with genuine worry in his tone. "It's okay, I'll call the school."

Fumi's sisters fervently nodded their heads but not without a semblance of empathy as their slight yet tight frowns and widened eyes betrayed.

Fumi acted reluctant by swinging her eyes upwards and to the side, biting her lower lip, hunching her shoulders, and finally lowering her head in submission before she almost imperceptibly nodded. A genuine sneeze and shiver sealed the deal as her Uncle arose from the table and walked towards an ebony and ivory rotary phone in the adjacent office.

Gen made Fumi's situation known to her school officials as she went to wash her hands in the nearest restroom. Her uncle was still on the phone as Fumi sat in front of her older siblings at the cherry wood table. She reflexively tightened her silk scarf with the rose print around her neck, even though the prominent marks which arose from the particular Sunday had disappeared, and she carefully massaged her slightly sprained left ankle.

"You know we care about you right?" Hana asked her little sister as she glanced at her twin. She quietly gulped as she resolutely placed a hand atop Fumi's. She went on as Arisa sighed and nodded in reluctant affirmation. "We realize that we may have been a bit mean to you because of your undue rudeness to Uncle Gen, especially after, you know...Mom and Dad...died. Sorry, that didn't really sound like an apology. Yes, I'm trying to apologize to you. What Arisa and I want to say is that we think we know why you were rude to our uncle."

Fumi's heart hammered as she forced her appearance to remain neutral. She glanced around to make sure that Gen had not yet returned from his call. *"Shut up you idiots, shut* up, *he'll hurt you if he finds out that you know,*" Fumi desperately and inwardly pleaded as she attempted to project those thoughts into her sisters' minds. *"Oh, my sweet sisters, you finally know,"* were the contrasting thoughts which intertwined with the panicked ones.

Hana continued, "It's because he took the place of Mama and Daddy whenever they got drunk and that broke your heart because it was you was the most attached to them."

Fumi's heart slipped and fell off a towering precipice as disappointment and gratefulness shocked her system.

Arisa spoke up, "Hey, no judgements from us...well actually our parent's favoritism probably compelled us to tease you especially harsh."

"Arisa," Hana chided her twin.

"Sorry," Arisa quietly replied after a few moments when she realized the full extent of her statement.

"Arisa did bring up another point, no

matter how rudely it came out," Hana went on. "We teased you, to make ourselves feel better. No, it was worse than teasing, we bullied you Fumi. Calling you names, making fun of your clumsiness even though it brought you injuries, and ignoring you at school even though you've always wanted to spend time with us. Oh Fumi, you've only been nice to us. We're so sorry."

Arisa whispered, "What convinced us to get over ourselves and work towards treating you better..."

"Arisa," Hana interjected.

"...you're right," Arisa interceded on her own behalf to avoid further scolding from Hana. "What convinced us to treat you like our sister who we love, (yes I also admit that I love you and that is true), is that you've started treating Uncle Gen nicer and..." Arisa gulped as she lost grip of her tough exterior yet she held on to enough control to prevent herself from getting teary eyed. "...we noticed that you're not recovering. It's never taken you this long to get over something as pathetic as the cold. You're a brilliant actress but we can tell that you're not getting better...you're slowly getting worse. We're scared Fumi. Uncle Gen says you're fine but please tell us the truth, do you think that you'll be okay?"

Fumi was taken aback that her sisters had seen through her guise. Her non-abating sickness had not escaped her notice yet she didn't want to ruin her modified plan by letting Uncle Gen in on it.

Fumi steeled herself as she looked into her sisters' earnest and heartbroken eyes. She realized that Hana and Arisa's softening hearts could be used to reinforce her scheme. She replied, "I'm not sure. But I'll tell you what: I'll convince Uncle to take me in to see a doctor. I just ask that you let me join you on your walk to school; it's not that far. Please persuade Uncle Gen if he believes me too weak to do even that. I wanted to still go with you even though I gave in to taking the day off. But now I feel even more inclined to spend that time with you, brief though it is, since you've opened your hearts to me."

Fumi resumed her speech and she reverentially lowered it upon the last phrase, "By the way, in case there was any doubt at any point in our lives, Hana and Arisa, I love you too."

Fumi spoke nothing of her menstruation which prematurely arrived three months ago nor of its cessation that month.

***

Fumi's secret plan (one year in the making), had received alterations that morning but she was grateful since she knew that it was for the better. Her mind wandered as she, Uncle Gen, and her sisters walked hand-in-hand with one another on their way to Miyajimaguchi Elementary as Fumi and Yu-Ri boarded the train to the school which she classified as elitist despite her knowledge otherwise.

4

Five Months Ago: The Last Friday of Second Grade

Fumi inconspicuously massaged her belly while she sat at the rear of the classroom. She ached though her constipation which was initiated by her Uncle's assault from the prior week had finally relented on this day. However, she didn't scold the secret admiration which twirled within her as Kaya began reciting her story for the class though it did cower before a fear born fury as Kaya went on.

Kaya's short tale was about a warrior princess who was not aware of her heritage. She fought against otherworldly creatures who were seemingly bred for evil only to discover that some of them fought against tyranny. Yet the true kicker was that the person whom she *yearned to emulate and fell in love with was her uncle.*

Fumi astounded herself with the strength she manifested by not breaking her composure yet her rage experienced a blindsided collision by grief and longing when Kaya spoke the conclusion to Nicéphore. In the end, the warrior princess was murdered yet she reunited with her parents, who died before her, in a sort of afterlife.

Some of Kaya and Fumi's classmates looked bored to tears due to total incomprehension, while others appeared intrigued yet nevertheless confused by her story, and the rest seemed perturbed as well as baffled. However, their instructor, Sensei Ami, praised Kaya for her tale, especially the implications that people are not evil merely because they have a different ethnicity and for the portrayal of the two opposing kings.

Fumi zoned out when Kaya took her seat at the front of the class while Haru stood before them to recite his story. Fumi was scheduled to play one of her painful piano compositions on the classroom's upright piano next (she always deliberately displayed poor school results as to not draw praise to herself) yet she had told the teacher that she would be unable to play at all that day since she had a severe tummy ache.

Every now and then her consciousness returned to that present reality so she noticed that the boy was unveiling his third sequel to the baby prince and his lost cricket companion. Whenever she became aware of the present, Fumi looked around the classroom and was disgusted when she noticed that everyone including Kaya was enraptured by what she deemed a childish and derivative tale.

***

Fumi casually walked towards the derelict looking restroom in the eastern wing during the lunch hour. It was hardly used since it had notoriously poor plumbing and it was the only bathroom which was situated far from the places within the school which were regularly utilized. No one stopped Fumi from leaving the cafeteria since that Tuesday because it was easy to slip away from the packed room and no one noticed her walking down the wing since it was deserted at the lunch hour. That Friday was no different in those regards.

When she opened the door to the dimly lit aquamarine restroom, bewilderment and horror paralyzed her before mortification accompanied those blossoming emotions. The trio of sensations propelled her to sprint to anywhere away from there.

Fumi halted and caught her breath in the center of a semi-lit room which was painted in the colors of the object situated at the far end's outer edge. She took in her surroundings as she realized that she had almost bumped into two people who appeared as blurs on her subconscious trajectory towards this destination which was within the entrance of the western wing. Fumi quickly left the viewing range of the door window as she crept towards the entrance. She surreptitiously peered out and noticed an absence of anyone. Fumi waited a few minutes before she was satisfied that there were no pursuers. She walked towards the rear half of the room and sat down upon the polished piano bench. She shudderingly inhaled as the memory of what she saw in the bathroom several minutes ago arose unbidden: A profile of Kaya in front of the farthest sink with the sleeves of her kamino uniform rolled up; using a pair of scissors to cut lines into her upper arms before she realized that someone was watching her. The last image from that moment was of Kaya looking into Fumi's eyes as a soul who was lost, frightened, and in excruciation from unseen wounds.

Fumi pressed the keys with such artistry that the grand piano sang the composition as if its author were playing it himself. As her fingers effortlessly traversed through the Moonlight Sonata by Ludwig van Beethoven, she was transported to two years ago when her Mother taught her the composition:

It was on the last day when Mari was sober, the night before she witnessed something on the way home which caused her mind to snap (Goro, Fumi's father had lost his sanity the year before).

Mari had cheered her daughter Fumi on as the seven year old girl mastered the piece in twenty five minutes. She also promised to teach Fumi another piece as long as she improved her grades for the upcoming school term which opened during the following day.

Fumi's memory had a bright sheen and she witnessed her Mother smiling perhaps a bit wider than she had and ecstatically laughing as well as cheering possibly a touch greater than she did.

Within her memory, Fumi's fingers continued to dance upon the upright piano's keys as she glanced at her Mother's face. Reality seeped in to reveal that the brightness of Mari's eyes flimsily hid the anguish, her brilliant smile was stiff as a result of an effort to conceal her frown, and her shoulders were slumped even as she pumped the air at her daughter's display of a prodigious skill.

Fumi's memories jumped to and fro within the past : she briefly relived many of her rapes, entered her parents' cottage bedroom and kept her sisters from witnessing their parents' self-hanged bodies (which were still upon her discovery), as well as a suppressed year and a half old moment when she discovered Uncle Gen drowning the stray Kai Ken whom she had grown closer to than any person. She witnessed the murder at the time when the puppy's last breath of life escaped him. Her Uncle had awkwardly apologized as the dog's body floated to the surface of Gen's portable tub. He claimed that the creature had become rabid so she had better not make an unnecessary scene...or else. Fumi had mechanically nodded her head before she ran from the bowels of her uncle's wooded and expansive backyard to her immediate family within his house. Through the racking sobs, she claimed that she was merely distraught over her parents' continued binge drinking. Her parents scolded her by withdrawing their drunken displays of consolation as they left the house and they didn't return until the next evening.

Fumi shrieked in anguish as she escaped her memories and she left her portrayal of the sonata near its conclusion.

Through her tears and fingers she believed that she saw Kaya in her peripheral vision yet when she swung completely around, no one was there nor was there a shadow. No one would have heard Fumi's yell nor sobs, much less her piano playing since the room had been padded to be soundproof to everyone outside it.

She regained a semblance of composure a few minutes later and she began to replay the sonata from the beginning. This time, her tempo was slower than what the sheet music called for but the decreased speed aided in *soothing her nerves. With a calmer mind, Fumi's imagination soothed her heart...*

Kaya entered the room and beckoned to her as she paused in the center. Fumi rose to meet the girl who treated her with more kindness than any child had. A pair of emerald velvet curtains, overlaid with silver embroidery, drew apart to reveal a grand audience. The girls, clothed in golden lacy gowns, delicately wrapped their fingers around one another's hands as the houselights dimmed and the spotlight found them.

The white beam followed Fumi and Kaya through their waltz as the orchestra played the Moonlight Sonata. About a minute into their dance, the orchestra transitioned into a peppy rendition of the sonata as the girls segued into a ballet. They flawlessly mirrored each other even when they performed pirouettes, grand jetés, and assemblés.

When the musicians closed in on the finale, Fumi and Kaya rushed in from opposite ends of the stage and embraced one another.

They held each other as the music crescendoed and the audience looked on through blissful tears. The girls pulled ever so slightly away to look into each other's eyes and Fumi stroked Kaya's upper arms before she slowly leaned in to chastely kiss her partner. When Fumi's lips touched Kaya's cheek, the orchestra ceased playing abruptly to enhance the effect.

The musicians played the last few notes quietly (in pianissimo) as Fumi ended the kiss and fully hugged a beaming Kaya. The crowd gave a rapturous standing ovation as the girls faced them, bowed, and gestured to the orchestra pit to direct the applause to the musicians as well. Fumi and Kaya ran towards the rear door, hand in hand and blissfully laughed.

The two whose intellects were synonymous with one another exited into an open air yet secluded bedroom with sheets that were sapphire and honey hued. The girls jumped into the King sized bed as their gowns transformed into silken robes and they observed the luminous constellations which made the night sky like day despite the new moon. They cuddled as Fumi whispered to Kaya, the girl whom she loved more than any boy, "I love you."

"I love you too Fumi," Kaya whispered in reply...

Fumi shook in confusion and guilt as she eased herself from her daydream while she slowly opened her eyes.

5

Four Months Ago: Fumi's Run

With a free falling heart, Fumi met the eyes of her former friends in the distance as she imagined waving at each of them in greeting. Chizu, Danuja, Chieko, and Tamae scowled in reply before they entered through the front doors of their school. Fumi had grown incrementally cold within their social circle in an effort to protect them from her uncle's jealousy while giving herself time to terminate her bond with them. Their friendship was superficial since the first day of school yet it was the most authentically powerful bond that she had ever formed with any human besides her parents and sisters.

Fumi resisted the urge to tightly embrace

Hana and Arisa before they waved goodbye as they rushed to meet their friends on the expansive front lawn of Miyajimaguchi Elementary.

"Don't be late," Uncle Gen yelled at them after he chuckled.

"*I love you*" Fumi inaudibly told her sisters.

***

On account of Fumi's injury and poor health, alongside Uncle Gen's failing heart, niece and Uncle made their way back to the mansion at a leisurely pace. About halfway through on the road home, Fumi tripped her Uncle and unsteadily ran west onto a perpendicular path towards the police station. It took merely a few moments for Gen to scramble over his shock to realize where his niece was heading. Spurned by panic along with fury, he rose from the ground and sped towards Fumi as she staggered up the wide adjacent hill.

Fumi glanced behind and below to confirm that her lanky Uncle was rapidly closing the distance between them. She waited until he was a few places away before she put on a tiny burst of speed. Fumi's method was to maintain a slight lead over Uncle Gen to give him hope of catching her and her sprained ankle helped to give credence to her slower running speed; she didn't need to put on much of an act since invisible spikes stabbed and screwed themselves into her bruised ligament.

Fumi focused on the aftermath of her plan to open the floodgates of her hope and it catalyzed another dose of adrenaline as she allowed her subconsciousness to lead her feet. As her pain and nausea abated, the forefront of her awareness revisited the message that Kaya handed to her on their first day of second grade, her very first letter to her...

Dear Fumi,

You're probably thinking, "Why the heck did

this annoyingly cheerful girl write me, an ultimately serious individual, a letter?"

To that I'd respond, "Silly, why are you reading a lovely letter from someone who you claim to despise?"

You don't really hate me though, not thoroughly at least. I've seen hints of admiring smiles break free to play upon your lips last year as you observed my recitation of my stories and as I engaged in imaginary adventures with my friends upon the playground.

The regret which shone forth from your eyes as you ever so slightly averted them whenever you bullied me did not escape my notice either. Your behavior towards those who are unlike you who dare try to befriend you is cruel yet you are not a monster. From the moment I saw you, I sensed that you experienced trauma which may be separate from the passing of your parents and the unrest in this world. I'm still not certain of what is mainly hurting your precious soul but I think that I may have an answer based upon the way you have become especially sensitive to peoples' touch. Over the summer, I overheard my Mom and Dad discuss that sometimes young girls are uniquely assaulted, especially of late, though the phrase that they used was far more to the point. However, I don't want to presume that the experience of those people is the same as yours.

Regardless, though I cannot engage in a friendship with you as long as you are likely to bully me, I promise that I still love you and my affection for you is the same one that close friends share with one another, regardless of whether you ever fully love me in return. You can always come to me and let me know what's going on. I assure you that you can trust me.

Love, Kaya, your supporter.

Fumi tripped on the edge of the hill's crown and she sprawled upon the summit. Coughs racked her body as she quickly raised her head. She saw Uncle Gen crest over with a deranged look of agony and triumph. He lunged for one of her arms as his right hand clutched his sternum.

His hand clasped onto her elbow...or it would have if Fumi hadn't of rolled to the side. Instead, Gen lost his balance. He fell onto his chest as Fumi fiercely pushed herself back with her right foot and the dirt spread across her back. She braced herself for a fresh surge of torment as she rocketed into an upright stance.

"You've always been nauseating to look at, your caresses ever pathetic, and you unfailingly moan like a little bitch!", Fumi hissed at her uncle before she raced ahead.

Uncle Gen ferally screamed as he pushed himself up and gaspingly called for the few confused passerby to stop his niece. Fumi ducked under the grasping hands of an elderly woman, swerved around an ungainly boy carrying a potted bonsai, veered around a clump of baby violet orchids, and returned to the center of the lane. She guffawed all the while to make it seem that she was an unruly child who was running away from her relative merely to frustrate him.

Wails stopped Fumi at the opposite edge of the hill's precipice.

"What have I done, what have I done," Fumi moaned to herself to throw off any potential suspicion as her heart threatened to cheer especially loud since no one was running for help.

Fumi kept repeating that phrase as she cautiously hobbled the quarter mile to the center of the hill where strangers circled her prone Uncle. As she arrived at the periphery, she saw a senior man sternly look into Fumi's golden eyes and shake his head as his fingers stopped stubbornly searching for a pulse.

"No, no, no," Fumi whimpered as she knelt beside Uncle Gen. "I didn't mean too!

Someone get an ambulance, why is

everyone just standing here? SOMEONE GET HELP!"

A middle aged woman laid a hand upon Fumi's shoulder yet the young girl shrugged it off as she broke down weeping. Fumi felt as if she was floating towards the stratosphere yet she made it seem as if her tears were of mourning. She did her best to cradle her uncle as she sang *Yurikago No Uta* by Hakushū Kitahara, the lullaby which Gen had hummed to her that morning, a song by which he often sang to her after he had sexually abused her:

Yurikago no uta o
Kanariya ga utau yo
Nenneko Nenneko!

Nenneko yo
Yurikago no ue ni
Biwa no mi ga yureru yo
Nenneko Nenneko!

Nenneko yo

Yurikago no tsuna o
Kinezumi ga yusuru
Nenneko Nenneko!

Nenneko yo
Yurikago no yume ni
Kiiroi tsuki ga kakaru yo
Nenneko Nenneko
Nenneko yo!

A canary sings
A cradle song
Sleep, sleep,
Sleep, child!

Above the cradle,
The loquat fruits sway
Sleep, sleep,
Sleep, child!

A squirrel rocks
The cradle by its rope
Sleep, sleep,

Sleep, child!

Dreams in a cradle,
With the yellow moon shining down
Sleep, sleep,
Sleep, child!

Fumi wished that her Uncle had just enough life left in him to hear her subtly mocking tone as she sang the song; she hoped that he could hear it in Hell, if such a place did exist outside of this world. She too had an impulsive desire that his heart attack didn't kill him so that she could reveal the small shiv tied to her upper arm, beneath the kamino, and pierce his brain with it through one of his terrified eyes. Yet the prominent mood which had lifted the weight from her soul was gratefulness: thankfulness that Kaya, Hana, and Arisa were free.

The elderly woman who had made a grab for Fumi found her voice and announced, "He's dead because of her. Don't let her crocodile tears fool you."

The lady pointed at Fumi as she continued damning the little girl, "He's dead because of you!"

Fumi looked at the faces which surrounded her and they all appeared at least suspicious to her. A nun made her way from the nearby church upon the hill.

Fumi imagined her Uncle's ghost kneeling beside her and murmuring, "Do you think that anyone will ever believe that I raped you little one? No, the truth will remain our little secret you filthy lesbian. Look at how they see you as a sinner already and I as an innocent. Look at them! You will always be my prisoner sweet Fumi."

Fumi undid her scarf to reveal the faint bruises which her Uncle had left as a result of a particularly passionate moment during the prior night. Her euphoria died in panic and despair as the elderly lady attempted to clasp onto her again. She swung away from the elderly woman's clasp as she ran ahead without ever looking back. She didn't notice the nun's expression which was full of understanding as she avoided her grasp as well. The wizened nun pleaded for Fumi to stop as she attempted to run after her.

Fumi paused only when she had arrived at the outskirts of Ōno's hub at the edge of the hill. She quickly blended in with the bustling crowd within the Saeki District as her melancholy and dread numbed her further injured ankle as well as the fire combusting within her overworked lungs. Fumi aimlessly limped with her head downcast as she reflected upon the last time that she saw Kaya, on the final day of their second grade...

Kaya slipped her letter into one of Fumi's textbooks during a group class assignment. Such was her method of delivery. Fumi noticed that Kaya's facade was shaky unlike before and for the first time the latter soul couldn't meet Fumi's eyes.

Fumi walked a few paces behind Kaya, Eiko, Emi, and Kaede after the final bell rang.

She halted and hid as Kaya's three closest friends' parents exchanged pleasantries with the latter individual before they and their daughter bid adieu.

Fumi resumed her walk when Kaya sat on the lawn as she awaited for Daito to exit the building and for their parents to arrive. She returned the letter as discreetly as possible before she continued onward without slowing her pace.

"Wait, did you even read it Fumi?" Kaya inquired as she rose from the vibrant grass. "You didn't, did you? Please, Fumi, let me help you. I care..." she faltered as Fumi walked back to her.

Furious over Kaya's portrayal of her and of the young girl's decision to read the story to the class instead of handing it to her, Fumi had planned on spitting on the child's face in front of a crowd in addition to returning the letter unread. Yet that scheme dissipated when she saw the self-inflicted cuts upon Kaya's arms that morning.

"Besides," *Fumi thought*, "no one else seems to notice my nor my Uncle's depiction in Kaya's story."

So Fumi hoped that what she was about to say would be sufficient in keeping Kaya away from her for the latter's sake.

Kaya looked hard into Kaya's eyes as she softly yet firmly proclaimed, "You can't even help yourself."

Fumi rapidly spun around and briskly walked away.

"I'm sorry," Kaya shouted. *Her sniffles were the final stroke to break Fumi's fractured heart yet she kept her face forward and posture straight even as her own tears flowed.*

***

Fumi found herself being drawn by an approaching whistle. Her head felt light though she experienced her soul repeatedly stitching itself back together only for demons to ceaselessly rip it apart afterwards and despite the summer Sun, she shivered from the blizzard within her.

Fumi moved to the front of the crowd who waited to cross the tracks and she didn't notice the few people who cared enough to talk to her.

The steam driven train was thirty feet away when it appeared to pivot onto its flank as she threw herself upon her side after tenaciously sprinting ahead. The train's approach silenced the screeches of the crowd from Fumi's ears.

"You're finally free from me," Fumi inaudibly proclaimed as she imagined Kaya, Hana, and Arisa's smiling faces.

Fumi's body lay at the edge of the locomotive path after twisting alongside it several times while her blood poured from her open neck and onto the railway. The train continued to carry Fumi's head away as it continued to pulverize it.

6

Three Sundays Ago: The Preserver

Time: 5:01 PM Japan Standard Time (JST)

Haruto observed Kaya and Yu-Ri as they passed in front of him on the way to Miyajimaguchi Station. His heart slightly quickened its pace and his loins toughened a smidgen as he focused on the little girl. Haruto deemed her as perfect for his purposes: her eyes were uniquely lavender, her hair richly raven, her nails kempt, her smile dazzling, her lips naturally tinged ruby, and her cream hued skin smooth.

The thirty year old individual waited until they were a safe distance away before he finished the dregs of his black coffee, placed his payment on the outside table where he had been seated, and followed them.

Haruto knew that the young girl would be the best of his private collection of preserved innocence. The rich man, who had teetered on the edge of insanity for as long as he could remember, began his work shortly after the initiation of the unrest four years ago. He imagined how Kaya would outshine the three nearly flawless, eternally grinning, and wide eyed taxidermied children. He just felt slight regret that he would have to replace Kaya's already flawless eyes with glass replicas.

Haruto took deep breaths to steady his heart and loosen his loins as he carefully kept the distance between himself and the two people close enough to keep track of them while not betraying his stalk. He was determined to kidnap the child even if he had to wait more than a day to do so without attracting suspicion.

As he stopped at the station's newsstand at the periphery of the train station, he surreptitiously stared at the two souls by not looking directly at them. Kaya laughed at something her mother said as they waited in the ticket line deep within the station's foyer. Kaya clasped her own hands together, lifted her arms, and slowly twirled in a seeming display of gratitude for her brand new lavender dress.

Kaya's requested something of her mom. Yu-Ri handed a handkerchief from her purse and Kaya began to wipe some of her sweat away. When she lifted her long hair to wipe the back of her neck, he saw a prominent brown birthmark where her neck met her left shoulder.

Horrified and embarrassed that he was going after a girl who he now deemed blemished, he quickly sped away.

7

Three Sundays Ago: On the Train to Meet Erina

Time: 6:03 PM JST

The electric train pulled out of Miyajimaguchi station as Riku oversaw Daichi, Eiko, Chiya, and Kaede work on a project at the house.

Kaya turned away from the locomotive window where she had been vacantly staring at the proximate mountains who were beginning to blush violet from the Sun's descending approach. She won her wrestle with fear as she fought back visions of Fumi's mangled corpse. Kaya kept her smooth mask of well-being in place as she peered at her mother's fractured one.

"Let's create a story Mommy," Kaya

stated as she rubbed her Mother's arm.

"We have, dear," Yu-Ri answered her daughter. *"The Guardians of the Itsukushima Shrine, I'll Teach You to Exile Me, Mister!* and *Why Was That Little Piggy Eating Roast Beef!?* And may we never forget our very first story, *Our Very First Story."*

Kaya chuckled as she replied, "I mean let's create a story right now."

"Sweetie, we don't have much time and I'm not great with improvising you know," protested Yu-Ri. She expelled a great sigh as she stated, half to herself, "I'm chained by perfectionism." She swiftly displayed a smile to make up for the dejected tone though she overcompensated at that moment so she looked like she had been forced to hold her grin for nearly twenty five years. Yu-Ri's smile shrank to societally accepted dimensions nearly as soon as it had appeared when she realized her melodramatic act.

"I'll guide you Mommy," Kaya reassured her mom as she placed her hand in hers.

"Besides, fortyish minutes is plenty of time for this story to bloom."

Yu-Ri pecked her daughter upon her forehead as she tenderly squeezed her daughter's hand and stated, "Guide on."

A Journey To A Surprise Destination

The Tale that Kaya and Yu-Ri Wove
Three Weeks Ago Upon the Train

***

"Look Mommy, we're animated!", Kaya trilled as she jumped once, twice, and thrice into the air. She paused to admire her appearance, her mother's, and the location's again before she resumed, "Everyone and everything is colored with dynamic hues!"

Yu-Ri responded in pleasant shock : "We're cartoons." Oh, but that word implied childlike simplicity to most individuals upon hearing it yet what she saw were colors that seemed to contain at least one bucket of paint for every object, sentient and inanimate.

Breathless, Yu-Ri looked at the space right behind Kaya and herself: the point where they materialized upon this celestial body within this galaxy. She knelt down and sifted the pink sand, that had the texture of powder, through her hands. Yu-Ri brought the lavender fragranced and bright purple grains close to her nose before she blew them from her palms. They left brief tails of rosy scented and hot pink colored exhaust within the air as they metamorphosed by her hot breath. She looked around again at the gently watercolored stylized world as her daughter triumphantly threw handfuls of sand in the air. Yu-Ri laughed in exultation at the evidence that the Dimension Transit Door on Surreptitiously Surreal World in the Outer Milky Way Galaxy had successfully transported them instantly to the Tranquil Comet at the edge of the Anime Galaxy, five-hundred and fifty five million lightyears away. Having encountered numerous adventures across twenty-five planets of the Milky Way (if one discounted Earth of course); they were finally within their journey's finale.

Book III: Within The Anime Galaxy

Chapter I: Upon the Tranquil Comet

Yu-Ri walked up the gentle thirty feet slope to the shelf where ocean and sand met. Strolling ahead fifty feet, lost in tranquility, she arrived at the jagged line where the gentle waves eagerly reached as far as they could go before they reluctantly receded for another go.

Yu-Ri brought a hand over her eyes to shield them from the proximate and large rainbow colored day star to study the midnight blue lake which was impossibly contained within a ninety-degree angle with nary a waterfall in sight. The water was crystal clear for as far as she could see, from the lowest position on this plane and the perpendicular one, both at two hundred feet, to the extremity of the sloth paced waves on either seemingly lengthless shore. She too could clearly behold the creatures near the distant shore despite knowing that it was a clean sixty miles away. She could make out polka-dotted horses galloping within the lake, at the furthest distance where the body of water tenderly rolled upon the opposite shore above. Yu-Ri also witnessed striped storks ambling and sitting upon the sheer far-side lake bed as if they had all the time in their world except if it concerned gravity. She too saw bronze hued elephants cajoling with silver furred giraffes amongst bonsai trees, rose gardens, and fifty foot grassy hills within the bottom plane of the lake.

A wrinkled white catfish brought Yu-Ri out of her trance when it accidentally slapped her face. It turned around to face her and apologetically meowed as it flew upwards before it continued to magically speed ahead. Suddenly, she heard the top leaves of the widely spaced one hundred foot high bamboo stalks rustle behind her. Yu-Ri turned around and looked all the way up to behold a flock of catfish flying away.

***

Yu-Ri just finished bottling up water for herself and her daughter when Kaya ran up chewing something. Her heart quickened in fright at her daughter's expression. Kaya reached into her side pocket and brought out a basket that was the size of a postage stamp as her Mother gave a wide berth. Kaya lifted her hand, let the basket go, clapped underneath it as it fell to the ground, and ran away in a seamless motion. The basket increased to a size which could easily accommodate two before it hit the sand.

Kaya stopped chewing and blew out a luminous pink bubble which rapidly grew to eighty feet tall and fifty feet across, at its widest , as her mother brought out a non-sliding Bunsen burner from her flaxen pack. Kaya took the fantastical rose water flavored balloon gum out of her mouth and clasped the end of it. Kaya let go of the balloon over the basket and threads of reinforced gum shot out to clasp the handlebars as her mother placed the lit burner underneath. The flame shot up as it sensed the bubble's presence. Mother and daughter hopped into the hot air balloon as a fifty foot shark appeared in the distance upon their shore.

"Rise, rise, RISE!", Kaya and Yu-Ri commanded the balloon as the giant tiger shark with swiftly wagging tail pranced towards them at seventy-five miles an hour; his massive exhales made mini comets of the sand before him.

"My name is Chase!", the massively muscled

shark with four legs thundered as Kaya and Yu-Ri jettisoned upwards with ludicrous speed, at twice the shark's prance. Their ascent ended at one hundred fifty feet when Chase reached the area of ground where they had been a moment before. As Mother and Daughter commanded their vehicle to fly forward, Chase stood upright and waved as he proclaimed, "Well, I guess you gotta go somewhere fast. Have fun you two! Bye, bye. Don't forget about me, my name is..."

The last of his sentence was drowned out by Kaya and Yu-Ri's swiftly increasing distance from him.

Kaya retrieved her map from her pack and she perused the single sheet of papyrus. She tapped the inked image of Chase and a disembodied voice hastily declared, "Chase. A quadruped tiger shark from the East Neptunian continent of..."

"Friend or Foe?" Kaya interrupted.

"Still searching...ah, foe...depending on your interpretation of the definition," replied the map. "Chase and his greatly extended family are foes to all except themselves. They do not dine upon sentient organisms or directly injure them. Chase and his family who are all named Chase live for chasing. Fortunately, they can't jump into the sky more than two feet. Anyways, once the Chases capture their prey, they abduct them and take care of their necessities in their posh five star cave which ever expands to accommodate the new guests alongside their growing family. They also tell them that they're going to 'join good ol' Jonah soon,' as their saying goes. Yet they secretly leave clues to which the victims can use to escape. Yet the prey aren't too keen on leaving luxury unless one of their loved ones isn't with them or if they are deluded enough to believe the Chases' threats. Yet the sharks never mistreat them besides the pursuit because they haven't the heart for abusing their unwilling playmates nor do they have one to throw them out. Some even seek the Chases out and allow themselves to be pursued to enjoy the subsequent first class treatment. However that was..."

"Thank you," Kaya told Expository as she handed the non-sentient parchment to her mother.

"So that's why that sliver of the beach was blank," stated Yu-Ri. "It's a portal breach between this place and theirs."

Inked Chases were appearing next to the breach. "Their world must be very near this comet right now and they seem to have run out of people to chase back home," Yu-Ri continued.

"Are you sure you don't want my job?", Expository inquired from Yu-Ri's hands. "I was essentially going to state that."

Yu-Ri peeled her eyes from the beach area of the map and looked ahead as she chuckled. "Someone has been having fun with sprucing up this technology," she stated as she swept her vision to her daughter. Kaya was enraptured with the world around her.

Yu-Ri smiled. Loving this comet yet having had her fill and ready for the next adventure, she returned her attention to the map. The parchment showed fifty miles of the area of any place which it was in and the users' current location like it did in the Milky Way. Yu-Ri hoped that it would still show the edge of the next world's entrance if it was brought near the gateway of a portal.

The arrow which indicated the direction to their ultimate destination was absorbed by the depiction of the portal out of *The Tranquil Comet*, which approached their blips on the map as the

Chases' jump into the water diapered over the bottom edge. The sharks popped in and out as various creatures sped around in fright.

"Wow," Kaya breathed as she studied the creatures that she and her Mother approached upon their travel to the portal's gate. The underlake horses were massive, approximately two hundred feet long and one hundred feet tall while the underwater storks were a quarter of their size. They were standing still, annoyance and contemplation within their rainbow colored eyes, as they observed the commotion upon the farther shore whose peak was sixty miles from the perpendicular juncture. The mighty creatures rushed to quell the commotion as Kaya and her Mom arrived at the portal's gate. Yu-Ri was grateful that the map showed a slice of the world beyond.

"In ten seconds, slow down to five miles per hour before making a hard left!", Yu-Ri quickly shouted at the vehicle as they passed through the wall of water and into the planet called Mȳthologia.

Chapter II: Welcome to Mȳthologia

The hot air balloon decelerated and veered left soon after it and its occupants entered the celestial body on the opposite side of the rainbow star. In doing so, the travelers avoided a meeting with the Tengu statue's open mouthed face. The sculpted deity's skin was red as a candied cherry, with irises as yellow as daffodils, and beard as dark as a starless and moonless night. His forty foot fangs appeared sharp enough to wound the air, while the scowl that they adorned silenced any laughter that may otherwise have bubbled to ignorants' throats upon seeing his fifty foot long nose, and his stature was the same as the rocky glossy red hill twenty feet behind him. He too wielded a double edged sword in his left hand which rested at his hip while his right hand held a luminous shield in front of his torso.

So enraptured were Kaya and Yu-Ri with the two hundred foot statue that they didn't peek at the map: otherwise they might have avoided the ebony behemoth barreling towards them from behind.

The tip of the sable dragon's claw sliced the top of the family's hot air ballon and the being's momentum proceeded to carry him forward as the wind from his passing propelled the humans onward. The thirty foot long creature with crimson eyes whipped around as his wits caught up to him. He placed his hands upon his mouth as he uttered a high pitch shriek of dismay.

"Now you've really done it," the ebony dragon stated to himself as he shot towards his unintended victims about fifteen miles away.

The dragon found Yu-Ri and Kaya dead...well, he feared that he would. Instead, he found the tumbled occupants quite alive within a massive clearing of the valley not far from where they had tumbled. He soundlessly made his way towards the pair and the two strangers who tended to them.

The elder stranger was the first to see the approaching dragon on account of his rather large eye. As soon as the ebony animal entered the top of his periphery vision he proclaimed in a voice that was tinted with croakiness, "So, the clumsy boy is here."

The others turned their faces towards the sky

and saw him shortly after. They waited as the dragon soundlessly circled down towards them.

The dragon looked at the ointment covered injuries upon the two women, minor cuts and bruises which escaped his notice from high in the sky. He apologized profusely and he wept with joy as Kaya and Yu-Ri graciously accepted each expression of his regret. He introduced himself with a curtsey as he announced to the company, "My name is Johnny."

Johnny looked uncertainly at the elder being after Kaya and Yu-Ri introduced themselves for he was the sole one who wasn't smiling at him. The senior creature had one visible eye which had an orange iris, was prominently curved, and it filled half of his face. His short fur was powder blue and in his two four digit hands he leaned upon a cane of reinforced amber. The frowning and stooped elder being identified himself as a yamajijii and he gave his name: "Hansuke." He assured Johnny that he was happy that he was with them. Hansuke clarified that the facial expressions of his emotions manifested opposite to that of most creatures. So if he was upset, it would appear as a smile.

The black sheep with the opposable hooves

identified himself as "Brodie."

Johnny retrieved the hot balloon basket from the lower raspberry laden branches at the southern edge of the clearing, one hundred feet away, as Kaya and Yu-Ri thanked him.

"Good thing Hansuke was there to cushion our fall through the branches and to the ground," Kaya told Johnny with an enormous grin. "He could foresee where we would land," she went on as she playfully elbowed one of his forearms.

"Why are you being so kind to me?", the dragon asked.

"We know all about you, Johnny," Kaya replied as she used a piece of her discolored snowy smock sleeve to mop her brow. "I'll show you the map but first we must gather firewood. It's hot as a sauna in this place to my mommy and I but Hansuke said it's going to be freezing tonight. He also said that night would be here before we knew it."

"No, we don't want to do that!", Johnny asserted as he removed pieces of the torn balloon from the irregularly spaced lower branches which were a foot above his head when he stood upon his hind legs.

"Why not?", Yu-Ri inquired. "Hansuke said we shouldn't either yet he refused to explain. There's heaps of branches a few paces beyond this edge."

Johnny told the mother and daughter, "These unnamed trees are very protective of every part of themselves, except for the fruit, even those which they no longer use.

Here, observe." Johnny reached into the forest and tapped one of the misshapen golden branch mounds. The tree closest to the mound responded by blowing a cluster of raspberries at him. The fruit avoided a tree in the way to swiftly detonate on his face. Hansuke fell to his knees weeping in the center of the clearing as Brodie yelled, "He's really laughing!", beside him.

Johnny wiped the juice away as he explained amidst his chuckles, "The more determined you are to gather wood or leaves, the more viscous they will blow their raspberries. They never seem to run out of berries either."

"Hey, we have to think of something," Kaya spoke through her guffaws which were fueled by shame for laughing at the dragon's predicament, nervousness and amusement. "Is night really almost here? It's hard to believe since Spectrum

Sun is still positioned at noon."

As if on cue, the rainbow day star blinked out to reveal an ebony moon in its place. Black stars twinkled in the dim ivory night sky.

"What a peculiar atmosphere," Yu-Ri stated as she shook her head in wonder.

***

The companions huddled around the brilliant silver campfire which Hansuke snapped into existence and they shared a meal. The ten year old dragon had no need for the heat yet he hunched there just the same for the sensation of totally belonging and because he empathized with his new companions. He even hunched so his head would be in approximate line with the others.

Johnny told them about why he was fleeing in such a distracted manner. Just as the map had told Kaya and Yu-Ri, he fled from his small community because his parents told him that unless he became a proper dragon by joining the ballet then they no longer wanted him.

"But I don't want to dance for other dragons," Johnny stated. "I want to improve relations between my race and others like yourselves through socialization." He gave an enormous sigh before he said, "I feel like the black sheep of the family."

Brodie gave him a stern look before he winked in good humor.

Brodie stated that he was born into a clan of white sheep. His parents told him that he best be off unless he died his wool white. So he merrily went on his way, away from his family and neighbors who were indistinguishable from one another.

"You see, a Mȳthologia sheep has the same bone structure, facial features, etc., even down to the minutiae. So the shade of my wool came as a blessing though they deemed it a curse to their comfort. I met Hansuke soon after."

Kaya and Yu-Ri talked about their celestial body hopping adventures.

"We've met pirates who were really just irate pie people, ran from flies who lived within richly furnished Venus flytraps, created snow angels in steaming periwinkle snow, oh and so much more!" Kaya exclaimed.

Kaya and her mother talked about Exposition

which was gifted to them by Albert, an automaton, at the entrance of Machinery World. They stated that it was a great item because though they had traditional maps to go on, they were obviously nothing like that piece of technology. It wasn't uncommon for them to misplace the numerous tightly crammed pages and thus lose their ways so they wished that they had Exposition sooner yet they were grateful for getting it while still on their journey. They too were thankful that they always had access to food and drinking water amidst their adventures.

Hansuke explained that he was a guide, just like the automaton who went by Al for short. He stated that he's assisted, assists, and will ever assist every pilgrim upon the last leg of this journey to revelation.

"Though my ability to foresee is irregular, my master grants me the power of omni-time and the ability to be everywhere upon this planet at once only as far as it relates to guiding travelers on this metaphorical road."

"Ah, so that's who we're going to meet," Yu-Ri stated to her daughter. She turned back to Hansuke as she stated, "Someone like you yet more powerful."

The map coughed in an exaggerated manner from within Kaya's pack.

"Perhaps a...Wizard of Mȳthologia?", Yu-Ri proceeded.

"Oh, trust me, he's no wizard," Hansuke gently replied.

"Please don't tell my Mommy anymore about the destination," Kaya pleaded. "I want it to be a surprise."

"Don't fear little one, my lips shall contain your surprise," Hansuke replied as he frowned.

Raven hued fog with splotches of primrose yellow overtook all the area which the campfire's light did not touch.

"Stay near the fire and all will be well," Hansuke stated to the company.

Hundreds of white luminous beings of baby humanoid stature shone around and above them. The beings whose illumination was self-contained beckoned to them from the completely opaque fog as they innocently cackled.

"How cute, they think they're convincing," Brodie stated.

"Why aren't they showing up on this map

and why did they, as well as the fog, instantly appear?" Kaya inquired. "Did they enter through a breach? Yet I see no blank spaces upon the map either."

"They were invisible to all eyes here but mine until I conjured up the fog," an unfamiliar voice spoke from their midst. "They are able to hide from devices such as your map as well," the voice went on as the five friends looked around for the source of the voice.

"Jiminy Cricket!" Johnny exclaimed when he discovered the speaker. He jumped up in fright and most of him exited the firelight's reach. A few luminous beings rapidly grabbed his cheeks, tugged them, and shouted, "Coochie, coochie, coo!" The baby creatures fled as Johnny quickly sat back down.

The indigo praying mantis which had silently seated herself between Kaya and Yu-Ri took a sip of her itty bitty cappuccino after she straight faced told Johnny, "Not quite. The name's Dooie Exophina Machinatata. But honey, you can call me Deus Ex Machina."

Deus Ex Machina placed her unfinished cup upon Johnny's hand which lay palm up upon the ground before she announced, "Well, what are we waiting for? Aren't you excited to arrive at your destination? Of course you are! Or maybe I'm just speaking for myself...anyways, lickity split, time won't wait for you!

Except for you perhaps darling," she stated to Hansuke.

"It's good to see you again," Hansuke replied with an epic scowl as he clapped his hands.

"But we can't move until daylight," Yu-Ri protested. It was too dark before this fog, it's especially opaque now, and there are baby creatures acting like we're their newborn chubby kids!"

"Oh, silly you," Deus Ex Machina replied as she ran into the fog.

"Why aren't the flying babies going after her?" Yu-Ri inquired.

"They don't think she's a cute baby," Brodie replied in awe. "Deus Ex Machina has been granted immunity to all misfortune."

Two trees at the northeastern edge lit up in crimson brilliance and some of the trees behind those soon shone in their own colored brilliance. The babies fled from the trees whose collective light's intensity was just below the threshold for sunglasses, and from the clearing which held the magnificent rays. The fog vanished with their disappearance.

Soon, Deus Ex Machina reappeared in their midst and exuberantly yelled, "Well, there's your path, let's go!"

Johnny looked again at the mug that was akin to half a pea within his palm. He gingerly set the cappuccino down as he walked forward with his friends.

Soon enough, they exited, shivering, from the wide lit path into another expansive clearing where the Tengu statue stood.

"You could have flown just above the tree line, Johnny," Brodie told his friend, not unkindly. "I saw you having trouble twisting through some of the tree gaps and just barely getting by without touching the trees or bumping into us."

"I, um, ah…" Johnny stammered as his dark cheeks surprisingly turned a pink hue.

"No matter, what's done is done," Kaya responded as she placed a hand upon Johnny's forearm. She gave him a grin which further consoled his anxious heart.

"WHO DARES STAND BEFORE ME!" the wide stanced statue thundered.

The companions, except Hansuke and Brodie, trembled.

A few seconds later, Deus Ex Machina proclaimed, "Ha, ha, hoy! I'm just kidding friends, that was me within the statue's mouth. That thing has wonderful acoustics and I just couldn't resist."

"How fast are you?" Yu-Ri inquired after she got over her shock.

"Well..." Deus Ex Machina replied before she vanished within thin air before she reappeared several feet away and waved.

"A teleporter," Kaya exhaled amidst her laughter. You know, the map would have told us that if one of us remembered to look at it and touch her inked image.

"You know, Kaya," Yu-Ri stated, that map has been awfully quiet, even with Deus Ex Machina here..."

"Hmmm...I must have tampered with it so..." Kaya replied.

"...it only snarkily responds to me," Yu-Ri interrupted.

"That's it, I knight thee, Yu-Ri, Dame

Exposition," the map proclaimed. I can finally retire to merely being a map."

Yu-Ri chased her laughing daughter and quickly caught her. They rolled around guffawing with one another as the mother playfully rubbed her knuckles upon her daughter's head.

***

"Okay, are none of the remaining individuals entertaining selfish desires?" Hansuke asked at the monolithic door to the mountain behind the statue. Deus Ex Machina had just finished proclaiming hers, with a uniquely serious demeanor.

"It's okay if you are but reveal them now," Hansuke continued. "It can quietly be told to any single individual here. Only with confession will your passage be smooth. This portal has a potentially turbulent nature unlike the rest, which your map will tell you, though it will be silent about the exact nature of the tempest.

So, I ask again, are you ready to take this shortcut or should we head west upon the road over there for about a year to arrive at our destination if you have something which to unmask but refuse to do so? The babies will be the only trouble upon that path and we will have plenty of sustenance along the way, but I reiterate: it will take roughly a year.

A year here is seven hundred thirty days," he emphasized to the mother and daughter.

"*Interesting*," Hansuke thought as he caught sight of two individuals slightly hesitating when shaking their head with the rest. With his lower microscopic eye, he too saw the individuals' heart skip a beat with their denial.

"Proceed," Hansuke told them as his cheery expression transformed into a somber one and he opened the massive door with a tap of his cane.

They lined up abreast upon the doorway's edge and peered at the self illuminated pond within the mountain. The display of the massive pond contrasted with the plain cave that appeared about the size of Kaya and Yu-Ri's modest house.

The water displayed a the Spectrum Sun and a sky which shifted in primary colors depending on which angle you looked at it. Fenghuangs, beings whose appearance was a composite of various beings of land, sea, and sky, gracefully flew through the expanse.

The companions jumped one after the other into the portal (Johnny slid in due to his stocky size). Without getting wet, they sped through the transport in a single file line.

Chapter III: The Penultimate Adventure

Within moments, they were expelled into the afternoon sky on the other side of Mȳthologia. The fenghuangs expertly swerved out of their way and Kaya enthusiastically waved to one of the fish tailed, swallow faced creatures as she floated down to the side of the portal. She landed next to her mom upon the grassy shore and Johnny, the last one out, soon joined them.

They lay there upon the grass for a few moments, warming their bones from the night upon the other side, when Kaya and Johnny were sucked back into the portal in a blur.

Yu-Ri screamed her daughter's and the dragon's names as she ran to the pond's edge.

"They will be better than okay," Hansuke assured Yu-Ri as he stood a couple paces behind. "Yet the journey will be painful. You will only be able to retrieve them if at least a semblance of their desire is to be found. Otherwise, you will find yourself in a sleepless stasis within the portal until Kaya and Johnny finish their journey within. Not even I can tell for certain how long that will take."

Hansuke had closed his eyes when he recited those facts and when he opened them he found that Yu-Ri was long gone. "Oh," he numbly replied.

Yu-Ri had immediately jumped into the water, pleading for it to take her to her daughter and friend as she desperately hoped that she'd be able to rescue them.

***

Kaya clashed her intricately etched light green blade with Fumi's while ivory leaves periodically fluttered from the scarlet barked trees around them. The two girls in crimson lined ebony blouses broke from their lock before they furiously twirled and parried.

A gust of wind blasted a heap of white leaves from the hillside nearest them and Kaya took advantage of the distraction to trip Fumi onto her back. Kaya stepped onto Fumi's wrist to prevent her from raising her hazel handled blade as she pointed hers to the latter's throat.

Fumi sardonically whispered to a seething Kaya, "So, you've finally learned to save yourself.

But have you really? Do you really hate me?"

Kaya looked down at her arms as rivers of blood suddenly flowed down the length of them.

"Or do you really hate me?" the individual upon the ground inquired in a voice unlike Fumi's.

Kaya gave a start when she heard that voice and she backed away, sword held in front of her, when she looked upon the face of the individual whom she had pinned down: the being was a replica of herself.

Paralysis took hold of Kaya as her replica arose. The replica mocked Kaya and guffawed as she overlaid her hands over her frozen grip. Kaya tried to scream as the replica forced her to cut and stab herself, slowly and seemingly unceaselesly. Kaya wished for death's embrace as Kaya heard her mother call her name.

"Love yourself Kaya, as I love you," Yu-Ri proclaimed through her tears.

With immense effort, and aided by her Mother's stream of affirmations, Kaya broke from her paralysis and embraced her replica. After a few moments, the stunned attacker returned the tight hug.

Soon, Kaya found Fumi wrapped within her

arms yet she couldn't feel her. Kaya broke down and begged to feel her embrace even in this place, for she had never hugged her in reality. The portal didn't oblige.

Kaya trudged on by stating, "You left me."

"Kaya," Yu-Ri ever so tenderly admonished.

Kaya took a deep breath and several moments before she apologized to her sister-by-love. She explained that *Nicéphore* was meant primarily to encourage Fumi by sharing her and her mother's spirituality with her. Yet she authentically apologized for how she allowed insensitivity to leak through the tale and how she didn't stop pride from leading her to share that story with the class without seeking permission from Fumi.

The hallucination vanished when Kaya finished her apology. Yu-Ri rushed in to hug her daughter within the depths of the illusionary pond as she said, "I'm so proud of you. Now let's go get Johnny.

***

Johnny pounded his fists and feet upon the force field as he called out the names of his new friends. Kaya, Yu-Ri, Hansuke, Brodie, and Deus Ex Machina didn't hear or see him as they each walked by a mere centimeter from him. Johnny clawed at the glass, tried to fly over it, and weeped as they continued to walk until they disappeared into the lush meadow which surrounded them.

The real Kaya tried to rush towards her friend yet her Mother held her back and explained that she would just be soundlessly thrown back as she was when she tried to reach her. Kaya and Yu-Ri spoke the dragon's name as they tried to console him.

Johnny turned in the direction of the voices yet he saw no one. When he turned around again, he saw his parents and dragons near his age walking towards him. He clenched his fists and backed away as he shook his head.

Kaya and Yu-Ri ascertained the purpose of this hallucination and they encouraged Johnny to reopen his heart to the individuals who he balked at, whether they truly had his best interests at heart or not; that he could love them whether they accepted him as he was, regardless of what his life's passion was.

After much hesitation, Johnny walked forward

and easily slid through the force field. He flew towards the dragons who were about to disappear from his vantage point when they halted their walk and turned towards him.

Johnny took the seed of his affection for his parents and fickle friends and expressed his decision to love them no matter if it was returned. As he went on talking, his affection blossomed. After completing his trek towards peace with the injury within his heart, the vision vanished.

Chapter IV: The End

Johnny burst forth from the portal with Kaya and Yu-Ri tenderly clasped to his sides. They laughed in catharsis as they floated from the night sky to their cheering companions and a crowd of strangers.

"How long were we gone?", Yu-Ri asked her friends. "It was long wasn't it? You waited here all this time for us?"

"Though the amount of time outside of the portal doesn't always match the time within when the vortex is teaching, the time will never past twelve hours outside of it," Hansuke shouted amidst the cries of joy. "You were gone twelve hours." In a surprising display of strength he threw Yu-Ri, then Kaya, and finally Johnny high into the sky as he guffawed. The crowd applauded with enthusiasm as they grinned and Hansuke smiled in his own way.

"Who are you?", Kaya inquired of the nearest member of the strangers who exuded a comforting heat.

"We are heralds," the woman answered as the companions were lifted upon the hands of the golden clad, brilliantly illuminated, and semi-transparent humans of all ethnicities. The friends were effortlessly carried forward down the crest of the slope and up the next as fireworks altered the appearance of the ivory night sky into ebony, the sable stars into ones of various colors, and the raven hued moon into a sphere of white flames.

At the summit of the adjacent slope, two of the heralds gestured to the moon directly above them and the comrades thanked them.

Kaya told her mother that she wasn't ready to visit the destination since she was still processing her lesson from the vortex. The others stated that they had already visited the destination and were still digesting the experience, though they authentically declared that they would return another time.

Passionate adieus and wishes of reunification were exchanged between the family and four friends. They all put in as good a show as they could: Johnny quickly wiped away a tear as he waved, Hansuke doubled over with laughter, Deus Ex Machina sent them many cheerful kisses, and Brodie smiled as he neighed.

As Yuri and Kaya floated towards the portal which overlaid the image of the moon, she asked the heralds near her if she could share in one final adventure with Kaya, Johnny, Hansuke, Deus Ex Machina, and Brodie.

The heralds granted every companion, except the dragon, the temporary gift of flight. The six companions excitedly flew through the harmless fireworks as they twirled with one another, kissed each other's cheeks (Johnny kissed the rear of his pinky and tenderly placed it on his friends' cheeks), and soaked in one another's laughter.

Kaya felt her face part the air and she sensed weightlessness spreading its wings throughout her chest as she dove towards the ground. She curved upwards about fifty feet from an unoccupied space of the grassy floor as the final three minutes of the fifteen minute limit arrived.

Finally, Yu-Ri and Kaya waved goodbye to their friends as they floated again towards the portal. Yu-Ri would enter to this odyssey's final adventure while Kaya would enter to return home.

***

Yu-Ri found herself in the hospital holding a newborn Kaya. The melancholy which had afflicted her since her childhood had exploded tenfold since the birth of her daughter. She kissed her baby daughter's forehead and whispered apologies as she silently shrieked at herself for feeling so much sorrow.

Yu-Ri slipped from reliving that memory to ones where she was imperfect in caring for her daughter, though she ever toiled to do her best despite the emotional demon who held her head underneath water.

Another memory detonated, one where Yu-Ri began cutting lines upon her torso after her husband gradually grew less intimate with her: Riku grew frustrated since he didn't understand why his wife was becoming increasingly distant.

Previously unbeknownst to Yu-Ri, Kaya was outside a gap within her mother's bedroom door when she witnessed her most recent deed of self-harm: Yu-Ri was drunk on her latest suicidal impulse.

Yu-Ri's memories jumped to a fantasy that had been playing within her head, even within this moment, behind the forefront of her mind yet it was now integrated by a potential future which came not from her:

She placed a noose around her neck and she witnessed every person whom she loved, alongside countless people whom she didn't recognize, cease moving regardless of where they were. As she tightened the noose, some individuals took out daggers while others took out pistols. Yu-Ri tried to make herself stop as the implications manifested within her mind yet her body disobeyed. She kicked back the stool which she stood upon and she fell in slow motion: with the same speed the knife wielders brought the points of their weapons to their hearts as those with guns placed their weapons within their mouths as cavities started to spread within their own hearts. When the rope went taut, knives began to pierce while fingers pulled triggers. Yu-Ri felt no physical pain from her sluggishly paced suffocation yet her soul writhed as she witnessed so many people suffering.

With her last breath, she saw bullets leave the skulls of open chested corpses and screeching undying people with knives plunged past the hilt into their hearts.

The potential future of Fumi and every person whose life she touched was replaced with a verdant garden which was vibrant and teeming with life, most of which and whom she had never beheld: she could see the beautiful fingerprints and intricate speech which had created them; only one bore no markings of creation.

She perceived herself being tenderly and patiently molded and painted, minutiae by minutiae at the hands and words of The Timeless Artist: He included her asymmetrical features, the hair upon her upper lip, and the marks upon her belly which gave evidence of Daichi's and Kaya's birth.

The Timeless Artist wouldn't have registered in her memory if he passed her by on the street yet Yu-Ri could perceive an iota of the being behind the veil: a towering soul of dazzling universes whose designs were far more diverse than she could have imagined; universes flying outward through space, following and preceding others with the sensed essence of the Timeless Artist tirelessly creating throughout.

"Ah, my daughter," the all powerful artist spoke when he finished creating her. "You are perfection.

Yet what is this?", he inquired with a choked tone as cuts appeared over Yu-Ri's torso.

Yu-Ri knelt before the inventor and profusely apologized as she wept at his feet.

The Timeless Artist knelt down to face her and the being embraced her as he sobbed with her. He healed her wounds with a touch. and with each touch, he looked deep into his daughter's eyes as he told her, "I love you." With the last cut healed, he leapt up and joyfully shouted into the air, "I love Yu-Ri!"

The Timeless Artist danced with his daughter and their laughter unleashed blissful tears. At the end, he encouraged Yu-Ri to say: "Kaya loves me, Daichi loves me, Riku loves me," and so on until she had finished going through her family as well as friends. Then he had Yu-Ri go through it two more times and the feeling of being loved was re-enforced each time. Finally he had her do the same with his name.

"You will ever be perfect in worth," The Timeless Artist edified. "Always remember Yu-Ri, that your melancholy does not make you a burden. You remembered to put others before yourself yet you must also fully love yourself such as you do for them and I. Every soul is interlaced Yu-Ri, including yours."

The Timeless Artist and Yu-Ri held each other in an embrace for a few minutes as he whispered into her ear, "I am always with you. We shall be together in eternity at the latest."

***

Yu-Ri woke up upon Earth, next to Kaya, with a smile.

End to

A Journey To A Surprise Destination

8

<u>Three Sundays Ago: Arrival</u>

Time: 6:55 PM JST

Kaya and Yu-Ri held each other as catharsis continued to flourish within them. As the train pulled into the station, Yu-Ri tenderly rubbed her daughter's upper arms through her sleeves. She wiped her daughter's tears and then her own as she stated, "Hey, that is your best tale yet."

"I had the outline of it swirling within my mind for quite some time," Kaya stated with a laugh which broke through a sob.

"You shouldn't be that modest," Yu-Ri gently chided.

"Neither should you," Kaya replied. "You helped create it and the story is all the better because of it."

"I'll come back for you tomorrow evening but don't forget to call me tomorrow morning," Yu-Ri reminded her daughter when the train rolled to a stop.

"I won't Mommy," Kaya assured her. "Here, look..." Kaya stated as she retrieved a planner from her small suitcase. She turned to that day's date: August 5, 1945. Below it, Kaya recited what she wrote: "Don't forget to call Mommy tomorrow morning, as soon as you wake up." Then she turned to August 6, 1945 and read what she had written there: Good morning sleepy head! Call Mommy."

"I probably won't wake up till ten in the morning but I assure you that I'll call you right away," Kaya told her Mother as the train doors opened.

They hugged one more time. Kaya's hand traced the length of her Mother's arm, down to her palm, and exited along her fingers as she turned to leave. Yu-Ri saw Erin greet her from near the platform. Within moments, Erin took

Kaya on her way to her daughter's sleepover party.

Yu-Ri eventually got up to board the train that would take her from Hiroshima back to Miyajimaguchi where she had to work the night shift in the neighborhood's hospital.

1.5

Yu-Ri's Letter

Location: The neighborhood of Miyajimaguchi in Hatsukaichi, Japan

Yu-Ri was in her study room and two hours had passed since her composure failed her that morning. She steadied her hand before she dipped a pen within her ink pot. With immense effort, she gently yet firmly pulled the reigns of her speeding heart. She channeled the ache from within her heart, to her arm, funneled it into her pen, and poured it upon the blank page in front of her:

Dear Kaya,

Oh, how I love you.

Were you afraid when the sirens sang?

Or did you refuse to let go of hope as everyone cowered and ran? Did my love make its presence felt as the demon dove towards the Earth? Or did you feel alone as Hell was about to breach throughout the city? Dear daughter, did pain escape you when you vanished into blinding light? Or did you feel every atom of your being torn asunder as the colossal cloud rose into the sky; What was your crime?

Is there a part of you that exists which I could lay to rest; a semblance of solely you whom I could visit?

Dear Kaya, where have you gone?

Made in the USA
Monee, IL
23 December 2020

55373887R00277